RAVES F(

"IRRESISTIBLY ADDICTING."
—*San Francisco Chronicle*

"THE KING OF HIGH-OCTANE ADVENTURE."
—Brad Thor, #1 *NYT* bestselling author

"A SUPERB WRITER who knows how to tell a tale with STYLE AND SUBSTANCE."
—Nelson DeMille, #1 *NYT* bestselling author

"MASTERFULLY exhibits SUPERIOR CRAFTSMAN-SHIP of the English language as he weaves his IN-DEPTH KNOWLEDGE of many different aspects RANGING FROM ASTROLOGY TO INTERNATION-AL POLITICS throughout his books."
—*Sacramento Book Review*

"Brings COLORFUL CHARACTERS, SPEED AND SUSPENSE."
—*Chicago Tribune*

AND HIS ADVENTURES FOR THE AGES™

"*RAISING ATLANTIS* is BETTER THAN *THE DA VINCI CODE*... A GRIPPING PAGE-TURNER... ONE OF THOSE BOOKS YOU STAY UP WAY TOO LATE READING!"
—*CBS News*

"*RAISING ATLANTIS* is AN ENCHANTING STORY with AN INCREDIBLE PACE."
—*The Boston Globe*

THOMAS GREANIAS

GODS
OF
ROME

ATLANTIS INK

ATLANTIS Ink

Atlantis Ink
780 Fifth Avenue South
Naples, Florida 34102

Publisher's Note: This is a work of fiction. Names, characters,
places, and incidents are a product of the author's imagination.
Locales and public names are sometimes used for atmospheric
purposes. Any resemblance to actual people, living or dead, or
to businesses, companies, events, institutions, or locales is
completely coincidental.

Cover Design by Ana Grigoriu-Voicu
Interior Design by Book Design

Gods of Rome / Thomas Greanias -- 1st ed.
ISBN 978-1-7350856-4-7

The world and its pursuits pass away.
But whoever does the will of God lives forever.

—1 John 2:17

PROLOGUE

There is no remembrance of men of old, and even those yet to come will be forgotten by those who follow them. Even so I am writing this confession down on parchment in the hope that you might escape my fate.

I have come to the end of my life, but I have failed to finish my race. I have fought the wrong fight. I have used up my strength and have nothing to show for it. I have done more evil in the name of good than I ever imagined in my former life as Athanasius of Athens, a hedonist and playwright above all others in Rome when cruel Domitian was Caesar.

If I had my choice, I would have picked a different world stage for the performance of my life. But we do not choose the dates of our birth or death. Not even Caesar. On the day Domitian was born, the stars proclaimed the exact date of his death: September 18 of this year, the 96th since the advent of Christ.

Rightly assuming his astrological birth chart itself was an invitation to his enemies to fulfill the prophecy, Domitian devoted himself from childhood to executing any and all his paranoid mind suspected of less than absolute loyalty. He probably murdered his father, Vespasian, and later his brother, Titus, in his ascension to the throne. Not content with being emperor of the Roman Empire, he proclaimed himself *dominus et deus,* "Lord and God," ruler of the universe. As if that were not enough, he also assumed the official mantle of *pontifex maximus,* merging the rule of Rome with the religion of her gods into a terrible theocracy with a single test: those who bowed before him and proclaimed him Lord and God lived, those who refused died. It was said of Christians, in particular, that they could not or would not bow. This is why they were branded "atheists" and executed.

All but one, it seemed, by the time I arrived on the scene.

The last living apostle of Christ, John, was still rotting away in his island prison of Patmos. But his apocalyptic Book of Revelation had fanned a firestorm of fear across the empire with its horrific visions of the end of the world.

Domitian thought better than to make a martyr of the old man. Instead he saw a historic opportunity to let John die of natural causes—and with him the Church's superstition and vain hope in a glorious Second Coming of Christ. Outlasting both September 18 and the apostle would be Domitian's ultimate triumph.

Unfortunately, neither Domitian nor John had foreseen the rise of the supersecret organization that mocked Caesar with its name Dominium Dei, or "Rule of God." It was said to have started with a small band of disciples inside Nero's palace, left behind decades ago by the Apostle Paul before he was beheaded. Now it was out in the open, claiming to have infiltrated all levels of Roman government, ready to take over once Domitian was gone and establish a thousand-year "Reign of Christ." The Dei's assassination of Domitian's officials only made the threat more worldly and concrete. Of course, it wasn't the so-called Dei that the empire feared, nor any return of Christ, so much as Domitian's response to it and anyone he suspected of being part of it. And the fledgling Christian church, despite the Apostle John's denunciation of Dominium Dei, bore the brunt of Domitian's wrath.

Two kingdoms—one in heaven, one on earth—each vying for a single throne in the heart of man. And one day, out of nowhere, I found myself caught in the middle of these two great wheels of history: religion and politics, grinding against each other and turning to dust the lives of innocents unfortunate enough to get in the way.

To all who have ears to hear and eyes to see, this is my apology for the murderous events into which I was swept and later instigated as the steward of the world's most terrible secret, which I now share with you in the only way I know how.

1

They had finished their business with the priestess whores at the Temple of Artemis and were about to call it a night when Caelus suggested they try out a new secret club in town called Urania.

Virtus held up his hand. "No more, sir, please."

The bodyguard believed in beating one's body into submission. He loathed having to keep company with this Roman official and his insatiable wants. At some point there had to be a limit. Furthermore, this was their last night in Ephesus before sailing back to Rome. Why tempt the Fates?

But Caelus insisted. "Next stop, Urania."

Virtus sighed. How His Fatness had wormed his way into Caesar's court was a mystery to him. Yet it would be his own head if anything should happen to Rome's chief astrologer. So he wrapped his white toga over his shoulder's scorpion-and-stars tattoo—that of the Third

Cohort of the imperial Praetorian Guard—and slid his dagger into its secret fold.

The moment they stepped outside under the stars Virtus knew this was a mistake. The latest performance of *Oedipus Sex* had let out of the amphitheater, and the streets of this port city, Rome's exotic "gateway to the East," teemed with 30,000 revelers of every age, race and sexual orientation. Singing, laughing and snorting in every tongue, they made their way to the closest tavern, brothel and public toilet in sight. Some couldn't wait and took to urinating at the curbs. A few squatters, Virtus noticed with dismay, magically grew tails.

"The mob is too much, sir. I cannot guarantee your safety. We should skip the club, head straight to the ship and call your visit to Ephesus a great success."

"Urania," said Caelus, wading into the throngs before Virtus could stop him.

Virtus quickly caught up and stuck to Caelus's side. To most observers they looked like any other typical Roman homosexual couple in the crowd, an older man and his younger love, which was their cover. Praetorian protocol was to dress in civilian togas when accompanying important personages outside Rome. It drew less attention and allowed Virtus to scan the masses for any threat.

A street prophet wearing a placard emblazoned with the date September 18 immediately caught his eye. That was the date the stars predicted Caesar would die. Indeed, the official purpose of Caelus's visit was to meet with oracles and rogue astrologers in the eastern half of the empire. Whatever they privately believed about the star alignments, their job was to align their public forecasts with Caelus's, which was that Domitian was destined to reign for decades more.

Virtus gently steered Caelus clear of the street prophet. He decided the man was a harmless if stark reminder that dangerous elements of the underground had begun to come out of the woodwork six months before Doomsday. Local informants said the anti-Roman death cult Dominium Dei was active in Ephesus, and their members didn't wear placards to announce themselves.

The Dei had a penchant for abducting local magistrates and sending pieces of them back to their superiors bit by bit—a hand here or an eyeball there, often accompanied by a taunting note. Their only sign of existence, beyond the headless corpses of those Roman officials they left behind, was a black tattoo of the letter *Chi* under their left armpit. It was a twist on the death cross and a symbol of the astrological ellipses of the earth. Very clever, and as good as invisible to the naked eye. Even that scrap of intelligence had taken months to discover from the sole Dei spy Rome had ever captured—from Caesar's own Praetorian Guards, no less—and it came only after the guard had killed himself by sucking poison hidden in his signet ring.

Anyone could be a member of the Dei: your best friend since childhood, even your brother or mother. It was this ruthless reality that kept the empire on edge. His first-hand knowledge that the Dei counted their lives for nothing next to their cause only further unnerved Virtus as he and Caelus merged with the cross-traffic of Crook-ed Street.

Vendors clapped cymbals and called out to the crowd as it snaked along the thoroughfare under the strung-up torches.

"New versions of Oedipus and the Oracle! Ceramic, bronze and silver!"

A young boy from a nearby stand shoved a figurine in-to Virtus's hand and stretched out his own for payment. "Oedipus!"

Virtus looked at the souvenir idol. The face was cut to resemble the late emperor Nero, just like the colossus near the Flavian Amphitheater back in Rome. The Oedi-pus "comedy" tonight was a fiendishly clever, thinly dis-guised retelling of Nero sleeping with his own mother. It was a staple of the Greek playwright Athanasius of Ath-ens to take the classic tragedies and twist them into hu-morous, subversive commentary about contemporary Roman virtue in high places, or lack thereof.

"Did you see this, Virtus?" demanded Caelus, showing him the figurine of the Oracle from the play. Actually, it looked more like an orb than a figurine. "Did you *see* this?!"

Virtus gave the marble orb a closer look and with a start realized it was cut to look like Caelus.

Caelus waved his arms hysterically. "How does that Greek get away with it?"

Virtus had no idea. But he didn't like standing in the open with Caelus, flesh pressing against them on all sides. A blade could shoot out from the crowd and withdraw, leaving him to stand over the crumpled corpse of portly Caelus. A bad omen for Caesar, for sure, and for his own future.

"Entertainment is our religion, and religion is our entertainment," Virtus said, handing the figurines back to the disappointed boy. "The rules of mortal men don't apply to the gods of the cosmic theater."

Caelus, who clearly considered himself one of the gods, nodded as Virtus moved them along. "Well said, Virtus. You are wiser than you look."

Having cleared the river of revelers on Crooked Street, they turned north into the quieter, darker streets of Ephesus. It was a wealthier part of town, and they were free of the anonymous masses.

"See, Virtus, I told you we'd make it. The stars said so because I say so. Wait until you see the delights in store for us!"

Up ahead was a villa perched on a hill. It overlooked the sparkling lights of the great theater, library and harbor beyond. The entrance was a nondescript bolted door. One could have easily missed it save for the bronze celestial globe on a stone pillar in front, and the two guards posted on either side under torches, so frozen in bearing they could have been statues.

Ex-legionnaires, Virtus guessed, who either weren't satisfied with their pensions or enjoyed certain side benefits from their new profession in retirement. As for the celestial globe, it was often depicted in art with Urania, the muse of astronomy.

Ergo, they had found Club Urania.

Virtus didn't like the looks of the thick smoke that hung in the air above the courtyard wall, nor the loud and slurred sounds of men and women high on wine and aphrodisiacs wafting over as well. Rome pretended that the empire was one great banner cut from a single cloth. But establishments like Urania revealed its underside as a patchwork both of silk and sackcloth, its seams stretched to the point of tearing apart. That the only thing holding this world together was so thin a thread as this fat pretender Caelus, who existed solely to prove the prophecies about Domitian wrong, only heightened Virtus's unease.

Caelus, however, looked delighted. "The priestess back at the temple said you must speak into the globe. There must be a pipe inside that snakes into the villa."

Ignoring the guards, Caelus walked up to the globe in front of the bolted door. "Muse of heaven," he commanded, his voice winded from the short but steep climb to the villa. "Open the sky."

The door seemed to open itself, inviting them to step inside a secret world of unimaginable delights.

Poor Virtus didn't know what he was missing, thought Caelus, resplendent after an arousing ritual of mineral baths in progressive tubs of hot and cold water. The stoic simpleton could have joined him on Caesar's denarius but had chosen to stand outside in the courtyard with the chariot drivers and bodyguards of other dignitaries. He didn't understand that the spirit was freed from the body by indulging the senses, not restraining them. Life would pass the fool by and he'd mourn these missed opportunities to taste the nectar of the gods and feel like one himself.

Now Caelus lay naked on a gigantic divan in a circular chamber as two exotic muses imported from beyond the corners of the empire worked special oils into every crevice of his body, under every flab, even into parts unknown to him. Caelus could only stare up at the domed ceiling painted black with white points of light arranged like constellations of the zodiac and thank the gods for his good fortune.

The haze of the opium above the flicking candles was already taking effect. The mosaics of the nine muses on the walls seemed to dance like shadows, and the constellations drifted across the painted heavens above him. The muse working on his face cupped her hands over his nose and mouth so he could inhale some exotic extract, while the muse working his legs began to massage his loins.

And then they came, one by one: seven more naked muses with foreign tongues to take their turns on him, giggling as his blob of a body writhed and wriggled uncontrollably. Together they took him to a higher plane of pleasure beyond the bounds of any he thought this earth could offer.

Truly, I have been born again, he thought when it was all over and he was alone in the chamber, the muses magically gone.

His body still vibrating with a new energy and lightness of being, Caelus slid off the divan and walked under an archway to the adjoining bathroom, which was even larger than the chamber he had just left. It was arranged like a public toilet with a fountain in the center and around it a long marble bench in the shape of a horseshoe with neatly spaced holes. A small water trough like a stream ran along the base of the bench to wash patrons' feet as they sat down.

He noticed a small fish symbol scratched into the mosaic floor. It was the sign of those blood-drinking, flesh-eating Christians. They had usurped the new Age of Pisces in the stars as their self-fulfilling sign of ascendancy. He resented anyone who dared muscle in on his heavens, most of all these superstitious amateurs.

"I piss on Christ!" he proclaimed and painted the fish graffiti with his urine. "Swim in this!"

Out of the corner of his eye he saw something move in the water below the toilet bench. He leaned over the dark hole to have a closer look.

Was it a shadow? No.

A face!

All of a sudden the floor gave way beneath him. His head banged on the trapdoor paver, and he felt himself begin to slide. Then two sets of hairy arms reached up out of the darkness and dragged him down to Hades.

Caelus awoke in a dank, underground cell. Dazed, he squinted his eyes in the dim light. Next to him lay the bruised and bloody corpse of Virtus. Rats had begun to nip on his bodyguard's flesh.

What foul fate is this? Caelus wondered as panic seized him. He was on his knees now.

Virtus had lectured Caelus for his own safety about the so-called Ephesian Underworld—the network of mysterious tunnels that lay beneath the streets of the old city. The tunnels connected the cellars of certain downtown inns and taverns to the great harbor. Originally built to move goods from storage to the ships and avoid the cart and foot traffic on the streets, they were also used to abduct unwary visitors and sell them as galley slaves. Caelus had assumed this type of passage was reserved for prostitutes and female slaves, and that Virtus had only been trying to scare him.

Two looming figures emerged from the darkness, dressed in the armor and black robes of the *Vigiles Urbani*—local police known as Watchmen.

"This is a grave mistake!" Caelus screamed, the echoes of his cry bouncing off the rock walls and fading into the black void. "Do you know who I am?"

"The great Caelus, chief astrologer to Caesar."

Jupiter! They know who I am. This was not a mistake!

"Yes, I am. I am counselor to Caesar. And he will have your heads for this!"

Unfazed, the big Watchman pressed down on him and pinned his arm to his side while the smaller one, who was not small at all, produced a large sword. It hovered over his forearm for a moment like a snake.

"He's the one you want!" Caelus cried out, nodding to Virtus. "He's young, strong, perfect for hard labor. Let me go! My hands are of no use to you!"

"God has a purpose for everyone."

Caelus looked up in horror as the hulking figure above him raised his blade to reveal a black *Chi* tattoo under his arm.

"If your right hand causes you to sin…."

The blade came down, and Caelus wailed in unbearable pain.

The Watchman held up a finger in the dim light.

Caelus could see it clearly enough through the blur of his tears. It was his finger! His own finger and signet ring! The rest of his hand lay on the floor like a piece of red, bloody meat.

They've cut off my hand!

"Don't kill me!" he moaned, suddenly aware that he could see only one Watchman.

He heard a *whoosh* from behind and felt something strike him in the back of the head. He fell flat on his face into the earthen floor, then rolled over to see a headless corpse, blood spurting up from the neck.

They beheaded Virtus!

He tried to scream but heard only a whistle passing through his slack jaw. Then he recognized the medallion on the chest of the collapsing corpse and realized it was he himself who had been beheaded.

They've cut off my head! My head!

He felt the breath of life escaping him as this last, grotesque visage before his eyes began to fade.

Thus Spurius Balbinus, the spindly son of gypsies who had risen to become Caelus of Rome, Chief Astrologer to Caesar, passed from this world to the next.

And he never saw it coming.

2

The small, ornate box took three weeks to arrive in Rome. It was delivered to Caesar in his private box at the great coliseum known as the Flavian Amphitheater during the afternoon gladiator contests. As Titus Flavius Domitianus, the 11th emperor of the Roman empire, read the attached note, his fingers trembled: *Due to unforeseen circumstances, Caelus has retired forever. Soon you will join him. The next government of Rome will be ruled by reason, not by dark arts.* It was stamped with the *Chi-Ro* symbol of Chiron, the pseudonym of the mastermind behind the militant Christian group Dominium Dei.

Domitian opened the box and saw the severed finger and signet ring of his chief astrologer. Shaking with rage, the 44-year-old emperor rose to his feet on buckling knees and wordlessly exited the stadium through the *Passaggio di Commodo*, a newly constructed private tunnel that led back to the palace on Palatine Hill. Close behind him were three key *amici* from his inner circle: Titus Petronius Secundus, prefect of the Praetorian Guard; Titus Flavius Clemens, consul and his cousin; and Lucius Licinius Ludlumus, a scion of Rome's wealthiest family and the Master of the Games.

Only when they were a good distance into the tunnel, where he was sure they could not be overheard, did Domitian unleash his fury and scream, "Will it take the death of Caesar for anyone to believe the conspiracy is real?"

Dressed in royal purple and embroidered gold, the balding, pot-bellied Domitian was in the 15th year of his reign, longer than any Caesar before him since Tiberius. He was also the first to demand to be officially addressed as *dominus et deus,* or "Lord and God." But this humiliating assassination of his chief astrologer by Dominium Dei or "Rule of God"—itself a mockery of his own divinity—only made him more paranoid than usual. He was terrified that he would not live to see a day beyond September 18, the day the stars said he would die. Worst of all, the only credible source in his eyes to give him hope otherwise—Caelus—was gone, having failed to foresee even his own death.

"And you, my chief protector!" Domitian glared at Secundus. "Your Praetorian in plain toga couldn't even protect Caelus. How am I to believe you can protect me?"

Secundus, realizing his own fate was on the line, spoke in a brave voice. "My man in Ephesus was but one in a city of villainy. Here in Rome, however, Your Highness has thousands of Praetorian surrounding you."

"Surrounding me! Who will protect me from your men? You all want me dead!"

They continued to walk on in silence, only their steps echoing ominously like the inevitable march of doom. The tunnel was brilliantly lit by rows of torches on either side to ensure that no shadow could hide a would-be assassin. So great was Domitian's fear.

As usual, it was left to Ludlumus, a former actor and failed playwright, to break the silence with his gravelly yet soothing deep voice. "No doubt this lapse of security is unacceptable. Nor any doubt now that Caelus was a fraud. But neither tragedy should cast doubt upon your own destiny. If anything, your continued survival is proof yet again that the gods protect you, that you indeed are one of them. You cannot kill a god, despite what second-rate playwrights might like to believe."

"No doubt, no doubt," Domitian murmured, annoyed that Ludlumus would use this moment to take yet another swipe at his former rival in the arts, Athanasius of Athens. "But Rome must make retribution for this public act against Caesar. We must therefore produce Chiron and execute him in public."

Domitian often spoke of himself in the third person when he felt threatened. This usually foreshadowed an order of execution of some kind, the object of which was any unfortunate fellow in his sight. In the last few years alone Domitian had executed a dozen prominent senators and countless noblemen in his Reign of Terror, if only to confiscate their fortunes to feed Rome's swelling public debt. This was on top of the usual allotment of Jews and Christians. But the rise of this Dei insurgency was a new phenomenon altogether, and the shocking, public nature of Chiron's recent assassinations had unhinged the emperor.

"To be sure, it is time for Chiron to die," Ludlumus said, halting for a moment, and then stated the obvious for Domitian's own understanding. "But to kill Chiron, we must first produce him."

Domitian addressed his cousin the consul. "Clemens, what do we know about these butchers who call themselves Dominium Dei?"

"Not much, Your Humanitas."

Clemens often addressed Domitian as the Merciful One, mostly in hopes of eliciting mercy on the Christians, of which his wife Domitilla was one and himself an inquirer at the least and sympathizer at worst in Domitian's eyes.

"No? Do they not receive secret instructions from the apostle John from his prison on Patmos?"

"John is the last of the Jewish apostles, Your Highness. His influence is contained to Asia Minor. The Dei are non-Jews in make-up, the spiritual progeny of those Christian converts that the apostle Paul left behind before his beheading by Nero. For decades these followers, both slave and freedman, have kept their faith secret even as they have faithfully served the governments of successive Caesars. These recent public executions are a radical departure from their reputation."

"And you would know that because you are one of them?" Domitian suddenly offered, catching his cousin off guard.

"What?" asked Clemens. "No!"

"Everybody knows that your wife Domitilla—my niece—is one. Some even believe that you are this 'Theophilus' to whom the apostle Luke addressed his account of the life of Jesus."

"Caesar knows much," Clemens said, neither confirming nor denying the rumors. "But the Christians here in Rome consider themselves successors not of the apostle Paul but of the apostle Peter. They are not infiltrators. They seek no influence over the affairs of state. They seek only to live quiet, peaceful lives. To render unto Caesar what is Caesar's, and to God what is God's."

"Caesar is God," Domitian insisted. "On this matter there can be no confusion."

"You know they pay their taxes and pray for you and all in authority, Your Highness," Clemens insisted. "They publicly denounce the Dei and all violence."

"Violence!" Domitian erupted. "And what is this Book of Revelation they all heed if not violence of the most extreme kind to Caesar, Rome and the empire? The end of this world! A New Jerusalem! And heaven and earth! You don't think this superstition inspires animals like the Dei to take up the sword in the name of Jesus? Or embolden my enemies in the Senate? Perhaps even members of my own family?" He glared at Clemens. "My family!"

"Surely you don't suspect Domitia?" Clemens replied, diverting attention to Domitian's wife.

A startled Domitian glanced at Ludlumus and Secundus, both looking quite impressed by the feeble Clemens' unusually clever recovery.

"Nonsense," Domitian said. "After all I've done for her? I can't imagine why she would want me dead."

Domitian had pursued his second wife Domitia from the beginning years ago. She was married at the time, so he forced her husband to divorce her so he could marry her. Later on, she ran off with the actor Paris, and he had to have the thespian killed. Still, after some time, she came back to him of her own accord.

Clemens said nothing and could only genuflect before his Caesar. But was he bowing before his Lord and God as well? Domitian wasn't sure anymore.

"Clemens," he barked. "I want you to find this mysterious mastermind of all that troubles the empire. I want you to find Chiron."

"Find Chiron?" Clemens gasped. "How am I supposed to do that? Nobody knows who he is!"

"Surely one of your devious little Jewish and Christian friends will know his true identity." Domitian could see the pain in his cousin's face. "Yes, Clemens. You will give Secundus names, and my Praetorian Guards will beat these fanatics and kill them one by one until they give up the most dangerous man in the world."

They had arrived at the palace, entering the lower level in back. Here the offices of Caesar were filled with hundreds of slaves and magistrates who kept Rome's trade routes clear—the roads clean of dung for its armies and seas clear of pirates for its navies. As Domitian passed by, the business of Rome suddenly seemed to pick up, with much scurrying and paper shuffling, until Caesar and his *amici* went up a short flight of stairs to the private residence.

Domitian stopped outside his bedchamber and glared at his *amici*.

"Clemens, you will find Chiron for me. And you, Secundus, will bring him to me. Those are my orders. Now carry them out."

The consul and prefect glanced at each other, said nothing, and went their separate ways, leaving Caesar alone with his Master of the Games.

Ludlumus said, "You know the consul is never going to find Chiron, Your Highness. Even if he did, he would never willingly give him up."

"Somebody has to die for this. Somebody big," Domitian insisted. "We must have retribution. And it must be public, as a warning to others. Once we produce Chiron, his execution must be public, humiliating and painful."

"I'll conjure up something nice for 80,000 spectators."

"See that you do, Ludlumus. And find out how Epaphroditus allowed that finger to ever reach me that my eyes should see it."

Ludlumus paused. "Your Highness had his primary secretary executed last year. Something about his assisting Nero's suicide 28 years ago."

"Exactly. That's what I meant. Epaphroditus would never have allowed this misfortune to disturb me. Now leave us."

By "us" Domitian meant himself, of course, and Ludlumus left and closed the door behind him, leaving Domitian to himself.

Domitian, Rome's Lord and God, removed his short-cropped wig and looked in the mirror of polished brass. He was painfully self-conscious about his baldness and had hoped the publication of his popular book on the subject of hair care would make him less so. But it hadn't. The fleshy face and protruding stomach didn't boost his spirits either these days. They made him feel weak.

Domitian looked around his bedchamber, dominated by his bed, couch and statue of his favorite goddess Minerva with her sacred owl. His chamberlain Parthenius had laid out a lavish spread of sweets for him on the table by the couch. But Domitian wasn't hungry, the vision of Caelus's finger filling his head. Who knew what his enemies would do to him?

And who were his enemies?

Everyone.

He knew he paled in comparison to his beloved father, Vespasian, the first Flavian to be Caesar. His brother, Titus, was also beloved by Rome's aristocrats, thanks to his military success in the Judean War. Titus's untimely death two years into his reign as Caesar only swelled public affection for Domitian's brother—and cast suspicion that he, Domitian, was behind it. True enough, perhaps, but not enough to explain the pure hatred he endured from the noble class.

No, Domitian concluded, the noble class of Rome hated him because he refused to promote lazy and entitled family, friends and political supporters to run the offices of government simply because they were his family, friends or political supporters. His administration was a meritocracy, and it was effective only because he installed the best people into the best positions to build up the empire with great public works, like the new Circus Maximus under construction down the hill, and the network of new highways being laid in the empire's eastern half of Asia Minor.

For this he was hated, because these useless aristocrats were worthless and had nothing to contribute to the world other than their money, which is why he was so often forced to relieve them of it along with their lives. Now they drooled over his prophesied demise and were attempting to sway those closest to him in his personal staff, and even his family: Domitian's second wife, Domitia, was in a league of her own concerning suspicion, closer to him than anybody else.

He walked to his bed and lifted his pillow to make sure the knife he kept was still there. It was.

Good.

He moved to the couch on which he liked to take his rest during the day, and removed from beneath it a two-leaved tablet of linden-wood. On the wood he had scratched his list of those he suspected were conspiring against him.

Domitia's name was at the top, followed by his two Praetorian prefects: Petronius Secundus and his colleague Norbanus. An emperor could never trust his own Praetorian Guards, who as Caesar's "protectors" had a long history of deciding in advance who should become emperor and then, once in office, how long that emperor should live.

Then there was his cousin Flavius Clemens, of course, and his wife, Domitilla, who was Domitian's own niece. Domitian had already proclaimed their two sons his successors since he and Domitia had none of their own. So clearly they were the most obvious beneficiaries of his demise, although Domitilla was the strong one in that marriage. Clemens was too weak and ineffectual to be any kind of threat. Only his able administration of the countless papers the government required to handle the Jews kept him employed, so long as he made sure the Jews paid their extra taxes for being, well, Jews.

Finally, there was Ludlumus, his Master of the Games. It was hard for Domitian to believe that Ludlumus could possibly think any successor would be as good to him. Nevertheless, although he trusted the ghoul, Domitian at bottom didn't like him, so his name was on the list.

These top names were on the left eave of his wooden tablet.

On the right eave he kept the names of those who had no reason to wish his demise but were close enough to him on a daily basis to inflict bodily harm: Parthenius, his chamberlain, whom he had honored by being the only servant allowed to wear a sword in his company; Sigerus, another chamberlain; and Entellus, who was allowed to enter his chambers with petitions requiring his attention.

He clapped the eaves shut like a book and slipped the tablet under his pillow on the couch. Then he set his throbbing head on his pillow and, afraid to even shut his eyes for a moment, stared at his statue of the goddess Minerva and prayed for her protection. She was the only one he could trust now. Soon his eyelids began to flutter, and he was drifting off to sleep, dreaming of the day he would kill them all.

3

It was a glorious day for an execution.

Less than a week after the unfortunate incident with the finger of Caesar's astrologer, Ludlumus paused at the private entrance to the Hypogeum beneath the Colosseum. He drew out an Etruscan dagger from a fold in his fashionable robe and ran his finger along the fine blade. He felt no prick, only the cool trickle of blood. Very nice, he thought, as trumpets announced that the execution was about to begin. He sucked his finger dry, slid the dagger back into its hidden sheath and walked inside.

The Hypogeum was a vast, two-level subterranean network of tunnels, animal pens, prisoner cells, shafts and trap doors that powered the scenery changes and special effects of the Games. Beastmasters, sword handlers and stage hands stood at attention as he walked past the sophisticated systems of ramps, winches, capstans and hoists—modern technology that could launch animals, prisoners and gladiators up into the arena.

It was dark but beastly hot down here. With so little natural light, the torches burned all hours of the day and night. It was the very pit of hell, and he reveled in it, his home as master of the underworld.

He proceeded past a series of chambers that rattled violently from the force of their snarling occupants: lions, tigers, leopards, bulls and buffalo. Then there was the smell of excrement, blood and death.

Glorious.

The holding cell at the end of the corridor was guarded by two Praetorians. Gazing out from beneath their shiny bronze helmets with hinged cheek-pieces were alert eyes, sweeping back and forth, looking for trouble. The Praetorians were dressed in full armor and carried side arms—a sword and dagger—and each held a javelin upright in front of him, spearheads gleaming.

The guards recognized him on sight as he approached. "Sir," they said in unison, smacking their boots together.

"At ease, fools," he told them, stopping in front of the cell door. "I bear no military rank."

Their faces were glazed over with perspiration from the heat. His own face was cool and dry.

Ludlumus said, "Caesar insists I spend a few moments with the prisoner before his execution."

The first Praetorian opened his mouth to protest but wisely said nothing. He instead motioned his fellow legionary to unlock the cell door.

"I'll need a recorder," Ludlumus demanded, and the first Praetorian followed him into the cell.

The prisoner was clad in leg irons and propped up in chains against the far wall, his head hanging down. Too weary and battered from torture, he was already half-dead and seemed resigned to die. But when he looked up and saw the tall Roman, he came to life as his former self: Titus Flavius Clemens—soldier, millionaire, consul of Rome and now accused Christian.

"Ludlumus!" gasped Clemens. "Domitian must be stopped! For the sake of Rome! He'll kill the entire Senate!"

"Speak for yourself," Ludlumus said. "The emperor wants me to record your confession before you die. He's especially interested in the names of any friends of yours we might have missed."

Clemens' face turned bitter. "Our self-proclaimed 'Lord and God' Domitian killed them all."

"Not all of them," Ludlumus said. "Your wife Domitilla has been banished to the island of Pontia."

"And my boys?"

"Young Vespasian and Domitian will live in the palace under the care of Caesar as his designated successors. Caesar has brought in the grammarian Quintilian to tutor them. His will purge them of any superstitions they have been exposed to by you and your wife."

"Rome will not steal their souls, Ludlumus."

"That remains to be seen. But for the sake of their lives, Clemens, tell me, who is Chiron?"

"I told you, I don't know! Nobody does!"

Clemens looked confused and scared. His eyes darted back and forth between the guard and Ludlumus.

"I didn't hear you, Clemens," Ludlumus pressed. "Who is Chiron?"

Clemens looked flabbergasted, as if he could not believe Ludlumus would do this to him. "How long have we served my cousin together, Ludlumus? You know there is no evidence linking me to the Dei. Killing me does nothing to hurt them."

"God has a purpose for everyone, Clemens. Isn't that what you believe?"

Ludlumus shook his head and removed the torch from the cell wall. He then moved closer to Clemens, lowering the torch.

"Guard," he ordered, "remove the prisoner's loin cloth."

The guard, stunned by the request, hesitated.

Ludlumus snapped, "Do it!"

Reluctantly the guard put down his tablet, walked over to Clemens and began to strip him of his only remaining dignity. "I'm sorry, Consul," the guard mumbled, shame-faced.

"Ex-consul now," Ludlumus rebuked the guard. "Now stand back."

Ludlumus stepped forward and stuck the burning torch between the prisoner's legs, scorching his genitals until the consul of Rome screamed like a wretched animal. Only then did Ludlumus pull the torch back. "What is the true identity of Chiron?"

"Acilius Glabrio," Clemens said, barely loud enough for the guard to hear him. "Acilius Glabrio was Chiron."

"Nice try," Ludlumus replied. "But I already had a word with the former consul before his death. I assure you, he's not Chiron. Try again."

Clemens refused to talk, and Ludlumus applied the fire.

"My God!" screamed Clemens, writhing in agony, his chains clanging. "You're the devil!"

"Save your breath and tell me what I want to know." Ludlumus applied the fire yet again, this time for a long minute, until the sweet odor of burnt flesh filled the cell. Clemens was crying now, weeping with inhuman suffering. Ludlumus noticed the Praetorian staring at him in horrific disbelief. "What are you looking at?"

The guard said nothing.

Ludlumus produced a wax tablet and shoved it into the guard's face. "Sign this."

The guard took it and read the writing. "What is this?"

"The prisoner's confession."

The guard looked puzzled. "But he hasn't confessed anything."

"You do make things difficult, don't you?" said Ludlumus as he pulled out the dagger and whipped it across the young soldier's throat, catching him just beneath the chin strap of his helmet. The guard opened his mouth but produced only a gurgling sound as he collapsed to the floor.

Clemens stared at the fallen legionary and then at Ludlumus. He lifted his gaze to the ceiling, screaming all the louder. "God in Heaven! Have mercy on me!"

Ludlumus, meanwhile, calmly took the slain Praetorian's hand, pressed the ring finger to the wax to get the impression from the insignia and slipped the tablet inside his toga. He then unhooked the keys from the guard's belt and unlocked Clemens. The consul fell to his knees, too weak to stand.

"It's a good thing the guard got your confession down before you killed him, Clemens," said Ludlumus, tossing the knife his way. "And I'm lucky I called his friend from outside to come in, or else you would have killed me." With that Ludlumus called out, "Guard, help me! The prisoner is loose!"

There was a rattling of a key in the lock, the door swung open and the other guard rushed in to see Ludlumus stagger to his feet.

"The prisoner killed him and almost took me too!" Ludlumus cried out.

The guard ran to his fallen colleague, saw the knife and then kicked the defenseless Clemens until he was flat against the wall. He turned to Ludlumus.

"Are you all right, sir?"

"I'm fine," Ludlumus replied. "Just make sure the prisoner's on in five minutes."

Ludlumus left the cell and emerged a few minutes later inside Gate XXXIV of the Colosseum. More than 80,000 fans had packed the stands today. Ludlumus was pleased with the turnout as he walked past the Doric columns to his section. The arena was surrounded by a metal grating, twelve cubits in front of the first tier of seats, which protected the public from the wild beasts. On the first tier ranged the marble seats of the privileged. Above those were the second and third tiers for the ordinary public. Even the plebes in the top gallery would be able to follow the drama that was about to unfold below them.

The imperial box for the Emperor, his family and invited guests was the easiest place to pick out because it had the best seats in the stadium, on the first tier on the northern side of the arena, and was protected by a bronze balustrade. The imperial bodyguard detail wordlessly allowed Ludlumus into the box. There he took his place at the right hand of Domitian.

Domitian said, "That didn't take long."

"Long enough. He killed one of your guards. With the very dagger you awarded him upon his consulship."

"I never thought he had it in him," Domitian said.

"The Dei will do that to a man, I suppose. But I did extract a confession."

Ludlumus produced the wax tablet and handed it to Caesar.

Domitian looked at the confession, his face turning livid. "But I'm throwing a party for him tonight!"

"Mmm." Ludlumus did his best to look devastated. "Although he's a good decade younger than I am, I once considered myself his protégé in the theater."

"Terrible. But you look like you are holding up well under the circumstances."

"Thank you, Your Highness."

Ludlumus noted with satisfaction that a low stone wall had already been set up by the propmasters. A fresh layer of white sand glistened in the sun, all the better to show off fresh blood. Now a warrior in armor walked into the arena to the frenzied applause of the crowd. "Romulus! Romulus! Romulus!" they all chanted.

Instantly Clemens was launched into the scene from a hidden elevator shaft.

The mob now chanted louder. "Remus! Remus! Re-mus!"

Ludlumus glanced at Domitian, who nodded approvingly at the send-off he had prepared for Clemens in this re-telling of the founding of Rome. Romulus and Remus were brothers. As legend had it, Remus mocked the little wall his brother Romulus had begun building for the new city, jumping over it and back to show just how puny it was. Romulus didn't like that and killed Remus on the spot. For this re-enactment, Ludlumus had the propmasters dress "Romulus" in the royal purple and gold as a stand-in for Domitian, while Clemens, as close to a brother as Domitian had left in this world, stood in for himself.

Ludlumus was quite proud of his work here. Only a former thespian like himself would appreciate the scale with which his beastmasters cleared more than 5,000 wild beasts from the morning's animal acts off the arena floor in order for the propmasters to erect the scene for today's lunchtime execution and, when that was over, the afternoon's gladiatorial contests.

Sadly, Clemens didn't seem up to the demands of his role. Standing wobbly on the floor of the great stadium, he barely had time to brace himself before the first stab from the sword of Romulus struck him. The blade went clean through him and out his back. Slowly Romulus withdrew his blood-tipped blade. As it was the only thing keeping poor Clemens up, the late consul collapsed to the ground, dead.

Ludlumus held back a smile as he watched the arena attendants pick up what was left of Clemens. Their assistants carried the corpse off while they hastily turned over the blood-stained sand for the next act.

It was all over too soon, Ludlumus lamented.

Athanasius of Athens would not die so easily.

4

he dreams were different, but the girl was always the same. Young, maybe 17, long black hair, dark eyes, and tears of blood trickling down her tragic face. Sometimes she was the harlot Rahab in ancient Jericho, and he was the enemy spy sent to bring down the walls. Other times she was a beauty named Aphrodite in a future Greece under the rule of Germania. This night she had no name, but he knew it was present day. She was in a cave somewhere, calling out to him in the darkness. She possessed the secret of the ages, a mystery he had to unravel, or his mission would fail and the world would be doomed. In the haze of dream, he stumbled down an endless cave, his hands feeling the walls as they narrowed, his feet tripping over jagged rocks. "I'll find you! I'll find you!" he cried out, and then slipped, tumbling over and over into space.

Athanasius of Athens awoke from his nightmare, gasping for breath, the sound of trumpets outside piercing the air. He sat up and let his eyes adjust. Shafts of sunlight streamed through the drapes and marble columns onto a vast mosaic floor. He looked over at Helena's empty side of the bed and put his hand on it. It was cool to the touch.

What time was it?

He put on a robe and walked onto the balcony of his hillside villa, taking in the spectacular view of the city below. To the west were dazzling white terraces and marble columns cascading down the cypress-covered hills to the Circus Maximus and the winding Tiber beyond. To the east was the intersection of Rome's two great boulevards, the Via Appia and the Via Sacra, and, in the middle, Rome's great coliseum, the Flavian Amphitheater. The roar of a crowd wafted up on the wings of the breeze. The lunchtime executions must have begun.

He frowned. It must be noon already.

On his better days the playwright Athanasius religiously followed a strict regimen. He would wake before dawn, leave Helena in their warm bed and put in a good hour or two writing his next play. Then he would leave their villa on Caelian Hill and head over to the Circus Maximus to run laps and maybe shoot some arrows—he was a marksman archer—before the heat of the day set in. He found his best ideas flowed while he ran, and it kept alive his fantasy that at age 25 he could still run the marathons he once did as a boy outside Corinth back in Greece. After lunch he would enjoy the baths, a relaxing massage, and perhaps take in an afternoon rest with Helena before answering letters, supervising rehearsals at the Theater of Pompey, or attending to the problems of everyday life, which he limited each day to the single turn of an hour-glass. Then he and Helena would enjoy dinner with friends in the city or stroll along the Tiber and watch the imperial barges delivering the world's luxuries to Rome. They would cap off the evening by attending various parties and then retiring to bed with each other.

It was, in short, the perfect Epicurean life he had always imagined as a boy, filled with friends, food, freedom and sex. Lots of sex.

Those were the good days.

On his bad days, he slept until noon, hung over from a late party or a nightmare induced by his creativity-enhancing leaves. Having missed his peak writing time, and not feeling up to laps at the Circus Maximus, he'd still have lunch with friends, go to the baths, enjoy a massage and a nap, albeit alone because the ever-practical Helena would be upset with him for his lethargy. All the same, they'd go out to dinner and perhaps see one of his own productions, just so he could validate that he existed. Then on to the can't-miss parties where the wine would loosen his lips and he'd talk about his writing and productions and delight the great of Rome with his humor and wit, praying to the Muses that he'd remember what he had said the next morning so he could write it down. He rarely did, of course, and too often the first time it all came back was while attending a rival's production when he heard the actors utter his stolen lines.

This was one of the bad days. He could feel it.

It was noon already, after all.

Helena was in the courtyard, where she emerged dripping from a bathing pool. Behind her was a gigantic, half-finished sculpture of herself in the guise of the goddess of love. The sculptor Colonius had been taking his sweet time with the hammer and chisel, Athanasius thought, and was months behind. He could hardly blame him.

Helena caught sight of him and wrapped a clingy gown around her supple, golden body. Then she turned to face him with her two round breasts and a smile.

"The toast of Rome has awakened!" she announced.

A true Amazon in height, she stood almost a head taller than him in her bare feet, and he was by no means average. She was a sight to behold with her hair of gold, flawless features and eyes of sapphire blue that betrayed an intelligence her beauty often masked to mad distraction. He had fallen for her instantly. The miracle was that of all the senators, noblemen and charioteers to choose from, Helena, the glory of Rome herself, had chosen him.

"My Aphrodite," he said.

"This year's model." She kissed him on the lips. "But I'll always be your Helena."

"You let me sleep in. Half the day is gone."

"And half your delirium. You know how you get before an opening. I spared us both."

She was right about that. Tonight was the premiere of *Opus Gloria*, his greatest and most controversial work yet, and he was a wreck. He needed it to be well-received, to secure his marriage to Helena. Her well-connected Roman family was quite wealthy at one time but had lost much of their fortune. If not for the modeling that her beauty brought her, and she had earned quite a bit from it, she would have been penniless by now, or married to a man she did not love. All the money in the world would never quench her fear of poverty, Athanasius knew, but they had agreed that the success of *Opus Gloria* would go a long way and be enough for them to marry. Next month would mark a full year living together, when Roman law regarded them as married. But she had planned a huge, multi-day wedding celebration, and he had planned to take her to Greece afterward to meet his mother and cousins, where there would be another wedding party.

So in truth the affections of Helena could not be bought, but they still had to be paid for. Thus the significance of *Opus Gloria* and his success in this Roman world, which would mean little to him without Helena by his side.

"I suppose you are right," he told her and kissed her back.

She smiled. "Repeat that line over and over in your head tonight, and all will be well."

He laughed. If only his father were still alive to meet Helena and see his success as a playwright. His father always told him to take pride in his heritage and "show the Romans what the Greeks are still made of." His memory made Athanasius suddenly reconsider the staging of tonight's performance.

Helena saw it in an instant. "Now what?"

"I still don't know why we should have to go to the Palace of the Flavians tonight to see my own play," he said. "Caesar and the rest should be coming to the Pompey to see it. That's the proper venue. The stage has already lost its place to the Games of the Flavian Amphitheater. Soon it will drop behind the races of the Circus Maximus when its latest incarnation is completed. If it falls another notch, I might fall off with it."

"Oh, Athanasius. Only you would find a way to diminish your achievement. You are bigger than the stage. What playwright wouldn't give his right hand to enjoy a venue at the palace? Besides, you heard what Maximus said about the Pompey. It has too many sinister associations for Domitian. Why would he want to celebrate your opus at the very place where Julius Caesar was assassinated backstage? It might give people ideas."

"Yes, well, we can't have any of those running around on the loose."

He thought again of his father, and then of dear old Senator Maximus, who had become something of a surrogate father to him. The senator was a Hellenophile and early fan of his plays, navigating them through the government censors and political traps of Roman high society. Even so, the roar of the mob in the wind was a grim reminder to Athanasius that the fading art of his scripted comedies was no match for the so-called "reality" of the Games. They were as bad as religion. Indeed, they were the new religion of Rome. He dare not speak it aloud, for who knew who was listening? But he thought it. And Rome had yet to invent a way to read minds. There was still free thought, if not expression.

"You hear that?" he asked Helena, lifting a finger to the breeze as another cheer rang out in the distance. "You know what that is?"

She shrugged. "The last of Flavius Clemens, I suppose."

"That's right," he lectured her. "First it was the Jews. Now it's the Christians. Who's next?"

Helena smiled brightly. "You?"

"Laugh all you want, Helena. You haven't heard Juvenal's jokes about Greeks in Rome."

"He flatters you by imitation, Athanasius, and everybody knows he is not half the wit you are." Helena ran her soft finger down his cheek and gazed at him lovingly.

"There is no pleasing you when you are in a mood, Athanasius, is there?"

"No."

"Then relax yourself before tonight. Join your friends at Homer's for lunch. Go to your favorite bath. Take a massage. Then enjoy the premiere of your greatest play ever."

"And then?"

"Let your work do its work. Let your rival Ludlumus burn in jealousy at what you can do with words that he cannot do with a thousand Bengal tigers. Let Latinus and the rest of your actors take the credit. Let the world and even Caesar himself forget September 18th and the sword of Damocles that hangs over Rome. This is your night to be worshipped, to join the pantheon of the gods of art."

"And then?"

"And then you get to go to bed tonight with the goddess of love and wake up tomorrow on top of the world."

She was heaven for him, it was true. "Well, you do have that effect on a man."

"A performance not to be missed," she told him, and kissed him on the lips again, warm and wet, full of promise.

5

She looked on with great affection as Athanasius walked away, but she felt a dark cloud of fear forming over her head and frowned. This bothered her even more because she knew frowning was not good for her. She may be the face of Aphrodite, but she didn't wake up that way. It took eight girls—now waiting for her in the bathhouse—to fix her hair, paint her lips and buff her nails for her to reach perfection for this evening. And this wasn't ancient Greece. It was modern Rome. Sculptors like Colonius were no idealists. The first tiny crease around her eyes would become a giant crack in marble and spell the end of her reign and the start of another's.

Not that Athanasius would care. He was the kind who, once smitten, would love her forever.

And that was the problem.

Athanasius seemed to think they had all the time in the world. Money and power meant nothing to him. Life was all about his works and the world's recognition of his merit as a playwright. The fortunes that came his way passed through his hands like water from the aqueducts passed through the bathhouses and homes of Rome into the central sewer to the Tiber. And yet he'd be happy scribbling away on his plays from a cave, eating wild mushrooms and smoking his leaves for inspiration.

She, however, would not.

Her beloved was a proud man who so desperately wanted to win the acceptance and respect of a Rome that spurned him. But he never would, even with his marriage to her. She knew that the only thing that made him acceptable to Rome was the popularity of his comedies—and the money they brought the state in ticket sales and merchandising. It was the same with her beauty. But Athanasius simply could not accept the reality that the mobs who flocked to the Games of the Flavian by day were the same who filled the seats of his Pompey at night.

"Ludlumus and I are not in the same business," he had once declared to her. "I am playing a different game, and those who see my plays are the better for it."

All of which led him to push the bounds of acceptability in his plays, to point out Rome's tragic flaws and weaknesses in hopes of strengthening society. This, in turn, only raised the ire of the pontiffs, augurs and astrologers he mocked along with the gods. For all its violence and lust, Rome was actually a conservative and religious society. It could only wink at its wits like Athanasius for so long before it lost its patience. It was time for him to pick a different theme for his productions.

Having waited until the servants confirmed to her that Athanasius had left and her attendants were waiting in the bathhouse, she turned in the opposite direction and walked past the great marble image of herself as goddess and under the peristyle into the villa.

Helena entered the library, which intimidated her with all its shelves of books and scrolls. Athanasius had one of the largest personal collections in Rome. It was a secret part of him she could never get her arms around.

She found a silver tray with a cup and pipe on her beloved's desk. She picked them up, one at a time, and lifted each to her nose with a frown. He had been drinking kykeon and smoking blue lotus leaves again, no doubt to lift his senses and enhance his creative spirits while he wrote.

"Oh, Athanasius."

Those creative spirits were going to ruin them. It was a miracle that *Opus Gloria* had even passed the censors, let alone get this kind of launch tonight at the palace. That scene of Zeus taking the form of a swan to rape Leda, or rather the other way around in this new telling was… so disturbing, to say the least, and certainly sacrilegious, worse even than the ridicule and death the gods had endured in his previous works. Only the intervention of his lead actor, Latinus, who reminded his friend Domitian that Athanasius took care to mock only the Greek gods, not their Roman successors, and the magistrate Pliny the Younger, who promised that the women of Rome would buy the uniquely shaped figurines of Zeus-the-Swan in droves, saved the production.

Helena felt the old confusion rise up inside her. She adored Athanasius. He was talented, athletic and compassionate. He was also incredibly handsome and a god in bed. Yet the very qualities she loved—like his dangerous curiosity and insatiable quest for truth—were what she most feared. Even his beloved mentor Maximus had once confided to her: "You just have to control him. Sexually, psychologically, financially. For his own sake. And you'll get by."

She glanced at the titles of his stacks of books and scrolls. There was Aristotle's *Poetics*, along with the complete works of Euripedes. There were also the classic Greek comedies of Hermippus and Eupolis, and Athanasius's favorites from Aristophanes, *The Clouds* and *Lysistrata*. There were others too: books about the arts, history. One was about the ancient Israelite invasion of what was now Judea, and another about Rome's campaign in Germania.

So many old books and crazy ideas that filled his head.

The pile of scrolls collapsed from her touch to reveal a scroll hidden behind them all. This one was in common Aramaic, which she understood enough to read the title: *The Revelation of Jesus Christ*.

She went cold. Officially banned by the empire, this was the book about the end of the world written by that crazy old "last apostle" John imprisoned on the island of Patmos. No wonder poor Athanasius had been having nightmares. What was he thinking? She knew that, to the love of her life, pure and undefiled religion was attending the Olympics in his native Greece and smoking psychedelics. All other religion he pilloried in his plays. To him this was a harmless curiosity, of course, a chance to "break the code" that rumors suggested was bound in the sinister symbolism of this evil tract. Wasn't the antichrist supposed to be Domitian, after all?

Everybody knew that Athanasius was a closet atheist who did not believe in the gods. Not all atheists were Christians, and certainly not Athanasius. But all Christians were atheists by Rome's standards, because they rejected religion altogether in favor of a superstition that required neither sacrifices nor idols of any kind. These were the very things that greased the wheels of commerce—and made life for her and Athanasius possible. Yet all a disgruntled servant or paid informant had to do was tip the Praetorians, and they were finished. At the very least, their new hillside villa, one of only 2,000 single residences in a city of squalid apartment blocks, would be confiscated.

"You live in a fantasy world, my love," she murmured to herself.

She produced her divination dice, which she used for every decision of her life. Each side had a sign of the zodiac. She would throw them to decide what to do with the scroll. Burn it now? Or ignore it and confront Athanasius tomorrow? Whatever the outcome, she knew she would have to avoid any row with him before the party tonight.

She pushed up her python lucky charm bracelets on each arm—double the charm to keep evil away—and rolled the dice in her hands. She looked up to heaven to utter a silent prayer and then said, "Fortuna!" as she cast them onto the desk.

A six.

She smiled with relief. She would burn the scroll, place the ashes with his lotus leaves on the silver tray, and let the servants carry them out. Perhaps Athanasius would never even notice. Perhaps a new idea would grab his attention, and these visions of the end of the world would disappear from his memory along with his nightmares.

A young voice from behind said, "Mistress Helena, your dress for the evening has arrived, and the girls wish me to tell you that they are ready for you now."

She stiffened. It was the servant boy Cornelius. He was a holdover from Athanasius's previous household staff and always seemed to regard her as an interloper. The boy fancied himself a protector of the great playwright's papers. How long had he been standing there?

"I am not ready for them," she said imperiously. She then rolled up the Book of Revelation, laid it aside on the desk and slowly turned. "I'm just tidying up for Athanasius. You know how he hates it if I throw papers out. Please take his tray back. Tell the girls I'll be with them in a moment."

"Yes, mistress."

She watched him take the silver tray and walk away. Then she took the scroll and buried it in the pile behind the poetics. She would have to burn it tomorrow. Or not, she realized with pleasant relief. After tonight it wouldn't matter.

6

In the days of the old Republic, perhaps he and Helena might have built their home here on Palatine Hill. Or so Athanasius fancied as their carriage curved past towering walls with cascading waterfalls toward the summit. The spectacularly lit Palace of the Flavians on top was the ultimate symbol of imperial excess in Rome, having literally taken over the entire hill and pushed out any and all private residences.

As they pulled up to the columned portico, Athanasius saw the Praetorian security detail in all their splendor: gleaming spears, dress parade black uniforms and capes with purple trim, and shiny sidearm swords. They were patting down guests for hidden weapons before entering. He also saw the black cutouts of snipers against the night sky—archers on the rooftops.

"You were right, Helena. The Pompey could never match the warmth of this reception for my audience."

"Athanasius, please," she said, smoothing the folds of her fashionable stola dress. "Remember our company tonight."

There were indeed plenty of purple stripes on many of the fine togas in the line to get inside—senators and magistrates. Plenty of gold stripes, too, on the military officers, and a rainbow of tunics on proud display from the celebrated charioteers. Fashion-conscious women had their hair dyed honey gold and piled on top with ringlets like Helena's. He wouldn't be surprised if it was Helena's hair on some of them; every time hers was cut it was sold for wigs and extensions. Diamond and sapphire brooches held up shimmering stolas, draped to emphasize heaving bosoms.

"I don't see old Max yet," he said, scanning the crowd. "Could he be inside already?"

"You know he hasn't been well lately, Athanasius, especially after his last visit to the palace."

"I forgot. But this is my night. He'll be here. I know it."

When their turn came, a footman announced their arrival while their names were checked off the guest list on a tablet. Once inside the expansive audience hall, however, the lack of any real reception for Athanasius hit him hard with the crushing reality that nobody was here to see his play. They were here to be seen. That included his lead actor, the comic Latinus, whom Athanasius was able to pick out through the towering Phrygian marble columns. He was standing under the extravagant frieze on the far wall, easy smiles as always, talking to their mutual lawyer, Pliny the Younger.

"Latinus should be backstage in the courtyard getting ready for his performance," Athanasius complained to Helena.

"This is his real performance, Athanasius." She sounded frustrated with him already, and the evening had barely begun. "And it's yours too. We need to play to our audience before and after. *Opus Gloria* is simply the middle act. You must accept that and let your work speak for itself. Here's your chance."

Athanasius turned to see the Empress Domitia floating toward them in a splendid, bejeweled dress. "Our guest of honor has arrived!" Domitia said as she embraced him and then kissed Helena. "You are the image of perfection, Helena, as always."

Domitia was flanked by two boys. She cheerfully introduced them as Vespasian and Domitian. With a start Athanasius realized that these were the sons of Flavius Clemens, the consul executed just that morning. They had a dazed look about them, understandably, and he could only imagine their terror now that they had to live under the same roof as the monster who had murdered their father.

"Helena, I have several very muscular gladiators and charioteers who wish to meet you in person," Domitia said with a wink. "You don't mind, Athanasius?"

"Not at all," he said as the empress dragged a reluctant Helena off and he waved her away with a smile.

He grabbed a crystal glass of wine from a floating silver tray and headed straight toward Latinus and Pliny. By the time he arrived, however, Latinus had managed to escape before Athanasius could scold him.

"You needn't worry, Athanasius," Pliny assured him with a wry smile. "Latinus is already putting on his fake breasts, face paint and costume."

Pliny was his friend and lawyer. But he was also a government magistrate and liaison for his public art with the Flavian administration. His job, everybody else had apparently agreed, was to even out Athanasius's complaints with calm explanations and assurances, and make sure the money came in as fast as Athanasius could spend it on Helena.

"I only hope he didn't have too much of this wine before the show." Athanasius swirled his wine and noticed the seal of Caesar engraved into the crystal. You could buy or free a few good slaves for the price of a single silver utensil, porcelain plate or crystal wine glass from the official collection at the Palace of the Flavians. You could also get your hands cut off if you stole it. He took another sip. "It's fabulous."

Pliny nodded. "Domitian's favorite. From some vineyard in Cappadocia, I think."

"Where is the Emperor? I don't see him."

"State business. He'll be down shortly and take his mark like Latinus. We're all actors tonight at the palace."

"My feelings exactly. Everybody would be in a better and more relaxed mood at the Pompey. Why the change in venue? You know we had to strip things out that would work on the stage at the Pompey but don't work here."

"The Pompey," said a deep, gravelly voice from behind with disapproval. "The greatest line ever uttered on that stage was 'Et tu, Brute?' Nothing you could pen will ever rival that."

Athanasius knew it was Ludlumus before he turned around to see his smirk.

The tall, silver-haired Ludlumus was a fixture in Rome, the son of prominent senator Lucius Licinius Sura, and a failed actor who had risen to run the Games.

"Pliny, why don't you tell Athanasius the real reason we're here instead of his precious, creaking, collapsing Pompey theater."

Athanasius felt his stomach sink in anticipation of new insult. But the well-mannered Pliny couldn't bring himself to deliver the bad news.

Ludlumus, on the other hand, was only too happy to be the bearer of bad tidings. "The reality, Athanasius, is that we make more money from tourists who come to see the Games in the summer by opening the Pompey to them at night. They pay to wander the empty stage and seats in hopes of seeing the ghost of Julius Caesar, not one of your ridiculous plays they could catch at any little provincial theater back home."

Athanasius looked at Pliny, who seemed embarrassed for him, and rightly so. It was probably Pliny's idea in the first place. He was fascinated with ghosts and always asked Athanasius to put one or two in his plays.

There was the sound of trumpets from the courtyard, informing guests that Caesar had arrived and that the play would begin shortly.

"Don't worry, Athanasius," Ludlumus said with a smile and wrapped a heavy arm around his shoulder. "You may be destined for insignificance, your name and plays forgotten, but tonight we honor your art, so-called. I am determined to finally make you interesting. Allow me to introduce you properly before the show."

They walked outside into the open-air peristyle, joining Helena and Domitia and the rest of the guests under the stars. The darkened stage was set up in the middle of the lit waters of the enormous fountain like an island. Latinus was already on it with his mask. Athanasius could see his silhouette with long hair and comically large bosoms.

Still, no sign of Domitian. Athanasius suddenly wondered if Domitian wished to dishonor him publicly by his absence. Then another trumpet blasted with the tone that cued the arrival of the emperor, and Athanasius was relieved to see the imperial procession of the Praetorian Guard led by the prefect Secundus enter the peristyle.

"And now for the evening's entertainment!" Ludlumus announced, and gestured to Athanasius as the Praetorian surrounded him. "I present to you Chiron, the mastermind of Dominium Dei!"

At first Athanasius wasn't quite sure what to think. Did Ludlumus just accuse him of being the head of the supersecret Christian sect Dominium Dei? Was it a nasty joke to steal some thunder from his play? Athanasius had heard all about Domitian's macabre party for the Senate the month before from old Maximus, who with the other senators was brought into a darkened hall filled with coffins, each engraved with a senator's name. Suddenly men in black burst out with swords and torches to terrorize them before taking their leave.

Surely this was an encore performance of sorts, Athanasius thought, and began to play the good sport and laugh out loud. "It seems my play has competition for your amusement!" he said. "Me!"

This prompted other guests to join him, which helped him feel better.

"Poor Latinus worries I want to replace him!" he called out.

The laughs kept coming, but then so did the Praetorian Guard with chains and leg irons. And neither Ludlumus, nor a stricken Helena nor even Domitia were smiling.

Jupiter! Athanasius thought. *They're serious!*

Domitia glared at Ludlumus. "What is the meaning of this?"

"Do something!" Helena ordered him.

"Out of my hands," Ludlumus said in what sounded like an earnest tone. "Caesar's orders. I only carry them out. I am truly sorry, Helena."

Helena rushed to embrace Athanasius before being pulled away by the Praetorians, who proceeded to clap him in leg irons and chains. The laughter began to die down as the picture before the party took an ominous visual shape of the playwright in chains.

Athanasius could no longer deny the sinking reality that his life was now on the line, and that it would take every bit of wit left in him to save it, starting with a simple declaration to all in earshot.

"I am innocent!" he stated simply and confidently.

Pliny rushed over to him.

"Say nothing, Athanasius," Pliny instructed as the Praetorians began to march him off toward the throne room inside. "Permit Domitian to be merciful to you. It's not over for you yet."

"Over?" Athanasius repeated, his voice rising. "I'm innocent. I'm not this villain Chiron. I've never killed a man, or torched a public building, or committed any crime of any kind!"

"I know, Athanasius. I'll find you a good lawyer."

"But you're my lawyer!"

As he was dragged away, Athanasius looked back to see Helena collapse to her knees. She had to be held up by a stricken, disbelieving Latinus, his own lip paint smeared and fake bosoms all disheveled.

7

The journey to the throne room was short and silent. The guards pushed Athanasius forward like a sheep to the slaughter. Dazed and humiliated, Athanasius caught curious glances from party guests, who whispered "conspirator" as they followed the procession.

How ironic, he thought as he looked around, that his arrest should have a more distinguished audience than any of his plays. If only Helena weren't here to witness this piece of theater.

A trumpet blast directed all eyes to the throne, where a resplendent Domitian now sat down in full dress imperial attire. No longer the host of a social gathering, he was the Emperor of Rome and ruler of the world. He looked around sharply at his groveling subjects and raised his right hand solemnly. The murmurs fell, a deathly silence filled the great hall, and a shiver passed over Athanasius.

The imperial throne room was the grandest of the palace, perhaps the entire empire. At the end of it, seated on his golden throne of judgment, was Domitian. To his right in rapt attention stood his favorite Egyptian Pharaoh Hound Sirius. To his left stood Ludlumus, his Master of the Games. Off to the side, behind a long table, were Caesar's notorious *delatores*, or informants, and the malicious *accusatores,* or prosecutors. They were mercenaries who papered over Domitian's executions in the guise of legal proceedings. They cared nothing for justice but only for themselves. Their heartless cruelty greased the wheels of tyranny with the blood of others.

So the jackals had already assembled, Athanasius thought as the Praetorian Guards brought him before their Lord and God. He looked around the throne room he had heard so much about but had never seen before. There were few pillars, and the ceiling was so long and high that only some miracle of invisible engineering held it up. The effect, intentional no doubt, was to diminish the spirit of any mortal man who had the terrible misfortune to enter this chamber.

The murmuring voices of the party guests outside in the peristyle rose and fell like the chorus of a Greek tragedy, which Athanasius realized was clearly in the making should his wit fail him. He looked over his shoulder as the great bronze doors closed with a definitive finality, shutting out his view of an ashen Helena and Latinus.

"Athanasius, I will defend you," whispered a voice, and Athanasius turned with relief to see Maximus at his side. "I am sorry I arrived late to your party, but hopefully I am in time for your trial."

"Surely this is a joke, Maximus. Like that party with the coffins that Domitian engraved with the names of senators."

"I'm afraid not, Athanasius," Maximus said in a low voice. "I just found out from Pliny like you did. Now listen to me. This is no time to say something clever or treat this like a joke. Because I assure you that while this sham of a trial may seem pure fiction, a death sentence from Caesar is not. Just answer the questions directly, Athanasius. Or look to me, and I will answer for you. The gods be with us."

Athanasius nodded and turned to face his accusers just as a gong sounded.

A curtain parted and out walked none other than the notorious prosecutor Aquilius Regulus. He was that rare senator who played to Domitian's worst suspicions and prosecuted his own colleagues. Athanasius had thought the unsavory character had long ago retired from criminal prosecution, but apparently the trial against Chiron was too tempting for this political mercenary to resist.

"He's the one who should be prosecuted," Maximus whispered.

Regulus stood behind a table across from Athanasius. He slapped a thick stack of papyrus papers on the table.

They had been watching him for a long time, Athanasius realized with dread, and even Ludlumus seemed surprised and delighted at this turn of events, as if he couldn't have planned it any better. Athanasius half-expected his rival to announce: "Behold, citizens of Rome, Regulus versus Maximus in the ultimate battle before Caesar for the life of Chiron!"

Instead, a solemn and suffocating silence filled the vast throne room. There was only the sound of Regulus shuffling through his voluminous papers, as if he were having trouble deciding where to even begin, the evidence being so overwhelming. At last he gathered himself, loosened his jaw like a would-be Cicero about to deliver an oration for the ages, then cleared his throat.

"You are the playwright Athanasius of Athens?"

"Yes, I am."

"Or are you?"

"You just said so yourself."

"No, I asked you."

Athanasius sighed. Games. They were not limited to the arena. "And I answered yes."

"Mmm..." Regulus murmured, like he was just warming up. "Are you a playwright, Athanasius? Or are you really an actor with two masks? In the mask of comedy, worn on the public stage of society, you are Athanasius of Athens, Greek playwright, citizen of Rome. In the other mask of tragedy, worn in the shadows of the underground, you are the notorious Chiron, general of Dominium Dei, the most wanted and dangerous man alive, perpetrator of murderous acts and conspiracy."

"I am not!" Athanasius declared for the record, fearful that any attempt at cleverness in his reply at this absurdity might pass over the dim heads of those assembled.

Maximus said, "You've heard the accused's plea, Regulus. Now where is your proof behind this baseless accusation?"

"Let us begin, as the playwrights are fond of saying, *in medias res,* in the middle of things." Regulus held up with a flourish a singular document for all to see. "The confession of the late consul Flavius Clemens, who plainly identifies the accused as Chiron."

There were several dramatic gasps from the other prosecutors for effect, as if they had not seen the confession before its introduction here at this mockery of a trial.

"I am not Chiron," Athanasius repeated. "And I doubt that is the true confession of Flavius Clemens, even if it bears the stamp of his signet ring. How convenient he's no longer here to be cross-examined by my counsel. Even so, your argument has no logic. I am not even a Christian. So how can I be Chiron?"

Athanasius glanced at Maximus, who nodded as if he had already prepared a line of defense for the charge of atheism.

"Lord and God Domitian and distinguished gentlemen," said Maximus, addressing Domitian with all the authority of his status as an elder statesman of Rome. "There is a simple test called the *tyche* that the court of Caesar has devised to determine whether one is guilty of atheism like the Christians. And that is simply to allow the accused to bow before Caesar and address him as Lord and God. It is said and has held true now for some decades that the Christian believer will bow before no other god but Jesus."

Domitian nodded his consent, and two Praetorian Guards brought out an altar and set it up.

Athanasius nodded eagerly, confident that he would be cleared. No *tyche* was going to keep him from Helena, and the public knew he was an atheist at heart. This memory would fade in time, and he would win them back.

Domitian led him in an invocation of the gods and the offering of some incense and wine to an image of himself. "Now the anathema."

"I curse the name of the dead Jew known as Jesus the Christ!" Athanasius said loudly with a ringing voice, and then bowed low before Domitian. "There is only one Lord and God of the universe, and his name is Caesar."

The echoes of his curse faded, and the entire throne room grew very quiet. However much the public at large despised Christians, they harbored little respect for hypocrites and turncoats. While he may not have been a Judas to the cause of Christ, everybody pretty much knew he had betrayed his atheism. The time to repair this damage to his reputation and his plays might take longer than he expected. But he had passed the test.

Then came the sound of clapping hands.

"Bravo, Athanasius!" said Regulus, who then picked up a scroll from the long table and pointed it at him like a priestly augur. "But if you are not a Christian, then how do you explain this?"

With a flourish Regulus unfurled the scroll to reveal the title letters of the Book of Revelation. More gasps at this seemingly incontrovertible proof that Athanasius had just lied to the face of Caesar.

Athanasius could only imagine the Praetorian had taken it from his study almost as soon as he and Helena had left the villa for this debacle of a premiere party. If so, all of this had been a set-up from the beginning. The ending, therefore, Athanasius was beginning to believe with a sinking feeling, was already written.

"And how do we know this evidence wasn't planted?" Maximus asked, cutting off Athanasius before he could reply. It seemed Maximus would rather he explain nothing at all and instead cast doubt on his possession of the scroll altogether.

Regulus gestured to a side entrance and cried out, "The witness!"

The blood-red tapestries parted, and there stood Helena.

8

In the name of all the bogus gods, Athanasius swore to himself as Helena was ushered into the hall. They were going to make her blame him and suffer for it. Her eyes were swollen from tears, but she held her head high and tried not to look at him.

"Helena of Rome needs no introduction, of course," Regulus stated, and then addressed her like a physician at the deathbed of a child. "I am so sorry your betrothed has put you in this position. But could you clearly acknowledge for the court that you are indeed Helena of Rome and will testify truthfully?"

Her long and lovely throat contracted as she swallowed and said, "I am, and I will."

"And have you ever seen this Book of Revelation in the villa you share with the accused?"

"No."

Regulus didn't like the answer and repeated the question. "I remind you that you are under oath before Caesar, beautiful Helena. Can you say without a shadow of a doubt that you have never seen this banned book of lies in your home?"

She feigned a careless shrug. "Do I look like much of a reader?"

Her response prompted some laughs among the magistrates and irritation on the part of Regulus.

Good girl, Athanasius thought.

"I'm disappointed, fair Helena," Regulus said. "Next time take a keener interest in the secret affairs of your lover. That way you won't repeat your mistake with Athanasius. Next witness!"

Out from the same side entrance came Athanasius's faithful secretary, Cornelius, an orphan whom Athanasius bought and freed the same day. The boy couldn't read, which was why Athanasius had him organize his papers. What could he possibly have to say?

"You are Cornelius, slave of Athanasius of Athens?" Regulus thundered, going in for the jugular.

"Secretary," Cornelius replied proudly, upgrading his status for the court.

Regulus asked, "Have you seen this scroll before?"

"Yes," Cornelius answered, to Athanasius's shock.

"And where did you see this scroll?"

Cornelius pointed his finger at Helena. "In her hands today in my master's library. She said she was tidying up. But I saw her hide it among his scrolls."

"Enough!" Athanasius shouted. "The scroll is mine. If Helena found it in error and put it back among my many books, it is no fault of hers. She could not have known what it was. The fault is all mine. Please excuse her and my faithful secretary Cornelius."

Regulus, smiling in triumph, dismissed Helena and the boy. The boy suddenly looked downcast and very sorry he had said anything at all. Helena, weeping again, couldn't bear to even look over her bare shoulder at Athanasius on her way out of the throne room.

"Well, now," Regulus said after they were gone, gathering steam. "Now that we've established that you do indeed have in your possession this banned Book of Revelation, could you please explain why?"

"I'm a playwright. There are a lot of revelations out there. I'm intellectually curious. That doesn't make me a Christian."

"Mmm. Tell us then, Athanasius, if you are not a Christian, what do you make of this so-called Book of Revelation?"

"Looks like a lot of third-act trouble to me," he said, eliciting a couple of helpful snickers and a trace of a smile from Domitian. "Jesus has not returned as promised, the Christians are losing hope, and now the last living disciple who was with Jesus is old and about to die. It only makes sense to leave the faithful with this hope of a *deus ex machina.* It may be good superstition, but it's terrible dramatic writing."

Regulus, however, was not amused. "What about these mysterious symbols you have drawn in the margins?"

Regulus pushed the open scroll to his face, and Athanasius pulled his head back in annoyance. He looked down and saw that the annotation symbol was indeed his:

"There is no mystery here," Athanasius answered. "It's been a common mark for Greek scribes for several centuries now. It's a *Chi-Ro* annotation, a combination of the Greek letters *Chi* and *Ro.* I use it to mark passages in my own works and those of others that I might want to review later."

"Mmm." Regulus made it sound sinister. "Has not the Dei adopted the *Chi* character as its symbol of the death cross? And is there not a little-known story somewhere in Greek mythology—in which you have inferred to us you are so deeply steeped—about the centaur Chiron who sacrifices himself to save others? Much like Jesus in the Christian superstition?"

"I vaguely recall something like that. There are so many versions and re-imaginations of classic myths, I'd be surprised if there wasn't one. That doesn't make me Chiron of the Dei."

"No, of course not," Regulus said. "You've already cursed the name of Christ and stated for the record that you are not a Christian. You are Athanasius of Athens."

"That is correct."

"Yet isn't it true you are actually from Corinth?" He glanced down at a paper. "From a family of...potters." He looked up. "Wait, that's only half the story. Your mother's side of the family are...tanners. They own a large tannery outside Corinth."

"That's right. So what?"

"So why lie?"

Athanasius refused to be humiliated before Roman high society for the proud work of his ancestors back in Greece, even if he had in fact hidden it from most when he went to university in Athens and then onto Rome as a playwright. Great playwrights came from Athens, according to Rome, not Corinth.

"I wanted to make good in Rome," Athanasius said. "Is that a crime? So I became Athanasius of Athens. So what? End of story."

"Or not," Regulus accused. "Your family's tannery turns sheepskin and hides into leather coats, boots, pouches and the like?"

"Yes."

"Are the hides skinned from animals at the tannery?"

"Some. I don't know the percentages. I was a child."

"As a child, did you ever hunt down any of these animals? Say, with a bow and arrow? You are, I'm told, a champion archer. You've even hunted with Caesar at his Alban country estate?"

"Yes, and I let Caesar win. What is your point?"

"My point," Regulus said loudly, as if drums were rolling in the background, "is that you're not a playwright." He paused for final effect. "You're a butcher! A butcher like Chiron and the Dei who have been chopping up Roman officials like so much meat."

"I am not!" Athanasius shouted, breaking character of the cool wit and lunging for the prosecutor in his chains. Maximus pulled him back.

Caesar looked down from his seat of judgment at Regulus, who wandered over to his voluminous stack of scrolls and tablets and removed the tiniest little sheet of paper. It was so slight he held it delicately like a feather, lest a sudden breeze should blow it away.

"Oh, really?" Regulus intoned. "Then how do you explain this?"

Regulus held it up for all to see and said, "Behold the sign of Chiron! See it on his note to Caesar! The note that came with the severed finger of Caesar's astrologer!"

At the bottom was a large *Chi-Ro* symbol as signature.

There were moans and murmurs as Regulus walked a circle to show the Chiron note in one hand and marked-up Book of Revelation in the other.

Maximus shrank back, as if this note were the final nail in a coffin for Athanasius of Athens, a coffin that had his name engraved on it long before this trial.

"We have the confession of Flavius Clemens," Regulus reminded Domitian and all assembled, summing up the state's case. "We have the testimony of the accused's slave, the Book of Revelation in the accused's possession, and the accused's use of the symbol of Chiron. Above all, we have the confession of the accused that he is indeed not who he has pretended to be all these years— a playwright with hands free of callouses or any sign of a common laborer—but rather a butcher with blood-stained hands."

More deadly silence, itself a verdict.

At that point, Maximus did the only thing possible.

"The state makes its case on two rather flimsy pieces of circumstantial evidence," Maximus began, taking a last stab at casting doubt on the state's case. "First, the so-called confession of Flavius Clemens could have been coerced while he was in custody, or the former consul may well have pointed the finger at Athanasius merely to divert Caesar's attention from the real Chiron."

Athanasius nodded. He liked this tactic.

"As for the second piece of evidence, mere possession of the Book of Revelation doesn't make Athanasius a Christian any more than the chief prosecutor's possession of Cicero's book *Consolation* makes him an orator and philosopher."

Even Domitian smiled at the dig, giving Athanasius a flicker of hope.

"So it is obvious the chief prosecutor knows his case has feet of clay, or he would not have attempted to bring the twin charges of atheism and conspiracy against the accused. If he were confident in one, he would not have brought the other. So he brought them both. But Regulus cannot prove the accused is a Christian after the accused dramatically testified publicly that he is not, surely obliterating any support from that underground if he ever had it. And he cannot prove the wild speculation that the accused is Chiron beyond the testimony of a dead man, which should not even be admissible. As it is, Regulus has neither leg to stand on. So we rest our defense before Your Humanitas and throw ourselves before the mercy of the judgment seat of Caesar."

Domitian rose to his feet and stepped down from his throne to render his final judgment. Each footstep sounded more ominous the closer he came. As he stood before

Athanasius, Domitian grasped his chains and looked at him as he would if forced to put down his hound Sirius. The balding head beneath the wig, the weak eyes, the cruel smile—he was a piece of human excrement and seemed to know it.

"Your final word, Athanasius?" Domitian asked. "What say you?"

"There are no gods in heaven—nor on earth," Athanasius told Domitian for all to hear. "You are no god, and I am no Chiron. There are no well-devised conspiracies by masterminds on earth. There are only men, and most of them are fools."

Athanasius could see the fury in Domitian's eyes, mixed with fear.

"We despise those who despise our laws and religion," Domitian announced. "But let us show mercy on the man Athanasius himself. Let us not fight the conspiracy of those cowards who hide in the shadows and carry out justice in the dark of night. Let us deal with this justly in the light of day."

Athanasius braced himself. It was common knowledge that Domitian's rehearsed preamble about mercy was an omen that foreshadowed his most ruthless sentences.

"Therefore, we will not allow this man to die by crucifixion or old-style execution upon the Gemonian Stairs."

Athanasius breathed a momentary sigh of relief. In an old-style execution, the condemned man was stripped, his head fastened to a wooden fork and he was flogged to death. It was a long, drawn-out ordeal. Perhaps Domitian would only exile him. There would still be a chance for him and Helena. There would still be hope for his life.

"Rather," Domitian continued, "allow him to die with dignity. Allow Athanasius to die in the arena. Allow him to die for our pleasure and as a warning to others who would defy our ways."

Athanasius felt ill in the pit of his stomach. His head started spinning. "No, your excellency," he said with shortness of breath. "No."

"He shall die tomorrow morning," Domitian announced. "After a night in the Tullianum prison."

Well, that was that. Only those sent to die went to the Tullianum, and he had never heard of a last-minute reprieve.

"Furthermore," Domitian said, raising his right hand in divine retribution. "Your Lord and God decrees that all inscriptions referring to Athanasius of Athens must be effaced, and productions of his work cease immediately from any public venue, and all copies of his plays be removed from every library throughout the empire and burned. May his memory be erased from our generation, and may the next never know the name of Athanasius of Athens."

"No!" Maximus cried out and rushed to Domitian, falling to his knees. It was a spectacle that Athanasius knew only put the senator's own life in jeopardy. "Mercy, Your Humanitas! Mercy!"

"Caesar shall show his mercy to the people of Rome by condemning to death the treacherous Chiron of Dominium Dei, who calls himself Athanasius of Athens."

Athanasius glared at Domitian as the Praetorian moved in to take him away. If he was indeed lost, Athanasius decided to make the most of it while he still had a voice, a last chance to inspire the silent majority around him with a call to action.

"Let no one mourn for me!" Athanasius shouted, shocking the magistrates. "For surely you shall follow me, all of you, as long as this monster lives!"

He saw Ludlumus and the prefect Secundus exchange cool glances. Not that they or anyone else besides Helena and Maximus would dare intervene on his behalf.

Domitian himself looked bewildered at this public challenge, but glancing around seemed to realize he had already meted out his justice and there was nothing to be gained from arguing with a condemned man.

"The man who killed the gods in his plays can't save himself!" Ludlumus announced to nervous laughter.

"Your gods won't save you, Domitian!" Athanasius shouted to the back of Caesar as he was dragged out the side exit. "Neither will the stars! You mock those you will follow shortly, and we will be waiting for you!"

But the doors had closed, shutting him off from the ears of everyone forever. The last thing he saw was Ludlumus waving goodbye with an old hand signal from the theater:

Exit, stage left.

2

The death march to the Tullianum prison ended in the Forum at the base of Capitoline Hill, where the ancients used to quarry. The prison was really nothing but a hole in the ground to hold very important prisoners until their execution. Common-day criminals were usually marched up the hill's adjoining Gemonian Stairs and beheaded, their skulls bouncing down the flight of stone steps like so many melons. So in some ways his stay at the Tullianum was an honor. He was about to join the ranks of foreign generals like Jugurtha and Vercingetorix, and domestic conspirators like Publius Cornelius Lentulus Sura and the apostles Peter and Paul.

The prison was underground with two levels. The guards were on the upper level, the prisoners kept in the lower level. The walls were made of blocks of volcanic tuff rock. To Athanasius, who was being processed on the upper level, the effect was that of standing in the bottom of a small pyramid with a flat top.

"Interesting accommodations," Athanasius quipped to mask his horror. "Do you have any better?"

The warden, a surly old fart with a face that looked like a smashed melon, told the Praetorian escort that the prisoner's armor had arrived. With a mixture of dread and curiosity, Athanasius suddenly wondered what cruel fate Ludlumus had devised for him in the arena tomorrow.

The guards unlocked his chains to strip him of his toga and tunic. Now he stood naked but for his loincloth. They slipped a red tunic over his head, and over that a centurion's *subarmalis* or leather armor.

"Look at this, Chiron," the warden said, reading from a note. "You get a 'belt of truth' and 'breastplate of righteousness.' Me thinks this is some of the 'spiritual armor' that one of our former inmates, Paul, used to instruct his followers in Ephesus to sport in spiritual battle. Too bad it couldn't save his head from Nero's ax man. But I'll bet you make a fine spectacle in it tomorrow."

They tied a legionary belt around his waist, then strapped him into a heavy *lorica segmentata* with polished armored plates. Athanasius knew the gleaming plates were for effect in the arena, to shine under the beating sun and highlight his own blood once the blade of a sword or spear had slipped through the plates.

Ludlumus was going to make him fight to the death. The depths of this impending public spectacle of his humiliation had now moved him beyond self-pity and a sense of loss to pure, unadulterated rage. He knew in his heart that this was the last moment before the arena that he would be free of chains, and despite the odds of one man against four guards—two Praetorian, two prison— and a warden, he would get no better.

The warden said, "You'll get your 'shield of faith' and 'sword of the spirit' tomorrow, just before you're launched into the arena. For now, take the 'helmet of salvation.'"

Athanasius took the centurion's helmet from the warden. It had brass accents and the infamous red plume. The plume, he knew, was less for décor than for the optical effect of making a centurion look taller.

"You know, I wore a helmet like this once to a costume party with my girlfriend, the model Helena," he told the guards, and he could tell by their response that they all knew of Helena and had probably fantasized about her every time they passed a statue in her image. "Funny thing is, my eyes still only reached the tip of her nose, and I was staring at her nostrils the whole evening."

They started laughing at the comic playwright, who was certainly different from the usual vermin. Then Athanasius smashed the helmet into the warden's head. The warden cried out as his face split in a bloody gash.

"A considerable improvement," Athanasius said, grabbing the sword from the warden's side and spinning around in time to drive it into the gut of the oncoming Praetorian from behind. Athanasius put his foot to the stomach of the Praetorian and pushed him into the other one. They both fell back onto the stone floor.

The two remaining prison guards circled Athanasius with a long chain between them, lingering beyond the reach of his sword. They crisscrossed him with the chain, tightening it around him.

Athanasius rushed the closest guard while he could and tackled him to the ground. As they struggled, he heard the clank of chains from behind, followed by a blow to the back of his head, and he blacked out.

Athanasius awoke in the darkness of the dungeon below, chained to the wall in his heavy armor. At one time prisoners had to be lowered through the floor of the upper room. But he had a dim recollection of being dragged in his armor down a flight of stone steps to this dungeon, all to the murderous threats of the bellowing warden.

His head throbbed inside its "helmet of salvation," and his shoulders drooped from the weight of his armor. His body felt dead to the world, his spirit crushed from the realization that he was about to depart this earth with so many unfinished dreams. The end always came more swiftly than the characters in his plays ever expected, and so it was with his own life.

In the silence he heard only the distant sound of running water somewhere, and then made out a small cistern drain in the dimness. It was probably connected to the Cloaca Maxima—Rome's central sewer known as the Great Drain.

He ran his dry tongue over his teeth, touched his fingers together and squeezed his toes to confirm he still possessed these and other bodily appendages. The warden and guards would have killed him on the spot were he not already condemned to a public execution. To deny the mob its entertainment seemed a worse crime than murder in Rome.

Athanasius ruminated over his sorry twist of fate and what would become of Helena. I have become the very tragic hero that I mock in my comedies, he thought. Now only my ghost will haunt the Pompey like Julius Caesar—if Pliny can figure a way Rome can profit from it. Athanasius could already hear the tour operators: "He killed the gods in his plays only to be killed by their wrath. Hear ye and be warned, citizens of Rome!" That's how he would play it, and raise the tour price. Two ghosts were better than one, and the new one should at least bring a sense of humor. Yes, Pliny would make sure of it.

But the thought passed as he realized the cold, cruel truth that while it might keep him alive to some, his body would decompose in the earth, or be fed to dogs, and the glory and immortality he sought as a playwright would die with him in the grave.

It's over. The show is over, like Ludlumus said.

Oh, Jupiter, he prayed. Spare me, and I will serve you. I will never mock you again under any name. I will write plays for you, and mock those like me who mock you. People will buy your idols and make sacrifices to you.

He knew it was the kind of pointless prayer that Helena made to gods who were not there but figments of imagination. But he took comfort in knowing she was praying for him too.

And then, as if by magic, he heard a noise outside the door. A key rattled in the lock.

A faint flicker of hope began to stir inside him. Perhaps Domitian wished to show himself generous and merciful! Perhaps Pliny and Maximus had bargained him a reprieve, an offer to write a glorious ode to Domitian in exchange for freedom! Or even just Helena to say her goodbye. To see her face one last time would be enough.

Yes, perhaps salvation had come.

The door swung open, the light of a torch splashing on the dirty floor, and in walked Ludlumus.

"Third-act trouble, Athanasius?"

Athanasius propped his tired back against the wet wall and spoke in a dry, cracked voice. "You're the one who will pray for *deus ex machina*, Ludlumus. It's only a matter of time before Domitian does to you what he's done to me."

Ludlumus shut the door and hung the oil lamp on an iron hook nailed to the ceiling. The effect cast light on him like an actor on the stage. He removed a clay tablet and stylus from the fold of his toga. "So that's your confession, Athanasius? You are innocent and Caesar is guilty?"

"Yes."

Athanasius could feel Ludlumus stare at him thoughtfully, and then watched him put away the tablet and stylus. Whatever was about to be said, he realized, was not going to be recorded.

"And how did you come to this conclusion?" Ludlumus demanded.

"There is no Chiron, is there, Ludlumus? You invented him."

Ludlumus actually clapped his hands. "Bravo, Athanasius."

Athanasius began to breathe faster, his mind racing. His hunch about Chiron was right, but it didn't explain everything. "Why? How? You certainly didn't invent Dominium Dei, did you? How could you? It's been around for decades."

"True, but instead of the Dei infiltrating Rome, Rome has infiltrated the Dei. Now Caesar can assassinate senators or other threats to the empire and pin the blame on Christians, whom we then feed to the Games. It's all economical."

"Economical?!" Athanasius exclaimed.

"All right then, let's call it...poetic," Ludlumus said. "Like the poetry of the Flavian Amphitheater itself. Rome's temple of death was financed with the treasures that Vespasian looted from the Jews after Titus destroyed their great temple almost 30 years ago. Of course, the Judean War cost a million lives on both sides. So to pacify the mobs back home, the Flavians built their eponymous coliseum as a political weapon. By making the Games the center of our universe, they've practically been getting away with anything else ever since."

"So the Dei is an imperial organization, not Christian," Athanasius stated for his own understanding. "Only the Christians don't know it, do they?"

"No. Too bad you won't live to tell them."

Something wasn't right, Athanasius thought. But he couldn't put his finger on it, and he couldn't let Ludlumus go yet without learning of Helena.

"What is to happen to Helena? Tell me, Ludlumus. You owe me at least that much."

"Why torture yourself even more, Athanasius?" Ludlumus asked, although he seemed quite pleased to go on. "If you must know, Domitian is confiscating her instead of the house on Caelian Hill. She will be allowed to keep it, but must remain on call for whenever her emperor requires her affection."

"No!" Athanasius screamed until his throat went raw and twisted like a rag. And then the tears that he had been holding back for hours burst forth like a flood, and he sobbed.

"If it's any consolation, Athanasius, I finally made you interesting. Helena and all Rome now think you are Chiron. As for the Christians, some might even mourn you as a hero."

Athanasius lifted his head and through tears of rage looked at Ludlumus. "Caelus the astrologer."

"What about him?"

"That business in Ephesus was something else. Something that went wrong. Domitian didn't want him dead. Not his precious astrologer."

Ludlumus paused, as if mulling over whether he would answer, then apparently decided that Athanasius was a dead man and it didn't matter. "We control the Dei at the very top. But as you can imagine, there are far more dupes who have no idea who they are really working for. Some true believers took matters into their own hands with Caelus."

"So that's what rattled Domitian, and why you had to produce Chiron in public. You, Domitian's little dog."

"You have it all wrong, Athanasius. My stage is much bigger than the arena now. Your trial tonight should be proof enough for you. Think about it. Caesar says he is Lord and God. Yet the Games control his destiny; if he loses the mob, he loses Rome. I am the Master of the Games. Therefore, I control Caesar. And if I control Caesar, then I, Ludlumus, am the true god of this world and hold the keys to Hades."

"Then I'll go and prepare a special place for you down there."

Ludlumus yawned at the empty threat, signaling that confession time was over.

"I had it in the back of my head to come and free you, Athanasius. To call it all a big mistake. To keep Chiron out there, and to make Domitian look merciful. If only for Helena's sake. But once again you've proven that any thought that comes into your head must come out of your mouth. Now you have to die. You know too much. Far more than I would have given you credit for. Interrogator!"

The door opened to reveal several torches bobbing in the stairwell, and a decorated Praetorian saluted. "Sir!"

"Cut out his tongue and bring it outside," Ludlumus instructed as he stepped out. "I'll have a man from the palace kitchen waiting for you. Domitian would like to eat it with his favorite wine tomorrow evening to celebrate Chiron's death. He will then enjoy the model Helena for dessert."

"Yes, sir."

"Oh, and no further questions for the prisoner—or you might as well cut out your own tongue."

"Understood, sir."

With that Athanasius watched Ludlumus turn his back on him forever and stride out while the Praetorian interrogator marched in, his black cape fluttering as he closed the door behind him. Slowly, carefully, he removed a short, thick blade and let it glint in the dim light.

"Trust me, Chiron," he said. "This won't take long."

10

Athanasius watched the Praetorian interrogator place his torch in a metal holder on the wall and face him. There was something familiar about the man as he moved, but Athanasius wasn't sure what it was exactly. He was one of those sinister political officers whose uniform and helmet signaled the high rank of tribune. But he was young, mid-20s like himself, which hinted at family connections. His rank did not represent the number of soldiers under his command, but rather the value of the information he handled on a daily basis for the empire, information extracted from very important prisoners like foreign generals or alleged domestic conspirators such as Chiron.

"My name is Quintus Marcus, and I will be your interrogator," he said with a soothing voice, making his introduction.

Perhaps this interrogator was one of Rome's professional maniacs who considered his particular line of work his "art." Indeed, the manner in which the interrogator carried himself, the way he crouched down and slowly unrolled a leather wrap on the floor to reveal several additional knives to choose from, conveyed the distinct impression that he put exacting care into his work.

"Now pay attention, Chiron. This is important."

Slowly Marcus rose holding the short, thick knife. So, Athanasius thought glumly, he was sticking with that one.

"The formal method of interrogation, recently amended by the palace, requires the interrogator to first cut off the prisoner's genitalia and stuff them down his throat," he explained as Athanasius couldn't help but squeeze his legs together. "Once the prisoner has swallowed some of what he is choking on, and regurgitated the rest, he'll usually be in a mood to talk. Then, and only after you are absolutely convinced that the prisoner has given up all the information he knows, you can cut out his tongue. Or, if ordered, slice his throat open to kill him. But you must be certain he has already swallowed everything or you might get some of it all over yourself."

Athanasius had no doubts as to the sincerity of his words and felt bile rise in the back of his throat. He swallowed hard and clenched his jaw so tight he felt a tooth crack. The welcome pain diverted the terror that had seized his body. His hope was that the man was professional enough to make the actual cut clean and quick, once he stopped talking.

As if reading his mind, the interrogator produced a small brick that Athanasius, from his days in the family tannery, knew was a whetting stone.

"As I'm told you know, Chiron, a dull blade only makes your job more difficult. So it's vital your blade be in peak condition."

Marcus set his knife at an angle to the rough side of the stone.

"Now I run my knife across the stone at least seven times, sometimes a dozen if I must. Then I turn the knife over and sharpen the other side likewise."

This Marcus did before flipping the stone to its finer side and repeating the process on both sides of the blade. Each slow, measured stroke was hypnotic in its horror.

"Not quite finished yet." Marcus put away the whetting stone and produced a small iron rod. "After the stone sharpening, you must hone the knife by removing any burrs or rough edges. Only then is the job finished."

He ran the knife along the sides of the sharpening iron until he was satisfied. Then he put the iron rod away and wiped the blade with his black cape.

"Here," he said and held out the knife to Athanasius.

Athanasius stared at the glistening blade. "If you are suggesting that I should cut out my own tongue, my chains preclude such an act."

"Then we shall have to remedy that," Marcus said, and to Athanasius's amazement began to unlock his chains.

Athanasius looked down as Marcus bent over to remove his leg irons and realized he could bring his hands down on the back of the tribune's head or knee him in the face. But the act of being freed from his chains confused him.

"What are you doing?" Athanasius asked as Marcus stood up and the two looked each other in the eye. "What form of torture is this?"

"Take it," Marcus told him, putting his knife in his hand. "See how it feels for you."

Athanasius grasped the knife and felt its fine, balanced weight. "I don't understand. I could kill you with this right now."

"And go where?" Marcus asked him. "There are guards upstairs. Your only chance for escape is to walk out of here as me."

"You?"

"Now strip. Hurry. We don't have much time."

Utterly astonished, Athanasius didn't argue as he and Marcus quickly exchanged uniforms. Soon Athanasius was dressed as a tribune, and Marcus his interrogator stood clad in the mock Christian armor of a prisoner condemned to death.

"You'll need this." Marcus removed a key ring from his finger and handed it to Athanasius.

As Athanasius took it, it clicked open to reveal the seal of Chiron hidden beneath. "You? You're Chiron?"

"I tried to be. But the Dei smashed everything. Clemens, you, and soon enough me. I cannot hide for long as a Christian in Caesar's court. I know too much for them to let me live."

"The Dei is imperial," Athanasius stated, testing to see if Marcus possessed as much information in his position within the Praetorian.

Marcus nodded. "You know the Omega, but not the Alpha. But I have no time to explain if you are to escape. I'm already dead. You stay in here, you're dead too."

"Then tell me how I get out."

"By drinking this."

Marcus produced a small vial and handed it to a reluctant Athanasius.

"What is this?"

"Strength for your journey ahead. Go on. It will keep you awake."

It would be a strange trap indeed for Marcus to free him only to poison him, Athanasius concluded, and drank the potion in one gulp. "Foul stuff," he said, gagging. "Now what?"

"The Cloaca Maxima."

Athanasius started. The Great Drain was Rome's primary sewer and cesspool of all waste that flowed from the slums and latrines. Athanasius stared at the cistern in the floor, which was a very small hole. "I'm not crawling through that."

"No," Marcus said. "There's only a small tributary under there, and you would drown."

"Then how exactly am I supposed to escape?"

"You will leave this prison dressed as me and pray the guards don't look beyond your uniform and rank," Marcus told him. "You will cross the Forum to the Basilica Julia courthouse. Take cover under the building's long portico along Sacred Way, and follow it all the way to the end of the block, then turn right. Under the courthouse steps, on the south side of the building, is a loose grating over a service entrance tunnel to the Cloaca Maxima. An agent called the Ferryman will be waiting for you in a small boat. He'll take you down the tunnels and out to the Tiber. From there you'll follow the river to the port at Ostia where a ship will be waiting for you. On board is a trunk with further instructions and everything you need. You will open it with the key ring on your finger. If you don't run into trouble, you should make it in an hour."

This was not at all what Athanasius had been praying for. At least in the arena he would die in public and perhaps find some way to make a final statement for his life. This plan risked him dying in a gutter. An ignoble end, if ever there was one. And yet it was still his only real chance of escaping death for the moment.

Athanasius said, "So come morning, I'll be long gone by the time they come back down here. They'll find you in the cell, and you explain how I overtook and chained you? Is that it?"

Marcus shook his head. "No. You will lock my chains now and cut out my tongue."

"I will not!"

"Then we will both die for nothing," Marcus said, his patience finally wearing thin. "Athanasius of Athens, Chiron, must die tomorrow. If they know you have escaped, if this secret gets out, then they will use the Dei to hunt you down, slaughter Clemens' surviving children, and round up even more innocent Christians in reprisal. Is that what you want?"

Not really, thought Athanasius. But there was no guarantee that all Marcus described would come to pass anyway. "They will know that you are not me."

"Only if they look hard enough. But they have no reason to suspect anything—unless you fail to escape Rome without being caught or recognized. Even then, they'll be too concerned with saving their own heads to report their suspicions."

Suddenly, Athanasius knew why he'd felt strange with this tribune's manner when he first saw him, and it had little to do with the man's devotion to his craft or his superstition. Marcus looked more than a bit like him in build. Not quite exactly, but almost.

Athanasius stood flat-footed, unable to move. "Why, Marcus?"

"Because my Lord did the same for me. Now cut out my tongue, before a guard comes down to find out what is taking so long. Hurry, or we both die and my sacrifice is in vain."

As much as he wanted to live, and as innocent as he knew he was, Athanasius hesitated with the knife. "This is insane," he muttered. "There must be another way."

"There is no other way." Marcus was now barking orders to him. "You will cut out my tongue, per your orders from the Master of the Games and the Emperor Domitian. You will then use the hilt of your sword to beat my face black and blue to knock me out and dull the pain. Call it resistance. My face will swell under the helmet, and the disfigurement will complete my transformation. You will leave with my tongue and hand it to one of the kitchen staff from the palace waiting outside in the street. The emperor wants to feast on your tongue tomorrow evening to celebrate your demise."

Athanasius felt his stomach swirl at the thought but nodded his agreement to the tribune.

"Fine," Marcus said. "Now, cut my tongue off. I sharpened my knife well to make a clean, quick cut. I pray you really are a butcher."

Athanasius drew out the knife and, trembling, put it up to Marcus's mouth. Marcus stuck out his tongue. Athanasius pulled it out further with one hand, while his other hand held the knife just above the tongue midway. Athanasius stared into the serene eyes of Marcus, who blinked once, as if on cue to proceed.

Athanasius made the cut. It was a quick slice and went clean through the tongue until it hit a snag at the very end. Marcus's eyes went wild, and he threw his head back against the wall in a cry of agony.

Athanasius quickly raised the butt of his sword and smashed it against Marcus's helmet and face four times until he slid down the wall in his chains to the floor. Blood was everywhere. Athanasius leaned down to where the tongue dangled over the soldier's chin strap, hanging by a thread, and cut it off.

He looked at it in his bloody hand and almost let it slip away. He grabbed a small cloth strip from the leather pouch and wrapped the tongue. Then he used the inside of his cape to wipe the blood off his hands and breastplate.

Athanasius stepped out of the lower dungeon and locked the door behind him, sealing off Marcus to his fate. He felt the weight of Marcus's tongue, wrapped in the blood-soaked cloth in his hand, and walked up the narrow steps to the upper level. He kept his face down and held up the bloody wrap to draw the eyes of the guards. As he solemnly made for the exit to the street, it was all he could do to avoid glancing at the warden, whose bandaged face he was curious to see. He had almost reached the gate to the outside when the warden called out after him. "Tribune!"

Athanasius froze in the dim light and cocked his ear. He did not want to face the man.

The warden said, "You missed a spot."

Athanasius looked down to see a drop of blood on his breastplate. Without turning around, he bobbed his helmet up and down and used his free hand to grasp his cape and wipe off the blood. Then he waved off the warden and walked outside into the night.

Only when Athanasius had gone a good ten paces down the street did he dare look back. There was nobody outside the prison entrance. The warden had gone back inside.

Heaving a heavy sigh of relief, he turned to make a run for it and suddenly stopped. Blocking his way in the middle of the street was none other than Domitian's Pharaoh Hound, Sirius, who let out a slow, menacing growl and flashed his teeth, wet with hungry drool.

"Sirius! No growling!" came a muffled shout from out of the dark.

Athanasius turned to see a light in the public latrine near the Senate House across the street. It must be the kitchen staffer Marcus had said was coming for his tongue. He was apparently the royal dog-walker as well, and he was taking a dump on Caesar's time.

Suddenly Sirius started barking all the louder at him, his black eyes fixed on the tongue in his hand, and Athanasius knew he had only seconds to make a decision.

11

The public latrine near the Senate House was one of the most delightful in Rome. The lanky African palace slave named Julius wasn't allowed to use it during the day when the senators conversed and conducted all manner of business. So he made it a habit to indulge himself at night when the Forum was mostly deserted. The marble seats had back support in the form of beautifully sculpted dolphins. Above the seats were decorated niches with statues of the gods and heroes. And a cheerful fountain tickled the ears. Best of all, the water that ran continuously below was so fast in this part of the city, there was hardly any odor.

Life really didn't get much better, Julius thought.

He had been enjoying his nightly reprieve from walking Sirius when his de facto master interrupted him by barking loudly.

Julius cursed, stood up from his comfortable throne and washed his hands in a bowl filled with fresh water. He then removed his tunic from its hook on the wall, slipped it on and hurried outside to quiet Sirius before complaints were registered with the palace.

But when he stepped outside, there was no sign of the Pharaoh Hound, only a Praetorian tribune holding what must be the tongue of Chiron that Domitian had ordered be brought to the palace kitchen for preparation and proper seasoning.

"Per the emperor's request, courtesy of the Tullianum prison."

Julius took the tongue and looked around. "Where's Sirius?"

"Who?"

"Caesar's hound."

"What hound?"

Julius looked at the impatient tribune and realized his place. "My apologizes, Tribune. He must be chasing something. I'll be after him."

The tribune nodded and headed north toward the prison at the base of Capitoline Hill.

Julius had no desire to follow in that direction, and instead turned south past the Senate and down the Street of Bankers, whistling here and there. "Sirius! Sirius!" A moment later, when he looked over his shoulder, the tribune had vanished into the night.

Athanasius walked quickly past the prison. Here the Street of Bankers sloped up into Banker Hill Road, and he followed it around Capitoline Hill toward the home of Senator Maximus.

He knew he was blowing his rendezvous with the Ferryman and ignoring the instructions of his savior Marcus. But there was still a chance to make things right, if only he could expose Domitian's plot. Then he would not only save himself and get back his life with Helena, but also save Marcus from death in the morning, however unfortunate their business with the tongue.

He saw nobody at this hour on the street and trudged through the dark up a private drive off the road. He reached the gate of the estate, which was surrounded by a high wall.

He knocked on the heavy wooden door. There was no answer at first, and then a lamp went on somewhere inside the villa and the door opened to reveal a servant girl who obviously had been asleep. She didn't seem to recognize him in his uniform.

Good.

"I am here on state business and must see Maximus immediately."

He was led through a courtyard and stepped inside the front door of the villa without being invited in. The servant girl scurried away while he waited impatiently.

He looked around the reception hall and remembered his early visits to his patron Maximus when he had first come to Rome. He would arrive every morning to pay his respects to Maximus in the atrium and receive his day's meal. Maximus would then take money from a trunk guarded by his big Syrian slave Dillian to hand him to pay actors or rent a small theater in the commercial strips of Mars Field. Athanasius had already squandered his own money in several expensive flops, and Maximus urged him to start small and build his audience slowly. Like other wealthy patrons, Maximus said he wanted to make Rome great. Most others did it by erecting temples or building parks. For Maximus it was the arts, and he seemed to believe that in Athanasius he had found someone whose works could speak more loudly than stone.

It was Maximus, Athanasius now recalled, who first arranged his introduction to Helena. He had been pining for her ever since he saw her cheering her then-boyfriend and his chariot at the old Circus Maximus. He remembered telling Maximus, "If I could have a woman like that, I would have everything, including the recognition of my arrival in Rome." To which Maximus laughed and said, "On the contrary, having Helena at your side would render you invisible. I know you want to be the center of her universe, Athanasius, but don't fool yourself: Helena is the center of her universe."

All the same, they met, and Athanasius won her over with his force of personality and relentless charm. To many in Rome, she was undoubtedly his greatest achievement, more than his plays, because he had beat out a formidable field of muscle in the form of gladiators, racers and athletes, and money in the form of countless wealthy suitors.

Now he had lost her. He had lost everything. He desperately wanted to go to her now, but it would do him no good. They could not save themselves. They needed help, and Maximus was just the man.

A moment later Maximus's chamberlain Dillian appeared. The look in the big Syrian's eyes told Athanasius that he recognized him.

"This way," Dillian said and led Athanasius to the bedrooms in the back.

Maximus was sitting on his bed. He was dressed in his night robe, white chest hairs poking out from his barrel chest, and looking years older and far more frail than his stage presence only hours earlier in the throne room at the palace. Athanasius worried he had assumed too much, that his mentor could be of help to him. Perhaps he had made a big mistake in not following the interrogator's instructions.

"Is it really you, Athanasius?" Maximus marveled as Athanasius removed his helmet. "I can't believe it. How?"

"Dominium Dei is an imperial organization, Maximus," Athanasius said without preamble. "Domitian's spies have infiltrated the underground Christian movement. He is fanning a war between the church and the state, playing both sides against each other in order to destroy his enemies in the Senate and amass ever more power for himself. We must inform the Senate and confront Domitian publicly."

Maximus looked shocked, and yet slowly began to nod. "It makes a kind of wild sense. But we need proof, Athanasius, and the support of the Praetorian."

"I have proof," Athanasius said, thinking of Marcus in his cell. "But we have little time."

"I suppose we don't, Athanasius." But Maximus sat there on his bed, tapping his foot against the brass frame and bed's ivory feet. "But how do I know that Domitian hasn't put you up to this, to save your own skin?"

"What?"

"Going against him as a group would only prove his contention that there is a massive conspiracy. He could wipe out the rest of his enemies in the Senate and the Praetorian Guard, all in one stroke—because you got us, the true conspirators, to expose ourselves."

"A conspiracy of truth."

"Of course, Athanasius, of course. But the end would be the same—you dead, me dead, all of us dead, and Domitian triumphant and living long past September 18."

"But he is triumphant already. What other choice do we have?"

"Only one," Maximus said. "Dillian!"

Athanasius heard a footstep behind and spun around. The slave Dillian was lunging at him with a sword. Athanasius grabbed his arms, his fists sliding down to his wrists, bending them back until the Syrian released his grip on the sword and it fell with a clank to the travertine floor.

The slave tried to grab it, and Athanasius countered with a knee to his face. He recoiled in pain, his hands reaching for his face, exposing himself. Athanasius whipped out his own sword, and as the Syrian straightened up, plunged his sword into the slave's chest, driving him back against the wall. The light of life flickered in his dark eyes, and when Athanasius pulled the sword out, Dillian slid to the floor in a pool of blood, dead.

"Your first kill, Athanasius?" said Maximus from behind.

Athanasius felt something on his back and spun around to see old Maximus holding a tiny stick. His mentor had tried to prick him with it, but it had broken on an armor plate. Athanasius grabbed it from Maximus with one hand and shoved the old man back onto his bed with the other.

"Athanasius, please," Maximus said, his lips bloodied by the blow.

Athanasius sniffed the tip of the broken stick.

Poison.

"*Et tu,* Maximus?" Athanasius said, dropping the stick to the floor and moving in with his sword.

Maximus smiled as he looked at the corpse of his servant Dillian. "You surprise us all, Athanasius. You really are a butcher, aren't you?"

Athanasius put the tip of his sword to Maximus's saggy neck. "And what are you, Maximus? Who are you, friend?"

Maximus nodded as if to say, "I'll tell you," and Athanasius pulled back the tip of his sword slightly. Then Maximus wiped his bloody lips with the back of his hand and coughed.

"The Dei are everywhere, Athanasius. They cannot be defeated. You cannot defeat them. In a few short years they will take over the world."

"Names, Maximus. I want names."

Suddenly Maximus gagged and went limp, collapsing to the floor.

Athanasius stared into his face. The old man's eyes were wide—and dead.

Kneeling over the body of his dead mentor, Athanasius noticed the ring on Maximus's gnarled forefinger. It reminded him of the one on his own hand, the one Marcus had given him.

The finger was already cold when Athanasius slipped the ring off and noticed the tiny hole. He sniffed.

Poison. Just like the stick.

Athanasius could hardly believe it. Maximus had sucked poison out of his ring rather than reveal anything more about Dominium Dei.

What more could there possibly be?

Athanasius then peeled away Maximus's robe to examine his mentor's barrel chest. Something had caught his eye during their struggle.

There it was, under the left armpit: a jagged death cross tattooed in black on the pasty white skin. It was a *Chi* symbol—the mark of an invisible army with legions around the world.

Dominium Dei.

They were indeed everywhere.

A piercing scream filled the air. Athanasius looked up at the slave girl standing in the doorway, peering in. "You killed the senator!"

He heard movement through the walls. The whole house was stirring. Athanasius picked up his helmet. He had to get out of there.

"Silence!" ordered Athanasius, releasing his grip on the robe and slipping Maximus's ring on the opposite hand of the one with Marcus's. "This is state business."

"You are defiling him!" she screamed. Her piercing cry reverberated off the walls like an alarm, and suddenly the siren of a horn blasted outside, alerting the entire hillside.

Athanasius rushed past her as she flattened herself against the wall and ran down the hallway to the front door. Maximus's carriage was at the gate, but it was too late to reach it now. Already a squad of Urban Cohorts, swords and spears out for attack, were running toward the villa, attracted by the sound of the horn.

Athanasius turned back and ran through the rooms of the house, waving his sword and knocking slaves over. When he reached the back balcony overlooking the old Republic Wall, he leaped off it, landing on the hillside behind the villa and sliding down the slope toward the grim apartment blocks in the vast slums below.

Arrows zoomed past his head as he ran toward the roof of a long apartment block built into the hill.

He was almost there when an arrow struck his helmet, sending him tumbling down and crashing onto the red clay tiles, terrorizing the screaming family in the room below. He rolled off into the rooftop courtyard, found the narrow stone steps and commanded his tired legs to race down six flights. A moment later he burst out of the stairwell and disappeared into the dark alleys of the city's slums, cursing himself for missing his only escape from Rome.

12

Athanasius ran on through the tangled streets in the dark, racing past the archways of the booths and shops boarded up and bolted shut for the night. The apartment slums above the *tabernae* on either side rose up six stories tall. He could easily lose himself in this jumbled maze of alleys until morning, blowing any hope of making his rendezvous with the Ferryman. Even if he reached the Cloaca Maxima beneath the Basilica Julia, he doubted the Ferryman would still be waiting for him. But if he didn't try, he was dead already.

He looked up for breaks along the seemingly endless ridge of black rooftops for a clear line of sight to the Temple of Jupiter and the Arx atop Capitoline Hill to orient himself. He couldn't go back the way he came, so he would have to circle around the northern base of the hill to reach the west side of the Forum—through these infernal alleys with their forgotten denizens, the hundreds of thousands of people who were born, lived and died in this cesspool of human misery.

And now he was one of them.

All of a sudden, the blood-chilling blare of the First Spear horn thundered across the skies. It was the official signal from the Urban Cohorts headquarters to the roaming gangs of the district that there was a fugitive on the loose, and a reward for his capture, dead or alive. Even the official *urbani* patrols avoided this graveyard of danger at night.

Almost immediately shouts and torches burst forth from all directions. He heard the crash of pots and cursing and looked over his shoulder to see a gang of four shadowy figures floating toward him like malevolent spirits in their odd, mismatched pieces of old infantry armor. The gruesome sight made him recall one of Juvenal's few good jokes about life in modern Rome: that only the careless dared venture out after supper without having first made their will.

I am not going to die in this piss pot tonight, Athanasius vowed to himself, breaking into a sprint. Better to go out in a blaze of faux glory in the arena than go face down here in some ditch.

The apartment slums on either side of him closed in like walls, the snaking alley narrowing into a dirt path. Now he was splashing through an open cess trench that reeked with the foul stench of human waste, dumped from the pots of the inhabitants in the *insulae* above him. The goo caked his aching calves, and it was all he could do to keep his heavy legs moving and not turn his face up toward the windows.

The muck had slowed the ill-clad gangs behind him, however, and he could no longer hear their shouts. But at the end of the alley was a veritable bonfire of thugs at an intersection waiting for him. He couldn't go back, and he couldn't move forward. He looked around frantically until he found an open laundry pit between two buildings. It was filled with sanitizing urine.

There was no way around it, he realized. This was his only exit.

He waded through the knee-deep pool, stopping only to untangle soaked garments that wrapped themselves around his legs, like the long tentacles of some sea creature sent to pull him under, and for a moment he entertained the vision of being found face down in the very piss pot he feared. But he made it out the far end of the pool and emerged atop a weed-infested ridge.

There below was Jugarius Street, and on the other side the warehouse district that linked the Forum to the Tiber. The boulevard was filled with carts and slaves of the night. No daytime traffic was allowed in Rome except pedestrians, horses, litters and carrying chairs. Nighttime was for transport carts of all sizes, loading and unloading goods from barges at the port on the Tiber. Like magic, all the stores, stands and markets of Rome would be filled with the treasures of the world by morning. And, with luck, he would be gone with all the garbage from the previous day.

Athanasius slid down the hill to the shoulder of Jugarius Street. He waited for a break in the traffic and then ran across the street and made an immediate left toward the Forum, slipping between two convoys of full wagons. He had just permitted himself to take a breath when the wagon in front of him slowed down and skirted to the right to reveal a line of two-dozen heavily armed *urbani* coming out through the Arch of Tiberius. They were marching straight toward him, their swords and spears at the ready.

Athanasius slowed down as the unit's commanding officer, a centurion, saluted as he passed by. Athanasius nodded and looked back as the troops marched on toward the Tiber, no doubt to take up positions on the Sublicius Bridge and close off that exit.

Athanasius passed under the Arch of Tiberius into the Forum, turned right on Sacred Way and hurried along the portico of the Basilica Julia to the end. There, at the intersection at Titus Street, he heard the sound of running water and found the sewer grating at the base of the courthouse's marble steps.

Quickly glancing both ways to make sure he hadn't been seen, he pulled at the heavy grating. It lifted to reveal an iron ladder that led down to a lead door. The air was foul, ranker than the alleys of the slums. He lowered himself down a few steps, slid the grating back into place over his head, and then pushed the door open.

It was dark inside, the damp air wrapping around him like a wet blanket. He heard the lapping of water and took another step forward. Suddenly he felt a sharp pain in his chest as a voice said, "Hands up."

Athanasius squinted in the dark, and a moment later his eyes had adjusted enough for him to barely make out a short but muscular young man in a tunic pointing a crossbow at him. Beyond him a small boat bobbed in the water against the stone ledge inside the great tunnel. "Ferryman, is that you?"

"Chiron?" The Ferryman lowered his crossbow.

Athanasius then saw the bodies of two auxiliary *urbani* on the stone ledge, both with arrows in their chests. "You know where we're going?"

"Out the drain to the Tiber, then down to Ostia and your ship, the Pegasus. Pier 34."

Athanasius nodded. This was more than Marcus had told him. "They're locking down the city topside. Units are moving into position at the Sublicius, where the sewer lets out into the river."

"Then we'll have to beat them," the Ferryman said as he launched them off down the tunnel.

The underground river of filth was a good fifteen feet across under the semicircular arch of the vaulted stone roof. And the current was faster than he expected, powered as it was by the confluence of the city's eleven great aqueducts flowing into this section at once. It all came together here, this churning cesspool of waste being pushed out to the river.

"Hold on," the Ferryman said as they picked up speed and shot through the dark.

The tunnel began dropping the closer they got to the outlet, the current churning with such force that they were careening into all kinds of debris and against the stone walls and had to use paddles as bumpers. Several *stadia* ahead Athanasius could see the half-dome light of the end of the tunnel, the moonlit Tiber beyond. They crashed through the open grating gates and were suddenly into the river, paddling frantically to avoid the wakes of the big barges passing under the towering arches of the Sublicius Bridge.

Athanasius looked back in time to see the Urban Cohort units come to a halt atop the bridge. Archers jumped out and began to take their positions, but by then they were long gone down the river and into the night fog.

"The Lord is with you, Athanasius," said the Ferryman as he maneuvered into the downriver traffic of empty barges to Ostia, doing his best to keep their little boat from getting crushed between them in the dark.

Athanasius reached behind his back and felt for his knife. "So you know who I am?"

"My name is Stephanus. I'm the servant of Flavius Clemens, whose life was cut short by the antichrist Domitian who wants you dead too."

Athanasius eyed him. "Then you must know I cannot be Chiron, and that Clemens could not possibly have named me in his confession."

"I know that the Lord has plans for you, Athanasius. Plans for good and not for evil, to give you and all of us a future and a hope."

Athanasius loosened his hold on his dagger and brought his empty hands forward. "I have no future, Stephanus. I have no hope."

"You have stood up to the gods of Rome tonight, Athanasius. You are the one who will lead us to topple the empire and create a new Christian world."

"I thought Jesus is supposed to do that," Athanasius said.

"We must prepare the way."

"Isn't Jesus The Way?"

Stephanus nodded. "You are very clever, like Paul was. Jesus is indeed The Way, and He is not willing that any perish but all come to repentance."

Athanasius felt a bump and looked into the waters to see the corpse of some slave who had likely fallen off a barge. "Too late for him, I suppose."

"But not for the millions of souls under the boot of Rome."

Athanasius could barely see straight in the fog, let alone think with all this madness. Didn't Stephanus understand that he was leaving Rome, never to return because there was nothing for him left to return to? Domitian had stolen his future. "A million died in the Judean War, Stephanus, and a Christian war would cost tens of millions of lives."

"It need only cost one," Stephanus said with shining eyes. "September 18 is not so far away. Imagine Domitian gone and Young Vespasian succeeding him. We'd have a Christian emperor. A Christian Rome. A Christian world. No slave or free. Male or female. Jew or Gentile. All would be equal. There would be peace on earth. No more fears. No more tears."

No more tears? What naïve nonsense, Athanasius thought. Surely Domitian would have something to say about that, and about September 18. And if not Domitian, he realized, then Dominium Dei. Athanasius had seen the reach of the organization tonight with Maximus.

What good would it do the Christians to cut the head off a Hydra when another would simply take its place and make short order of any so-called Christian emperor, which itself was an oxymoron clearly beyond this simpleton's grasp.

Domitian, and Rome with him, was simply too powerful to fight.

Athanasius saw no future hope in this river fog down the Tiber to Ostia, only a glimpse of the harbor's great lighthouse at the end. The bonfire at the top of its towering edifice seemed to watch them like a great eye as they floated silently past the travertine piers toward the hulking Pegasus docked at Pier 34. Athanasius said goodbye to Stephanus, who prayed for his return to Rome and said that he and others would be awaiting his orders.

Athanasius wondered if he'd survive the night, let alone ever return to Rome. But at this point Stephanus was his only friend in Rome. So to amuse him he played the role of Chiron and said, "Tell your friends that Chiron lives and Domitian shall die."

"Amen," Stephanus said with gusto as Athanasius shoved him off.

As Athanasius crossed the rows of warehouses and winches to Pier 34, he took in the slaves and dockworkers loading and unloading the great ships. They were the true cogs of the Roman machine that worked around the clock to keep the empire going. Straight ahead of him a centurion stood at the gangway to the Pegasus. Athanasius realized he had no identification papers and tensed up as he approached. He had to instantly establish his identity before there could be any doubt.

"Centurion, is my trunk on board?" he said with a token salute that flashed his ring.

The centurion didn't have to look, transfixed as he was on the ranking shoulder straps. "Tribune, we were beginning to wonder."

"I'm here, let's go," Athanasius said gruffly.

Athanasius marched up the gangway to find a deck full of Roman soldiers waiting for him. He started, and then saw they were at attention, along with the ship's captain, a Greek who introduced himself as Captain Andros.

"Tribune, we have 80 troops, and a crew of 180 oarsmen, sailors and marines at your command."

Athanasius decided that in his present company the less he said the better. "Anchors away, Captain. I will retire to my quarters and will not be disturbed until morning."

"At your orders, Tribune. Your belongings have already been stored on board. Galen here will show you to your quarters."

Athanasius followed the wiry steward across the long deck, taking in the sea air, aware of the captain barking orders, of shouts returned, anchors pulled and the sudden quake of the wooden planks beneath his feet as two hundred oars hit the water. The Pegasus lurched forward.

His quarters were at the sterncastle, reached by two wooden steps and an outside door. There was a bed inside along with a built-in desk beneath a small window. On the desk was a tray with bread, cheese and a pitcher of wine. Beside it were shelves and a personal locker. The locker was open, and he could see a locked trunk. Athanasius looked up to see Galen staring at the ring on his finger.

"That will be all, Galen."

Galen nodded and left, shutting the door behind him.

At last alone, Athanasius exhaled and immediately poured himself a cup of wine and gulped it down. Then he took two big bites of the bread, almost choking on the mouthful as he did, and looked out his little window. He could see several chariots and units converging on the shrinking docks. But they were too late. The anchors were up and the loaded ship was pulling away from the pier, already out by three lengths of the Circus Maximus, clearing the stone breakers and entering the Tyrrhenian Sea into the gathering fog of darkness.

Jupiter, he had made it, he thought, as he watched the nightmare of this tragic day fade like the lighthouse of

Ostia in the fog. He felt his lips tremble. He wiped his mouth and saw blood, not wine. Then he stared into the wine cup and watched it fall as if in slow motion from his loosening hand and crash to the floor. And then he plunged into darkness.

13

Deep inside the cave a young woman cried out to him, "This way, Athanasius! Hurry!"

He tried to find her but stumbled in the darkness. The further he followed her down the endless tunnel, the further out of reach she seemed. *I have to save her!* At last he caught up to her in a dim shaft of light, grasping for her long, black hair. When she turned to look at him with her dark and haunting eyes, tears of blood trickled down her tragic face.

He stared back, suddenly aware they were not alone in the vast subterranean cavern. All around him were thousands of others like the young woman with bleeding eyes, their hands reaching out to him for help. He opened his mouth to scream, but the mountain above began to quake and the rock ceiling crashed down upon him.

Athanasius of Athens awoke from his nightmare, gasping for breath, aware of the smell of the salty sea and sound of scrolls shuffling. He blinked into the bright daylight inside his cabin aboard the Pegasus. He was lying on a cot, dressed in the uniform of a Roman tribune. Like a heavy stone fell the realization that the events of last night in the city of Rome were no nightmare and that his life as he knew it was over.

He looked over to see his steward, Galen, hunched over the open Chiron box, going through its contents while he nibbled on fish and bread.

Athanasius quietly swallowed, careful not to make a sound, waiting for the proper moment to stir to life and kill the swine.

Was it only yesterday I woke up in my comfortable bed inside my comfortable villa in Rome as Athanasius of Athens, celebrated playwright and hedonist? Was it only yesterday I woke up to the woman of every Roman's dream, Helena, and the premiere of my greatest production yet, *Opus Gloria?*

It was, he realized grimly. But then he had been arrested and sent to certain death in the arena. The absurd charge? That he was Chiron, the mastermind behind Dominium Dei, the mysterious and militant Christian conspiracy that had been blamed for the assassination of Emperor Domitian's chief astrologer and other Roman officials. Now Caesar, Rome's self-proclaimed Lord and God, had initiated a Reign of Terror, slaying any and all suspected enemies.

And by some cruel twist of fate, Athanasius had become one of them.

It was only by some miracle in the person of a Roman
tribune and Christian named Marcus that Athanasius had
escaped, alone with the secret that Dominium Dei was in
fact an imperial organization created to infiltrate and destroy the fledgling underground Church.

The last thing he remembered was making it to the
Pegasus before it set sail in the middle of the night from
the port of Ostia. I was poisoned, he recalled. Galen the
steward poisoned me. How did I survive? Then he remembered the elixir that Marcus had given him in the
prison back in Rome. It must have been an antidote of
some sort, something to coat his stomach in anticipation
of exactly this kind of betrayal.

Galen sat up suddenly and glanced over his shoulder,
sensing something. Athanasius froze, afraid he had made
some movement that drew the Dei man's attention.
Through the slit of his eyelid, however, he saw that Galen
was looking at the cabin door.

"Tribune?" asked a voice outside. It was the captain.
He then seemed to address somebody else. "Isn't this
unusual?"

"No," said a voice that Athanasius recognized as that
of the centurion in charge of transporting the 80 troops on
board to Ephesus. "I've found that imperial interrogators
like to keep to themselves, have food brought in. Don't

like to mingle with the rank-and-file, even the officers like me. They are political officers more than military, and as likely to interrogate us as the enemy. They don't want to make friends. I get nervous when they do want to join us in the galley. It usually means one of my men is under suspicion."

"Well, Galen says he is taking his food. I'll have him inform the tribune that we'll enter the Gulf of Corinth by nightfall and make our way through the canal in the morning."

The voices faded with footsteps, and then Athanasius heard the planks creak as Galen approached and stood over him. Athanasius could smell the wine on his breath. The man had poisoned him and was now eating his food, going through his papers.

Enough.

Galen said, "So you wouldn't eat your fish with the rest of us, would you, dear, departed general of the Dei. Now you are food for fish when I chop you up with your own knife, stick you in your box and dump you overboard. If only I had kept you alive long enough to tell me the key to the coded texts. Now they remain a mystery, and all I have is your gold."

Athanasius opened his eyes, shot up his hand and grabbed Galen by the throat. "Your prayer is answered, swine."

Galen's wide eyes seemed to pop out of his terrified face as he choked in Athanasius's vise-like grip. Athanasius stood up and quietly pushed Galen against the wall, pinning him at the neck.

"Who are you people?" Athanasius demanded.

Galen struggled, gasping for breath, saying nothing.

Athanasius said, "Who do you take orders from?"

"You," Galen said.

"Then why did you try to kill me?"

"That's how we advance."

"That doesn't sound very Roman to me."

"We are not Roman."

Not Roman? Athanasius thought. The Dei was imperial. That was the big secret. "If you are not of Rome, and not of the Church, then of what?"

"Ourselves."

"For what purpose?"

"Our own."

Athanasius looked into the weasel's eyes, saw the fear and felt he was telling the truth. "Why me?"

"I don't know."

"My family in Greece."

"They will be slaughtered, if not already. As will you!"

Athanasius felt a prick at his shoulder and saw a thin stick in Galen's hand. It had hit his leather strap and not his skin. Athanasius grabbed it with his free hand and waved it in front of Galen's face.

"That's twice you've missed, Galen," he said and stuck it into Galen's neck.

"No!" Galen moaned before blood began to trickle out of his nose and the corners of his mouth. His eyes rolled back, and Athanasius let go. The body crumpled to the floor with a thud.

Athanasius looked at Galen's twisted face, worried that the crew on the deck below heard the fall. He knelt over the body of the dead steward. With his right hand, he ripped the tunic away, exposing white skin and a twisted cross of black. The mark of Rome's mystical legion.

Dominium Dei.

Almost immediately there was a knock at the door, followed by a voice. "Tribune, are you alright?"

It was the centurion who had been with the captain.

Athanasius dragged Galen under his hammock. He looked in the brass mirror and ran his fingers through his unruly black hair. His face was pale, the blood drained, his eyes hollow and haunted. He was a mess.

He opened the door a crack to afford the centurion a peek at his desk but nothing more.

"Tribune, are you alright?"

"Never better, centurion. I just rolled out of the wrong side of the bed today. You know how it is."

"Yes, Tribune."

"But I'm still hungry. See if you can find my steward Galen for me. Oh, and tell the captain I'll be joining you and the officers for dinner tonight in the officer's galley."

The centurion gulped and nodded. "Yes, Tribune."

Athanasius removed the key ring from Galen's stiff finger and slipped it on. It looked different than before. Now that its key had broken off, what remained was a form of the Chiron insignia—the Chi-Ro symbol. Only it was flanked by the Greek letters Alpha on the left and Omega on the right. It also had a tiny jewel inside the loop of the Ro. Possibly an amethyst, he thought, taking a closer look. He couldn't be sure, and right now it didn't matter.

He walked over to the open trunk and looked inside. There was money. Lots of it. Gold, silver and gems. There were also scrolls. The scriptures of the so-called New Testament between God and man, comprised of four accounts of the life of Jesus by the disciples Matthew, Mark, Luke and John, the letters of Paul to the churches he established, and several from John, including the Revelation. Athanasius saw little use for them, so he set them aside and focused on three letters quite different from the others.

The first was on a heavy parchment, clearly official and with an imperial stamp. Athanasius read:

> *You will regard the bearer of this letter, my imperial interrogator, as my right hand, the hand of Rome, and do anything he instructs you without question, even so far as to take your own life.*

> *His Excellency Flavius Titus Domitian*

With a start Athanasius recognized the seal of Caesar, the same seal he recalled seeing at the palace only the night before. It felt like a lifetime ago.

Surely this was the key to open doors that Marcus had told him about.

But there was another letter, one written with symbols, the letter Galen had been trying to crack. The first line alone was unintelligible.

•> D• ^^ •| V D• > |•

This must be Chiron's letter with his "further instructions," Athanasius thought. Perhaps the real key unlocked this code.

But where?

He looked at his pouch with his knife kit and the elixir. He emptied it. There was nothing else there. Then he saw the tiny holes in the bottom of the pouch that he had first noted curiously back in the prison.

He removed the drawstring and flattened out the pouch on the back of a wax tablet. They created an odd pattern, as indistinguishable as the symbols on the letter from Chiron.

He picked up one of those poisoned little sticks and began to poke it though the holes of the flattened leather into the wax tablet. Then he removed the leather skin and stared. The dots were definitely set apart in groups.

Staring at the pattern for a while, a pattern of space between the dots slowly began to appear. He drew a diagonal line between two groups, and then another intersecting line. The Chi symbol. But what of the grouping above? He drew the Ro and stared at the symbol of Chiron. The key.

Within an hour he was able to assign symbols to their counterparts in the Roman alphabet and translate the text. But upon reading it, he wished he hadn't.

> *You are to direct the ship to make a stop on the island of Patmos. There you will present yourself with Caesar's introduction to interrogate John the Apostle and then in private tell him what you know. He will then provide you with instructions and introduction to find sanctuary in the church of Asia Minor.*

Athanasius was aghast. Go to Patmos? This was his mission? Escaping one prison in Rome only to march into the Roman garrison on the prison island of Patmos was not his idea of freedom.

Athanasius hoped Chiron's last letter offered a better alternative. It was made of a flimsy papyrus and appeared to list several recipes and formulas. But they were not for food, Athanasius realized as he deciphered it, but for poisons and explosives.

> *Below are instructions on the poison and anti-dote favored by the Dei, assuming you have survived their first attempt on your life. Familiarize yourself with the smell, texture and even taste of these ingredients and compounds, if not for your own use then for your protection.*

Athanasius felt light-headed. Surely this would not be his life.

One formula was for the Dei poison Galen had used on him, with various grades to delay the onset upon the victim by minutes or even hours. It appeared to be the standard formula found in Dei rings for suicide and on wooden sticks to quickly prick a target and kill him without a trace. The antidote, too, which Marcus had given him in advance, could be used as a prescription or remedy.

Most curious were the formulas for a flammable mud called maltha, which promised to stick to anything it touched, clinging to anyone who tried to flee, even to water, which merely made it burn more fiercely. Another compound, which combined quicklime, sulphur, naptha and saltpeter, promised to create a material capable of spontaneous combustion that could be thrown at enemies and explode on impact.

Athanasius put the last letter down and looked at the corpse of Galen on the floor and could picture his own face, his own end. He felt like falling to his knees and sobbing, but he was no longer prone to displays of emotion because he hardly had any left. The reality was that he had nothing more in life but these so-called presents from a dead tribune, given to advance him into a future of death. Yet they were all he had to work with, he knew. Somehow he had to put them to good use. Starting now, here on this ship bound for Ephesus.

Obviously, as Maximus and Galen had proven, he could trust no one in Rome or the Dei. If Ludlumus or Domitian figured out that he had in fact escaped and another man was executed in his place in the Colosseum, the Romans would surely go after his family in Corinth, if that order hadn't been given already. He had to get to them first and warn them to flee.

Several hours later, just after midnight, Athanasius was pacing the deck under the stars and found Captain Andros talking to the helmsman in the tiller house, his face dark and brooding like the Ionian Sea upon which they were crossing.

"That was quite a show you put on for the officers at dinner, Tribune," the captain said. "I didn't know a knife could do so many things to a fish."

Athanasius noticed the helmsman look away from him in fear and get back to his tiller. The Pegasus had a double-oar rudder system, with cables attached to the main tiller to allow the helmsman to turn both oars at the stern simultaneously. The system of levers and cables enabled him to control the Pegasus in strong currents and rough weather, although tonight it was smooth sailing.

Athanasius said, "I didn't want the troops to think the emissary of Caesar stayed mostly to himself and took his meals in his cabin. And I wanted to get a good look at them all. Has Galen turned up yet?"

"No," the captain said. "He must have grasped your suspicions and slipped overboard when we passed an island and swam for it."

Athanasius shrugged. "Small fish," he said. "I have bigger in Corinth. How much longer until we arrive?"

"Tomorrow morning we reach the Gulf of Corinth. But it will take another day to make our way through to the harbor," the captain said. "Then it is a full day to cross the isthmus to the Saronic Gulf and begin the second leg of our journey to Ephesus. You will have only ten hours in Corinth if you plan on doing an interrogation."

"A full day is more than enough time."

"You know Corinth then?"

"No, not really," said Athanasius quickly. He didn't want to give the captain the impression he was overly familiar with his hometown. "Stopped over once before, like now. But the local garrison will have someone waiting to drive me where I need to go."

"But, of course, Tribune," the Greek said grimly before leaving him alone to his thoughts beneath the stars.

Athanasius waited until he was gone before heading back inside his cabin to drag out Galen's corpse. He had wrapped him in a blanket and tied him to a two-handled amphora full of grain. He dropped him over the side, watching the Dei man quickly sink beneath the wake of the Pegasus to the bottom of the sea.

14

After her beloved's execution at the Colosseum, Helena was summoned to supper at the Palace of the Flavians. She had no doubt what the performance of her duties to Domitian would entail. She was surprised, however, to find his wife Domitia joining them in Caesar's private *triclinium* dining room. Now her agony was compounded; not only was Domitian taunting her, he was using her to taunt his wife, which explained the daggers in Domitia's eyes as Helena washed her hands with a cloth from an attendant and reclined with them both.

"Welcome, Helena, you look lovely," Domitian said as the staff began serving supper. "The chef has prepared a feast for us tonight. The first course features a delicately seasoned tongue paired with my favorite wine from Cappadocia."

With horror Helena understood they were to eat the tongue of her beloved, and she immediately felt the acid of her stomach race up her throat. It was all she could do to not vomit, and she doubted she would be able to stop herself for long.

On cue two servants brought in a beautifully decorated amphora. It had an ornate black-and-red design and two handles. With great pomp and ceremony, the servants unsealed the top.

"My wine comes straight from the vine, untouched by human hands, the nectar of the gods," Domitian told her, and then nodded to one of the servants.

The wine taster dipped a very small imperial cup that resembled a ladle into the amphora, sipped the wine and swallowed. Helena got the distinct impression that this display of approval was in fact intended to signal to Domitian that the amphora had not been tampered with in transit and that his wine was not poisoned.

"To a successful execution," he toasted after their cups were filled. He greedily gulped down his cup, then held it out for more.

Presently the flaming tongue arrived, delivered by a servant from the private kitchen they called Julius, which was the kind of name rich Romans reserved for their pets. The African servant's hands were trembling as he delivered the sizzling dish. The sound and smell were too much for Helena, and she quickly covered her mouth with a cloth and gave up her fig appetizer.

"I beg you pardon, Your Excellency."

Domitian smiled. "Now you have more room for the tongue."

Even Domitia could see beyond her own suffering to lay a soft hand on her back for comfort.

Domitian did the honors of slicing the tongue in half, one portion for himself and the other half to be divided equally between Domitia and Helena.

I cannot do this, Helena thought as she watched him spear a slice and shove it into his mouth, smacking his cruel lips in satisfaction. I cannot breathe. I must die.

"Really, you must try some," he said, waving another piece of tongue before her face. "Or must I give your slice of heaven to Sirius?" He motioned to Julius, who looked visibly shaken, and said, "Bring me my Pharaoh Hound. I have a treat for him."

Julius looked terrified and said nothing, only nodded and walked away.

A minute later it was the Praetorian prefect who returned with a grim expression.

"Wrong dog, Secundus," Domitian told him. "Where is my Sirius?"

"We seem to have a problem, Your Excellency. It appears the imperial Pharaoh Hound was attacked by an animal of some sort, his body found by a drain this morning outside the Senate."

Helena could see shock and sadness in Domitian's eyes for a fleeting second, only to be quickly replaced by rage. "And where was his walker, Julius, when he was attacked?"

The Praetorian, Secundus, paused, glancing at Helena and Domitia. "Yes, perhaps I can explain in a private audience with His Excellency."

"No," said Domitian, swallowing another chunk of tongue. "You shall explain it to me right here, right now."

"It appears there was a bit of a mix-up at the Colosseum today, Your Excellency. Even the Master of the Games was not aware of it. I only found out now, after piecing together several disparate reports."

Domitian chased his chunk of tongue down with another sip of his Cappadocian wine. "What sort of mix-up?"

Secundus cranked his neck just a bit and said, "The propmasters decided to salvage some of the armor used for the production of Chiron's execution, so they went into the Gate of Death and began to strip the corpse."

Helena thought she was going to die. Please, Jupiter, make it end.

"Upon removal of the armor, one of the propmasters noticed a tattoo on the shoulder of the corpse."

Helena stopped breathing. Athanasius had no tattoo that she knew of, unless they had cruelly branded him for show.

"This tattoo was of the third cohort of the Praetorian. One of our own, sir."

Domitian's eyes seemed to pop as the truth began to sink in. "What are you telling me, Secundus?"

"It appears that the man executed was not, in fact, Athanasius of Athens but the imperial interrogator sent to torture him in prison. Somehow the villain overcame him and cut out his tongue."

Domitian stood up, shaking. "You mean to tell me that Chiron escaped and I have been feasting on the tongue of one of my own officials?"

Helena was elated inside. Athanasius alive? Escaped?

"No, sir," Secundus said quickly, and she became subdued again. "I am only the messenger here, Your Excellency, and would never even consider bringing what I am about to tell you unless I knew for certain other parties were aware and that it will not remain a secret for long."

Domitian spoke in as low and cruel a voice now as Helena had ever heard him. "The Prefect of my Praetorian will tell me this secret immediately or die."

"Caesar's personal physicians, who know so clearly your love for the imperial Pharaoh Hound, examined him carefully in hopes of determining what sort of beast could kill such a divine animal, in order that Caesar could hunt the beast himself. It was my hope to have the beast ready for you before having to present this tragedy." Secundus swallowed hard. "Upon close examination, Your Excellency, your physicians found a half-digested tongue inside the animal's stomach, and its own cut off cleanly."

Domitian looked confused. "You are telling me that the monster who cut off my hound's tongue then forced him to eat it?"

"No, Your Excellency. Based on the eyewitness account of your servant Julius, your sharp-eyed Sirius spotted and detained a man dressed as a Tribune outside the Senate late last night. By the time Julius ran after him, chasing the yelps, he found only the Tribune, who said the dog had run off. In hindsight, it appears this Tribune was none other than Athanasius, and that he used the tongue of your interrogator to lure the dog and then kill him. He then passed along the dog's tongue to your servant Julius as that of Athanasius's, and the kitchen prepared it for you tonight.

Helena was in a daze. The Empress Domitia's mouth was open, desperately trying to keep its corners from turning up in a smirk.

Domitian suddenly fell over and began to wretch on the floor, sinking to his knees in the puddle and crying out, "Sirius! My Sirius! What have they done to you! Minerva, save me!"

Helena quickly got up and hoped to excuse herself from this scene. But Caesar pointed an accusing finger at her that made her freeze in terror.

"You!" he screamed at her. "And you, Secundus! Rest assured that this clown Athanasius, this amusement, this half-wit who calls himself Chiron, will suffer more than he ever imagined. Secundus, I want you to fetch me the Master of the Games. Ludlumus will answer for this. And round up the generals. The armies of Rome will search the far corners of the empire to hunt down Athanasius and bring his head to me on a silver platter."

"At your orders, Your Excellency," said Secundus, who vanished quickly.

Slowly Domitian rose to his feet, the bottom of his toga stained with the bits of vomit and tongue, and walked over to her and looked her in the eye. "Your beloved Athanasius couldn't die with honor in the arena, could he? Couldn't take the status that Ludlumus gave him as Chiron—a far better station than any playwright deserved—and thank the gods for making him more immortal than his forgettable comedies? No, he had to poke us in the eye and shake a fist at the gods. He had to mock us with this travesty, and in so doing merely tell us he is still alive and that our retribution was not too harsh but too light. You and I, Helena, will have to remedy that. I will see you in my bedchamber shortly."

With that Caesar turned his back on her and Domitia and stalked out to meet with his generals. Helena looked at the empress, whose expression of horror only further worried her as to what more divine misfortune could possibly befall her and Athanasius.

15

Much like Athanasius himself, his hometown of Corinth straddled two different worlds. The Greek city was built on the Isthmus of Corinth, that narrow stretch of land that joins the Peloponnesus to the mainland of Greece, about halfway between Athens and Sparta. The well-to-do city had two main ports, one on the Corinthian Gulf, which served the trade routes of the western empire, and one on the Saronic Gulf, serving the trade routes of the eastern empire. As such it was at the crossroads of trade, culture and religion.

The Pegasus had docked in the port city of Lechaion in the Corinthian Gulf. By nightfall it would be departing from the port city of Kenchreai on the Saronic Gulf on the other side of the isthmus. In between was the Diolkos, the overland stone ramp that connected the two ports after centuries of costly attempts to dig out a canal had failed. The Pegasus would be rolled across the isthmus on logs, as the ancient Egyptians had rolled blocks of granite to make their pyramids. The journey was a good 43 *stadia* and would take ten hours.

That's how long Athanasius had to warn his family and escape before anybody knew the tribune interrogator was missing when he failed to show up in Kenchreai.

As he walked down the gangway and around the harbor crates and cranes, Athanasius knew he was defying Marcus's instructions by visiting his family estate outside the city, just as he did when he went to Maximus. But a growing fear for the safety of his family had been gnawing him for days. He had to warn them, help them escape. There were thousands of islands in Greece, far away from the big ocean traffic, where he could lose himself, just like his forefather, the original Vasiliki, who had killed some ancient general who had taken his sister as a sex slave and then hid out in the Minoan city of Vasiliki in Crete. When he returned to public life, friends and strangers called him by his new name. He could do that, maybe someday get Helena to join him, after Domitian was finally dead.

He thought of his mother and two older sisters and two younger brothers and their families. More than two dozen nieces and nephews in all. How in the world could he protect them all or get them all out of Corinth? It seemed impossible. Whatever the case, he resolved to be steadfast and firm and demand the family flee. His plan was clear: to send them back to the islands from whence they came.

Even from the harbor he could see Corinth's acropolis in the distance, where the great Temple of Aphrodite once stood before an earthquake leveled it. Now there were several smaller temples dedicated to the goddess in the city, each with statues boasting the face of Helena. The first one greeted him and all visitors to the harbor as he walked toward the taxi station. The sight aroused both pride and anguish. He had hoped to return in triumph with Helena and the success of *Opus Gloria.*

Athanasius hailed a *cisium* at the station, put his sack of belongings in the compartment under the seat and told the taxi driver to take him to town, where he would switch to another cab. The *cisiarri* yanked the reins on his two mules, and the open carriage with two wheels started down the limestone Lechaion Way south toward the town.

They drove along the colonnade of Corinthian columns and pulled up to the Roman arch near the Perine Fountain. He got out, paid the driver and walked through the *agora* of public buildings and shops, passing the tribunal bema from which Paul the Apostle spoke to his parents' generation in Corinth some 20 years before he was born.

Athanasius headed straight toward his favorite temple of Aphrodite next to the city's theater, which could seat 18,000 and where he used to spend so much of his youth and staged his first play. Almost a hundred years before he was born, the Greek geographer Strabo boasted that the city's famous Temple of Aphrodite employed more than one thousand prostitutes. Athanasius recalled only about 300 growing up, less in number than the days of the year, which wreaked havoc with the math of a peculiar contest of religiosity among the local Greek boys that stirred quite the resentment among local Jewish and Christian girls.

He also recalled some tension with the Christian community in Corinth, mostly because the Apostle Paul had lived in the city for almost two years. Here he wrote his infamous Book of Romans, which was about as controversial as John's Book of Revelation. All Athanasius remembered as a child were the jokes about the Corinthians simply being Corinthians in response to the apostle's call for stricter sexual mores. His mother and father knew a couple who were Paul's right-hand leaders, a woman named Priscilla and her husband Aquila. His father thought it blasphemous that the new superstition allowed such lofty status for a woman. His mother, meanwhile, never got over how swiftly the superstition could carry her friend off to the far corners of the earth with this crazy evangelist.

Athanasius listened carefully to the conversations in the air as he walked through the public squares. No news yet about his death except that it was anticipated. He stopped off at the theater with a statue of himself, the hometown boy. He had hoped to bring Helena here to meet his family and show her that she wasn't the only one to get statues in her honor. He had also hoped to impress his cousins by presenting Aphrodite herself in the flesh.

Helena's statue was in front of the Temple of Aphrodite. There she was, a fifteen-foot-tall Helena in stone representing the goddess Aphrodite. Athanasius stood before her, thinking about the model for the even larger version in the works back in Rome and if it would ever see the light of day now that she was linked to him, the notorious Chiron.

"Now there's a handful," said a voice, and he turned to see a stranger.

Athanasius looked him over, and then around, worried about spies and assassins waiting for him. It was possible that news of his escape from Rome had outraced the Pegasus to reach Domitian's informants here in Corinth.

He decided it was best to simply get out of town, before some cousin or childhood friend recognized him. "Isn't she?" he told the stranger and walked away.

He hailed another cab, driven by a young man with smooth, dark features and a fixed smile for tourists. "Where to, Tribune?"

"The Argos Farms," he said, naming a neighboring farm past his family's estate. He would double back on foot to reach his home, cut through the groves to the stables in back and avoid the front drive off the main road.

The driver nodded. "That's a good twelve *stadia* outside town. It will take us an hour."

"I'll pay you for your way back too."

"At your service, Tribune."

Athanasius climbed in and off they went, leaving the statue of Helena and tourists behind. He was headed home.

Corinth and its outskirts had changed some since Athanasius last saw his hometown four years ago. The Romans were upgrading public buildings, and the roads were vastly improved. He doubted it would take even an hour to reach home, and he was right: Sooner than he expected they approached his family's estate outside town.

As they drove past his childhood home, Athanasius did his best to avoid looking at the two Corinthian pillars that marked the entrance to the long, winding gravel path lined with cypress trees to the villa. But something caused the cab's mules to skip a step, and Athanasius looked ahead to see traffic coming their way.

"We may have to pull over to let the caravan pass," the driver told him. "Perhaps they come from the Argos Farms?"

Athanasius couldn't afford to find out. Any member of the Argos family or their workers might recognize him, sitting in the open carriage in a tribune's uniform no less.

"Cut down the path ahead," Athanasius ordered.

"What path?"

"I'll show you." Athanasius decided to use the back road to the family tannery. The tannery road started at the northwest side of the property, a few minutes from the east gates. He would use it to quietly reach the estate. "Hurry!"

The mules kicked up and they went about half a *stade* before a narrow dirt path, barely visible, appeared between the trees. "Here?" the driver asked.

"Yes," said Athanasius, and tried to will the mules to speed up.

They turned onto the path and slipped into the trees just as the first of the wagons from the caravan passed by on the road behind them, affording whoever was looking a view of the carriage's backside.

They took a long path past the family's fly-infested and odorous tannery, which was kept a good distance away not only from town but from the Vasiliki estate, and finally rounded a cool glade and entered the sunny grove behind the family villa. Athanasius could see the stables below, and for a moment he was a boy again. He could picture old Perseus the stable hand, showing him how to properly saddle a horse or milk a goat. Such a different life it was, his childhood. As was his life now. So different had it turned out than expected.

"Athanasius!" called a voice, startling him and perking the ears of the driver.

It was Demetrius, his old friend and son of Perseus, coming out of the stables and waving his hands wildly.

"Demetrius!" Athanasius shouted, and climbed down from the carriage to give big Demetrius a hug and stop him from talking too much until the driver left. "You're even bigger than I remember. Where's your father?"

Demetrius looked down. "He died not long after your father." Then he looked at the driver who lifted the seat in the carriage to remove Athanasius's pack. "Where is she?"

"Who?"

"Helena, your bride. The whole family is inside waiting for you. Your mother has prepared quite the feast. Everybody is coming over."

"What are you talking about, Demetrius?"

"The message you sent your mother about your arrival today. What's with the Roman get-up? Is this one of your jokes?"

"I sent no message," Athanasius said, yanking his sword out of its hilt as he spun around and stabbed the driver in the stomach. The dagger in the driver's hand, lifted in the air to stab Athanasius in the back, fell to the ground with the body.

Demetrius stared at the driver. "What are you doing?"

"We have to get to the house!" Athanasius yelled over his shoulder as he set off in a run. "The Romans are coming!"

He was halfway across the gardens when he saw the first flaming arrow arc high into the sky and crash through the red-tiled roof. "Jupiter, no!" he yelled as dozens more from all directions flew over him and hit the villa.

An explosion of screams followed by fire and smoke blew out every window. Then a great column of fire burst up out of the roof and into the sky.

A door opened and in the frame he saw his mother, bent over, staggering in the smoke, helped out by one of the cousins. Then an arrow hit her in the chest and she fell.

"Mother!" he screamed.

Dozens of heavily armored Roman legionnaires with javelins, swords and shields approached the house in a line, moving in methodically to block any escape. But one of his nieces, he could not recognize which, managed to crawl out a window and make a run for it.

A Roman butcher—the very one who had shot his mother—chased her down. His face was unforgettable, marked by a vertical gash from his forehead to his chin, as if an ax had once practically split his head in two. And his demented expression was like some malevolent god who took pleasure only by inflicting pain. When he caught up to his prey, he raised his javelin high and with two hands plunged it into her back, once and again.

"No! Oh, no! No!" Athanasius screamed and then felt something large tackle him to the ground.

It was Demetrius, sitting on him, pushing his face into the dirt to muffle his cries. "Too many spears, Athanasius. You cannot save them, only yourself."

And then the words shattered through the shouts and screams as the villa came crumbling down. It was his mother, calling out to him.

"Athanasius!"

Athanasius couldn't move, couldn't even open his mouth, so great was the weight of big Demetrius upon him.

"You must run, Athanasius. Run away. As must I."

With that the heaviness was gone, and so was Demetrius. Athanasius looked around at the smoldering ruins of his family's villa, unable to comprehend the vision of tragedy before his eyes.

He tasted blood in his mouth where he had bitten his tongue and heard his hard breathing. Something inside him had crumbled to nothing, unleashing a fury that overwhelmed all his fears.

He quickly picked himself up, made his way back to the stables, pulled out a horse and rode away, allowing himself one last look at the destruction of everything left that he held dear in this life. He had thought he had lost everything before, but now the finality of yet another shock turned his grief into a wildfire of rage.

You're going to die for this, Domitian, he vowed to himself. *You and all that stinks of Rome.*

The port of Kenchreai hummed at dusk as the dockworkers loaded the last stores onto the Pegasus. Captain Andros was going over the charts with the helmsman when he heard his name and looked up to see the centurion approach, shaking his head. "We've waited as long as we can, Captain. No sign of the tribune, and we have to arrive in Ephesus by the 14th of the month."

The captain nodded and walked out on deck to give the order to lift the gangway. It was late indeed, and darkness had fallen across the harbor. He could hear the strands of music from the taverns welcoming sailors who had just arrived. Then he heard a shout. Coming up the gangway was the tribune.

"We thought you weren't going to make it, Tribune," the captain told him as the gangway came up.

The tribune, who looked unusually distressed, said, "Some interrogations take longer than others. I'll be in my cabin for the night."

"Of course, Tribune."

"Oh, one more thing," the tribune said, and Andros could feel another surprise coming in the pit of his stomach. "We will be making an unscheduled stop on the way to Ephesus. I have another interrogation to perform on Patmos."

"Patmos?" the captain repeated, unable to contain his dismay.

"Don't tell the crew until the last moment," the tribune calmly replied. "They might worry they are the troop relief for the island instead of Ephesus. Even the commander of the garrison on Patmos is not expecting me. Caesar is worried about spies in his ranks. Let us not give him cause to suspect any of your crew."

"Yes, Tribune," Andros said and watched the tribune march up the two steps to his cabin door. Andros was as superstitious as old men of the sea came, and he could only shake his head. This doesn't bode well, he thought as the tribune shut the door behind him. Not well at all.

16

For the better part of two days Athanasius lay on his hammock staring at the ceiling, contemplating his situation and how he was utterly alone in this world. The sad fact was that he had nowhere to hide—not Rome, not home in Greece, and not even the Dei. At this point he had no choice but to use the cover he had as an interrogator to visit the last apostle John in his prison on the island of Patmos.

But he would not be asking the last apostle to help him find refuge within the underground Christian movement as Marcus had anticipated back in Rome. No, he would break the old man out under the guise of a prisoner transfer to Ephesus for a trial before the governor. He could think of nothing better to drive Domitian insane than to make John vanish from custody and magically appear in the streets of Ephesus, publicly discrediting the Dei. The truth would destroy Domitian's lie to the Christians and expose the false accusations that Athanasius of Athens was Chiron.

Of course, the Romans could quickly kill him and John, but the damage would have been done. And if Athanasius could stay alive long enough—that is, outlive Domitian—there was yet hope he could one day return to Rome, reunite with Helena and wreak vengeance on his turncoat rival Ludlumus.

But what if John balked? There was always that remote possibility. In that case, Athanasius would have to persuade him in his own vernacular. To prepare for his visit with the last apostle, he decided it best to study what the apostle wrote.

So on his third day since fleeing Corinth, Athanasius dug out the scrolls of Christian scripture from Chiron's trunk. For hours he sat at his cabin's desk, studying the collected gospels, letters and Book of Revelation, pausing only to take meals at his desk, sleep in his hammock and relieve himself in the nearest latrine at the stern—an empty amphora, once filled with something else, that drained to the bilge at the bottom of the ship.

It didn't take him long to see why The Way had so spooked Rome.

According to the "good news," the only sacrifice to God that the Christian superstition required had already been made in this man Jesus. And the only religious sacraments he could find—communion and baptism—were not requirements of the faith but symbols of remembrance. They were certainly a far cry from the urban legends in Rome of drinking blood and drowning people.

As for money, Jesus didn't seem to bother with it, except to drive out moneychangers at the temple in Jerusalem who forced people to pay to pray. He also offended his rich followers by telling them their money would not get them into heaven and to give it away to the poor, not to the temple nor even to his own organization. All so nobody could boast of his charity to God. It was this kind of thinking that apparently set off his treasurer Judas, who later betrayed him.

Well, Athanasius concluded, without sacrifice or money involved, Christianity could not be defined as a religion at all. Indeed, it was antithetical to everything the gods of Rome demanded for survival.

Most galling of all, Jesus was quoted as saying that there would be surprises in heaven. Not everybody who used his name on earth would be granted admission. Meanwhile, he said that others who had never heard of him would be welcomed.

Athanasius now understood why so many disciples deserted Jesus toward the end of his life, and he could see why he would too. He especially took issue with the entire *deus ex machina* return of Jesus at the end of history.

Believing in Jesus, let alone waiting for him to come back, wasn't going to get him out of his mess. Only action.

There was a knock at the door. "Enter."

The steward who had replaced Galen in serving him walked in. He was the young, peppy anti-Galen. "Tribune," he said brightly, even as his knees practically knocked together in terror. "The captain wanted you to know we've spotted Patmos."

Athanasius went up to the deck to get a glimpse. It was just before sunrise, and the dark cliffs of the island rose from the horizon like a jagged rock jutting up from the sea. As they rounded a cape, Athanasius saw a small white harbor nestled at the foot of the gloomy mountain.

Somewhere in that mountain was a cave, he thought, and inside that cave a man who claimed to have seen the end of the world.

A voice beside him said, "Tribune, are you sure you don't want to skip this excursion?"

This time it was the centurion who had come to converse in private with him.

"Now why would I want to do that, Centurion?"

"My men are anxious to get to Ephesus. And the oarsmen, sailors and marines aboard are anxious. They don't like the thought of anchoring off an island prison."

"Perhaps they've done something to merit such fears?"

"Nothing, Tribune. Nothing at all. But you know men of the sea. They are a superstitious lot. The end of the world was revealed on this island."

"Only if you're superstitious, Centurion. I am not. Tell the captain to take us in, or prepare to explain to Caesar why you chose to defy the will of Rome."

"At your orders, Tribune," he said and left quickly.

The Pegasus was too big a ship for the tiny harbor, so it had to anchor some ways off in deeper waters. The centurion and two officers took Athanasius in on a smaller boat. On the way in, Athanasius couldn't help but notice another ship, rather sizable but small enough to anchor in the harbor. The name painted on the stern was Sea Nymph, and it flew an Egyptian flag. It had the forecastle and stern house for dignitaries, but only one row of oars to support the sails. Something about it seemed off.

The centurion must have seen him staring. "A floating opium den and whorehouse from Alexandria, here to entertain the garrison. Our timing was fortunate."

Indeed, it was. Athanasius could use such a distraction with the garrison while he extricated John. The oarsmen of his little boat seemed to put their backs into it, eager to reach the island now that it offered more than prisoners and prophets of doom.

"Your men will have to wait until Ephesus, Centurion. I won't be long. We have a prisoner to transfer."

Athanasius could feel the wind taken out of his two rowers, their disappointment palpable. "Such is life," he told them sternly, knowing it all too well.

The officers tied up in the harbor, and Athanasius and the centurion headed up the stone quay, passing the whitewashed barracks toward the square, where there was some commotion.

Athanasius reached the edge of the square and saw a prisoner tied to a post, surrounded by a small group of soldiers. The island's commanding officer—and de facto prison warden—was dressed in full regalia, minus a helmet, perhaps to impress the whores watching from the deck of their ship.

The commander snapped a long whip on the prisoner's battered back, leaving a deep red stripe among several others. The prisoner screamed in agony. The soldiers jeered. It appeared to Athanasius this was something of an entertainment between the rounds of real fun aboard the floating pleasure barge.

"Commander?" Athanasius asked aloud.

"Sextus Calpurnius Barbatio," the commander said, irked by this break in his rhythm. Then seeing the tribune rankings, Barbatio snapped to attention. "Tribune, sir. To what do we owe this visit? Surely you must understand that my men get first priority with the Sea Nymph.

Your men will have to wait their turn. I'm sure you'll understand."

Athanasius wordlessly handed over his imperial order with Caesar's seal to the commander, who gave it a glance and then, apparently due to poor eyesight, handed it to his aide to read to him. The aide did so in a low voice as Barbatio listened with a stone face.

Barbatio said, "How can we assist the tribune?"

"I'm here to interrogate the last apostle John."

There was silence in the square. Even the wailing prisoner stopped his cries.

"You will find the threat of physical torture and death useless on the old man," Barbatio finally said. "Even my own psychological efforts have failed thus far."

"And what are those?"

"We learned the whip does not work on the apostle, so we use it on the other prisoners every night before supper. Then I visit John to confess my evil and demand his forgiveness. I know he must, as many times as I ask. So I wait for the day he cannot bear the burden any longer and tells me what I want to hear."

"What is that?"

"The meaning of the Book of Revelation."

"Oh, you mean there is one?" Athanasius said, prompting some nervous laughter. Then he got tough. "Your failures are not my concern, Commander." He glanced at the brothel boat in the harbor. "Nor your lack of discipline. I have my orders, and so do you."

Barbatio, none too happy with the tribune's tone, nodded. "Cornelius here will escort you to the cave. It's a bit of a climb."

A young officer stepped forward, and Athanasius followed him toward some stone steps out of the public square and up the hill. Behind him he heard the music of Patmos play again with the snap of a whip and the cries of the prisoner.

Athanasius went up the long, zigzagging path toward the cave. He was almost out of breath by the time they came to the iron gate at the entrance, which was flanked by two prison guards. The guards opened the gate at Cornelius's orders.

"You'll wait outside," Athanasius said and stepped inside.

The cave was dark, illuminated only by a few flickering candles and a shaft of dim light from some crack in the ceiling. There was movement in the back. Athanasius waited for his eyes to adjust.

He could see the recess in the rock, close to the ground, where the apostle would lay his head when resting. But he was not there. There was another recess to the right a little higher up where the apostle would probably support his hands as he knelt to pray. But John was not there either. And there was a more or less level place in the rock that looked to be used as a desk. There were papers and writing instruments on it.

Perhaps another revelation? Athanasius wondered. One that could explain what had happened to the last apostle?

He took a step toward the desk when he saw a shadow move at the back of the cave. A flicker of light appeared. An old, bearded man with white hair emerged from an alcove holding a candle. He wore the simple tunic of a prisoner and broken sandals. He looked at Athanasius curiously.

"I haven't seen your face before, Tribune."

"No, but perhaps you've heard my name. Chiron."

The last apostle screwed his eyes and paused before answering. "I doubt that. Who are you, really?"

Athanasius looked around the cave and back toward the opening. Satisfied they were far enough away from being overhead outside, he said, "My name is Athanasius of Athens. I'm here to free you."

17

"I don't want to be freed," John the Last Apostle told Athanasius after listening to his sad story. They were sitting on the sleeping ledge of the cave. John had a gentle, soft demeanor, completely at odds with his character in the gospel accounts and the violence of Revelation. "I'm already free. You're the one who needs to be free. Free from this hatred I see in your eyes."

This was precisely what Athanasius feared might happen. "My hatred is reserved for Rome, old man, and for Dominium Dei. Not Jesus or The Way."

"You must love others, Athanasius, and forgive your enemies."

Athanasius resisted the insanity of John's easy words. "You don't know Caesar Domitian like I do, nor his vile master of the Games. They killed the consul, Flavius Clemens, your top Christian in Rome, I hear, along with

179

many others. They will keep on killing. They want to destroy your Church."

"It's not my Church, Athanasius. Jesus is the head."

"Then come with me to Ephesus and say as much publicly. Expose the Dei and Domitian. Leave the rest to us in Rome."

"You will accomplish nothing by killing Caesar."

Athanasius threw out the bait that Clemens' servant Stephanus threw him: "Even if Young Vespasian becomes emperor and bows before Christ?"

"That's his business," John said, unimpressed with the vision of a Christian world. "But you are gravely mistaken if you believe that turning Christianity into the official religion of Rome will save anybody. Jesus said his kingdom is in heaven, not on earth. I see great evil in this thinking of yours."

"And I see greater evil in an old man who would prefer to see his doomsday vision scorch the earth than lift a finger to help an innocent man."

"From what you told me, Athanasius, you don't seem so innocent. Senator Maximus's slave, the steward on your ship, the driver in Corinth. You've been busy, and there's blood on your hands. Why should I believe that you are not from the Dei? You could be a plant from Caesar to spy out the Church and destroy it."

"I am not!" Athanasius shouted and stood up. "The senator, like you, betrayed me. His slave tried to kill me.

The ship's steward thought he had, and the driver in Corinth was about to, before his friends the Roman legions slaughtered my entire family and razed the house I grew up in! My actions are justified! You don't tell me about calling down the fire! Because your good Jesus has already incinerated everything I held dear!"

His rant prompted the guards outside to open the iron gate at the mouth of the cave and walk in to see if everything was all right.

"Father John!" called Cornelius until Athanasius cut him short.

"Out!" Athanasius cried, brandishing his sword. "Or I interrogate you too, Brother Cornelius. Are you one of those secret acolytes among the guards here that I've heard about?"

"No, Tribune," Cornelius said, backing off with his torch. "My apologies, sir. Hail, Caesar."

Athanasius watched him retreat and turned to John, who was calm as ever.

John said, "Tell me about this girl in your dreams again, before your nightmare began. The only one I see in my nightmares is the Whore of Babylon."

"I told you, old man. I, too, have had visions of the future, and the ancient past as well. Comes with being an imaginative playwright, I suppose. But while the dreams change, the girl is the same. Barely a young woman, with long black hair and big dark eyes that bleed tears of blood. I have always fallen into a bottomless cave, but she calls me out into the light with a voice that sounds like running water." Athanasius sighed. "I don't know what I'm saying. My life is all a bad dream now. Your God is an illusion."

"No, Athanasius," John told him. "God is reality. Everything else is illusion."

He held his candle up to the crack in the roof of the cave, presumably produced in the rock by the exceptional physical and supernatural phenomena that accompanied the vision. This fissure extended across the upper part of the cave from east to west, dividing the rock into three parts and thus, Athanasius supposed, serving old John as a continual reminder of the trinitarian nature of God.

"Your coming to this holy place is not chance in your life, Athanasius. God, who wishes all men to be saved and to come to a knowledge of truth, who directs all things for man's spiritual benefit, has guided you here for you to listen, deep within yourself, to the secret echo of the words that Jesus spoke to the seven churches of Asia."

"Words that have been ignored."

"Yes, the light has been extinguished because their faith in God grows cold. But I know that you have seen in your mind's eye the heavenly vision revealed to me. I can see God's sovereign work in your life even if you do not. And if what you say about the Dei is true, it must be exposed to the churches of Asia Minor."

"So you will come with me?"

"No," John said, shuffling to his desk of stone. "But I will write a letter for you to take to the church leaders in Ephesus. They can decide for themselves if they want to help you."

This was not what he wanted, but it was clear he would get no better at this point. He had told John about the Dei, and the old man was writing in his own hand a letter acknowledging such for him to give to the leaders of The Way in Ephesus.

"And how can your disciples help me?"

"They can hide you in one of the churches in Asia, away from Rome's legions."

"You mean one of those seven problematic churches you address in your Book of Revelation? Some help."

"I did not address them, my son. Jesus did. And there is an eighth church I have in mind."

"An eighth church?" Athanasius repeated.

"Yes," John said, finishing up and signing his papyrus, folding it and sealing it with wax and a symbol. He handed it over. "If you open it, you can see I used the Caesar's own cipher. You know it?"

Athanasius knew it. The key was a square containing the 24 letters of the Roman alphabet across the top and 24 numbers down the side. Each numbered row or "shift" was its own alphabet, beginning with the next letter of the alphabet from the shift above. So alphabet 1 began with the B, which translated "A." Alphabet 2 began with a C, which also translated to an "A." And so on down the line for 24 alphabets.

"I know it," he told John.

"Then you know that neither you nor the Romans nor the Dei can break it without knowing the secret keyword." John handed him the letter.

Athanasius placed it in the pocket beneath his breastplate. "So what is the keyword?"

John smiled. The old man wasn't going to tell him.

Athanasius sighed. "Then who is my contact in Ephesus, and where do I meet him?"

Again, John was indirect in his reply. "You'll take the letter and go to the town library. There you will request the eleven-volume memoir titled *Miracles in Asia Minor: My Life and Times.* It is by Gaius Mucius Mucianus, who was once governor of Syria and traveled throughout Asia and wrote about it."

Athanasius vaguely recalled the name Mucianus from his lawyer Pliny's uncle, who apparently drew from this memoir in his own geographic text *Natural History.* "And then?"

"You will place the letter inside the eighth volume and return the collection. The following day you will return to the library and again check out the collection. Inside the same eighth volume you will find further instructions."

Athanasius didn't like it. John was proposing one of those drop-offs the spies used, and not direct contact. The old man really doesn't trust me, Athanasius thought. "So I'm to fend for myself for a night in Ephesus? What if the Romans get me?"

John shrugged. "They haven't yet. This is all in God's hands."

"And you've just washed your own hands clean like Pontius Pilate did with Jesus, is that it?"

John nodded. "You've been reading your Scriptures."

Actually, he remembered that one from the imperial Roman accounts of the trial of Jesus that he had read long before this nightmare. "How do I know you aren't instructing them to kill me or turn me in?"

"How do they know you aren't an assassin of Rome or the Dei to kill them all? They may not even recognize my handwriting. My secretary Prochorus comes by day to write my letters." John sighed. "I can't make them do anything, and Jesus won't make them do anything. This isn't the Roman army or empire. Each can do as he likes, and as you've read with the seven churches, most do. I can remind them of the true gospel of Jesus, warn them of false gospels, tell them to love each other. But I cannot offer them worldly wealth or comfort. We're all volunteers."

"I was conscripted."

"Yes, you were, weren't you? I told you, I see hatred in your eyes, if not for the Lord then for Rome. That in itself is a danger to The Way."

"Yes, quite," said a voice, and out of the shadows emerged the commander Barbatio, sword at Athanasius's throat. Somehow he had slipped in silently. He stared at Athanasius. "To think I can now have both the head of the church of Asia and the head of the church in Rome. I can only imagine Caesar's gratitude for your capture. How is this for a proposal, Tribune: You stay here, and I get off this rock and return to Rome?"

Athanasius nodded. "There is only one problem with your proposal, Commander," he said. "This little stick."

Athanasius held up a wooden stick to Barbatio's sword, and the commander laughed. "What do you think you are going to do with that?"

"This," said Athanasius and thrust his hand forward, driving the poisoned tip of the stick into the soft flesh beneath Barbatio's chin.

"Ach!" the commander gasped, clutching his throat.

Athanasius quickly grabbed him by the hair and threw him face down on the floor at John's feet, where he writhed in agony.

The last apostle threw his hands to his head. "This is not the way of Jesus!"

"Nevertheless, you said I'm God's servant," he said. "And right now this is the only way I know how to get out of here. So say your prayers. Silently."

He ran out of the cave at the same moment Cornelius and the two guards ran in with torches to see their commander face down on the cave floor with a halo of blood around his head.

Cornelius drew his sword and took a swing at Athanasius as he shouted to the others outside. But Athanasius blocked it with his own sword and smashed the hilt on the aide's helmet, sending him to the ground. Then Athanasius ran out.

Already a unit of archers was rushing toward the cave, brought on by the shouts.

Athanasius dashed around the hill, racing through rocks at the back, jumping into a trench and down toward the quarries below.

Arrows began raining down as he wound this way and that, not knowing where he was going. Once again he had blown his way of escape, just like he had in Rome, only this time it was worse: Unlike the dark slums of Rome, he was out in the open with no cover and no ship to go back to, because surely more legions were now waiting at the Pegasus. He had met the last apostle and had gotten a letter of introduction of sorts to open doors in the church, much like the letter from Caesar opened doors in the empire. But he had failed to take John with him, had killed the garrison commander of the island prison, and thus sealed off any way of escape for himself.

I'm going to die here before the last apostle, he realized as he ran.

An arrow glanced his calf and he went down, tumbling over and over until he hit a fig tree. He jumped up and darted into a grove of trees. Suddenly he came upon a break in the grove, where a narrow road cut across. He slid down through the brush and started to cross to the other side when a golden litter carried by four dark slaves stopped in front of him.

The veil opened to reveal the spitting image of Cleopatra. It was the madame from the Sea Nymph, the queen of the whores. "Need a lift, Tribune? Or do you want to stay here and die? Get in!"

18

As the litter moved off into the dusk, Athanasius and the woman dressed like Cleopatra sat cross-legged facing one another. "You're dirtier than all the prisoners here, Tribune."

The way she said "Tribune" told him she knew exactly who he was, or rather who he was not. "Why are you helping me, Cleopatra?" he asked her, using the same tone on her name that she had used with him.

"Call me Cleo, mistress of the Sea Nymph," she told him. "And who says I am helping you? I am helping John. My pleasure barge pays regular visits to Patmos. My girls service the guards, well, most of them. Some of the guards come aboard and slip my girls secret letters that we take to other ports of call."

"Like this one?" Athanasius showed her the letter that John had given him.

She looked it over and then nodded. "Exactly. I was waiting to receive something like this from Cornelius before you assassinated Barbatio."

"It wasn't an assassination," he insisted. "It was more of an accident."

"Too bad. He terribly mistreats my girls. I was going to have to do the honors of serving him tonight until you spared me."

Athanasius studied her as he pondered this unusual arrangement she had with the last apostle and his key leaders in Ephesus. "If you'll pardon my asking, Cleo, why would a man like the last apostle trust you?"

"A whore?" she said, raising an eyebrow. "For the same reason he probably trusts you. I tell him what his bishops and acolytes won't: the truth. Now you'll have to trust me too. Quick, crawl under my ass."

Athanasius cocked his ear to make sure he had heard correctly, then pulled back the veil of the litter slightly to see that they were entering the harbor. Night had fallen, and the torches were lit. Cornelius, awake and alert now, barked orders for the ranks to form lines. The last of the garrison's pleasure seekers were quickly disembarking the Sea Nymph and putting on their helmets.

He dropped the curtain and looked at Cleo. Her knees were drawn up to her heaving bosoms, and she had pulled back the cushion underneath to reveal a secret compartment. It was only a Roman foot or so deep but ran the length of the litter and was wide enough for him to crawl in and lie flat. She then rolled the cushion back and sat on him.

"Easy does it, my slaves," he heard her call out.

The litter stopped. Then came the sound of approaching boots and a voice.

"Madame, you are safe," said a loud voice, which he recognized as belonging to Cornelius. Perhaps he was playing to the troops. "There has been a tragedy. Commander Barbatio has been assassinated."

"Have you found the assassin?"

"We are turning the island over now. We have a centurion from the assassin's ship who can identify him. The captain refuses to help."

"Have you searched my ship? My girls could be in danger. I won't board until you've searched it from top to bottom."

"Search the whore barge!" Cornelius shouted, and Athanasius heard the thunder of boots going up the gangway to the boat.

There were holes in the bottom of the litter, through which Athanasius could see the ground and breathe quietly, but not without some struggle. Cleo had made a good play. The troops were bound to search the ship at some point. Better now than after he was on board.

A short time later there was more thunder as the troops came back down the gangway, and a voice said, "I have searched the whore ship from top to bottom, sir. There is nobody but the whores and crew on board."

"Very well," said the voice of Cornelius, and as the sound of boots faded away he addressed Cleo. "Such a tragedy, Madame."

"Yes, it is," she said in a droll tone. "Barbatio hadn't consummated our deal, and my girls only serviced the first round of the night. Barbatio had ordered five rounds. I expect to be paid in full. We made a special trip to Patmos. I have Nubian oarsmen, sailors and marines to pay, and girls to feed."

The voice turned stern as it addressed Cleo, again, it sounded to Athanasius, for public consumption. "You will be content to leave with your lives and return at a later visit to finish our business and get paid. Now be gone, and take your whores with you."

And with that Athanasius could see the stone of the quay give way to the wood of the gangway as the litter carrying him and Cleo was walked up to the deck. Minutes later he crawled out of his secret hold and stood at the rail of the Sea Nymph gazing back upon the dark waters. The black cutout of Patmos slowly began to fade into the night until it disappeared.

"Oooh, how it must hurt, Pharaoh."

Seated on a small divan in Cleo's private cabin aboard the Sea Nymph, Athanasius tried to relax as a girl named "Nefertiri" bathed his cuts in oils, dabbing them gently with a cloth. She seemed genuinely concerned for each and every scratch, blowing on and kissing them.

She offered him wine. "Medicine for your stomach, Great One, as we cruise the Nile on your royal barge?"

Athanasius, recalling his last experience with wine offered to him from Galen aboard the Pegasus, was inclined to decline, but took a small sip anyway, his bones and muscles feeling crushed and not wanting to spoil this little fantasy Nefertiri had created.

Then Cleo spoke from the door in Greek. "Phyllis, back to your quarters."

Phyllis sheepishly scooped up her assorted comfort potions and tools, then bowed before him and Cleo. She smiled at Athanasius on her way out.

Cleo entered and poured herself a cup of the wine. "Cornelius will see to it that the logs on Patmos will show that the Sea Nymph is going to Alexandria. But first we'll stop at Ephesus for you. We'll anchor offshore, and you can go in by boat. You will have to watch yourself going in. I think your Pegasus will beat us with its two additional decks of oars. Consider your career as a tribune over for now. You will have to put away your costume."

Athanasius nodded. He knew as much. "I don't suppose you have any other disguises for a man in my position?"

"Wigs, beards and dyes for your hair, too," she said as
she drank her wine. "Everything you could want. We
could even make you a woman, although I'm afraid you
might draw even more unwanted attention from some
men than you already have with the assassination of Barbatio. I can't imagine old John is happy with you. You
must be somebody special if he trusts you."

"He doesn't trust me," Athanasius said. "He thinks
I'm a spy from the Dei sent to destroy the Church."

At the mention of the Dei the blood drained from
Cleo's face and her hand holding her cup froze in mid-
air. For a wild moment Athanasius worried he had said
the wrong thing and might not reach Ephesus after all.
Women like Cleo could be quite cunning, and she did
have a deck full of Nubian strongmen at her call. But
instead she laughed and put the cup down, then lay on top
of him on the bed.

"I can look into your eyes and tell that you are not one
of them."

"And how is that?" Athanasius asked, shifting beneath
her.

"You don't have the empty, dead eyes of the Dei that
are devoid of any humanity."

Athanasius could see that he didn't have to worry about her killing him, although he did begin to worry about where this evening in bed was going. He could only think of Helena, and how important to his survival it was to hold onto his hatred of Domitian and Ludlumus. To let up for even a moment might deprive him of the full venom he needed. "You know the Dei?"

Cleo nodded soberly. "Who do you think runs the church in Ephesus?"

Athanasius bolted upright in her bed. "You're lying now."

She sat back, startled. "I thought that is why John is sending a man like yourself, to do what his acolytes in the Church cannot and smoke out the Dei."

"Who told you that the Dei was evil?" he pressed her. "I thought the Dei defended The Way and the helpless, and only attacked Roman power."

She said, "The Dei preys on the weak and helpless, on the least of these, to make itself more powerful. And it has compromised the church in Ephesus."

Athanasius said, "According to the Book of Revelation, Jesus lauds the church in Ephesus for its sound doctrine, for not falling into apostasy."

"Its doctrine is fine," Cleo told him. "In practice, however, it has been hopelessly compromised. John knows it. But Bishop Timothy, who is a disciple of Paul's, and his second, Polycarp, who is a disciple of

John's, apparently don't. I suspect John is sending you to Polycarp because he doesn't trust Timothy's disciples, who are thick with the Dei. I know these men, because they run me too."

Athanasius looked her in the eye. "Tell me everything."

For the first time since entering her cabin, Cleo smiled.

Over several hours Cleo explained to Athanasius what she knew about the Dei, working backward from her own experience aboard the Sea Nymph to the opium dens and whore houses the Dei operated in ports all around the Great Sea, to the flesh they shipped out of Ephesus— women to the temples, and men to feed the galleys, the mines and the Games in Rome.

"But where do these people come from?" Athanasius asked.

"There are caves in the hinterlands of Asia Minor," she told him. "Vast, endless caves where the Christians hide in underground cities. Tens of thousands of them. Most live there because they have nowhere else to live, and they crawl out into the day to work as field laborers if they can find work. Many others have moved there for protection from Roman troops, who have better things to do than crawl into holes in the ground. And a vast majority are convinced the world is about to end and have shut themselves in with their families and food stores in preparation."

Athanasius listened carefully. He had heard rumors of these underground cities, much like the urban legends of catacombs beneath Rome, where a growing army of Christians were breeding to one day surface and overwhelm the city like locusts. But he had chalked that up to Domitian's propaganda machinery, which always seemed to go into full motion just before the start of the Games every summer.

"What do the caves have to do with the Dei, Cleo?"

"I told you, the caves are where the Dei gets its flesh to feed the Games," she explained. "Masked men dressed like the Minotaur of Greek mythology make raids to grab young girls and men and terrify the population. The Christians think they are armed bands of local gypsies. But they are Dei. They drug the men and women with opium, and bring them to the port cities, the biggest of which is Ephesus. The women become whores, the men mostly slaves or gladiators, and are shipped out to the far corners of the empire, never to return."

More myths and mysteries, he thought. Each seemed to reveal yet another when it came to Dominium Dei. He had been led to believe that the Dei was an imperial organization. But Cleo was describing something else, something more like a trade organization based on commerce, not politics. "So the Dei sells opium and flesh for money?"

"No, secrets. They use their sex clubs and ships like this: The Dei employ young boys and girls to have sex with customers and blackmail them. The Christians are the easiest marks and make no trouble. Bishops who come to Ephesus for church conferences, for example, are often lured into compromise and then, once under the control of the Dei, are sent back to their provincial churches."

"None resist?" Athanasius asked.

"No," she said. "I tell my own girls that God has given them free wills. The only opium they use is for the pleasure of their guests. The ones who are Christians, they are ashamed to go back to their hometowns and families. The few who have are shunned and come back to me. Only one girl, a very young girl who was terribly mistreated, went back to the caves to warn the others and never came back. I heard she was alive, but that was months ago. Today, God knows."

"Why don't you resist?"

"I do," she said. "I stay employed by the Dei in order to help the real Church and men like John—and my girls. I cannot choose their life for them. But I can do my best to keep them safe as much as depends on me."

"Why are you telling me this?"

"Two reasons," she said. "The first is that you said something about the Dei being an imperial organization. Perhaps it is. But in Asia Minor it is very much associated with the Church."

"Why don't the bishops denounce it?"

"They do," Cleo said. "That is, they denounce murderous acts like the slaying of the astrologer Caelus, despite their belief that astrology is of the devil. But they don't know about everything else the Dei does. They don't even know that their prime benefactors are members of the Dei, because their society in the Church goes by a different name than it does in public."

"What name is that?"

"The Lord's Vineyard. It's a fellowship of tradesmen and commercial businessmen."

"And the Lord's Vineyard and the Dei are one and the same?"

"I think so."

"You think?"

"I know that the owner of this ship is a member of the Dei by the code name Poseidon. He is the Dei chief in Ephesus. I also believe he is a member of the church there, and a representative of the Lord's Vineyard. His daughter goes by the name Urania and runs a honey trap in Ephesus called the Club Urania, using her girls to nab men who go there. Her father then ships them off to Rome along with more girls and opium. If you find him, he might be able to lead you to the head of the Dei itself in Asia Minor."

"What's his real name?"

"I don't know," she said. "One of my girls claimed to have seen his face during a church communion. But before she could give us his name, she disappeared."

Athanasius nodded. "What is the second reason you are telling me this?"

"I was not always this way, and neither were my girls," she answered. "I want you to remember this, to remind the church leaders, if you live long enough to meet them. Now, rest up. You'll need it."

And with that warning, Cleo rose to her feet and left him alone in her cabin. As soon as the door shut behind her, Athanasius fell fast asleep.

19

When Athanasius disembarked from his tether in the harbor of Ephesus, he looked like a new man. His hair had been soaked in brilliantine and carefully cropped like a Roman nobleman's by Cleo's girls back on the Sea Nymph, now on its way to Alexandria. The papers he had forged himself stated that his name was Clement. Amazing how different he looked with so little effort and free of the weight of a tribune's armor. But then, as he discovered so often in the theater, a little was often all it took.

The first advertisement etched into the pavement that Athanasius saw upon his arrival was for the Club Urania that Cleo had warned him about. He read several more as he walked along, head down, unwilling to look up for fear of being recognized by any of the Roman troops on the docks who may have let off from the Pegasus anchored offshore. Captain Andros had beat the Sea

Nymph to Ephesus, and Athanasius wanted no interruptions between the dock and the city's library where he was to make the drop and connect with John's man in Ephesus.

The bustling city of Ephesus was almost half as big as Rome—more than 500,000 citizens—and was traditionally Greek, feeling more like home to Athanasius than the exotic "gateway to the East" it was to Roman visitors. Many came to see the city's famed Temple of Artemis, the largest building in the world and more than six hundred years old, and its many-breasted statue of the Lady of Ephesus that beckoned every sailor who stepped ashore.

Built on the slopes of Pion Hill, Ephesus served as the commercial capital of the Asian provinces. The roads were paved with marble and the colonnaded shopping streets with fine mosaics. Sloping up the hill to the grand villas overlooking the city was Curettes Way, named after the priests of the city who led the regular processions and festivals to honor Domitian. For a city dominated by Greek ethnicity, Ephesus took great pride as a steward of Roman religion and thus had a history of clubbing Christians, starting when the apostle Paul spoke in the theater decades ago.

Athanasius had been here several times before, mostly to launch various performances and sign off on the merchandise from the sleazy local idolmaker Supremus. He had also consulted on the design of the grand new library that had been proposed for the city by Julius Celsus Polemaenus, a local Greek who had become quite rich in Rome. The current library to which he was headed was small and only a single story. By financing a three-story edifice, Celsus was angling to win the governorship of Asia from Domitian in the near future. Athanasius had always considered the Celsus family sellouts for so easily embracing Rome and its religion and yet using their Greek heritage to win commercial and political advantage in their home province.

As he walked from the harbor up past the city's great bathhouses, Athanasius realized he couldn't fight the temptation to stop by the city's other great attraction—its 44,000-seat amphitheater, the largest in the world—if only to see if his *Oedipus Sex* comedy was still playing. So he marched up Marble Street to find out, passing the library on the way—and spotting a wine shop and tavern across from the entrance that he would be sure to return to after dropping off the letter.

Up at the theater, there was a crowd milling about, as the stage served the public as a forum by day if there were no performances or rehearsals underway.

A bad omen for him, he thought.

He stopped a stranger who was walking away from a conversation to ask, "Anything playing tonight? I saw no signs at the entrance."

"Nothing right now. Rome canceled Oedipus Sex along with its playwright Athanasius of Athens. It's too bad. I really liked the Greek rascal."

"So did I," Athanasius replied, and turned away.

So word of my demise has reached Ephesus, he thought. Perhaps that was a good thing. The general population wouldn't be apt to recognize him if they didn't expect to see him, even if the Romans were looking for him. The mind was funny that way with the eyes. He would need that luck now at the library.

Retracing his steps down Marble Way, Athanasius approached the city library with caution. It was a small but deep single-story building squashed between two larger ones. It had seen better days, and Athanasius assumed few denarii were going toward its upkeep what with the grand new library being planned, complete with a two-tiered façade and three levels of niches. He walked up three short steps and passed between the pair of Ionic columns flanking the entrance.

Inside was a large rectangular hall that faced east toward the morning sun. There were windows just below the vaulted ceiling to allow natural light, along with the central square oculus in the flat ceiling. The central apse was framed by a large arch at the far wall, and inside the apse stood a statue of Athena, the goddess of truth. Along the other three sides were rectangular recesses that held shelves for the nearly 4,000 scrolls.

He was greeted by one of two unarmed guards who watched for theft from patrons on the way out and was directed toward the main marble counter by the statue of Athena.

Like other libraries around the empire, Athanasius knew that this one existed for the benefit of students and traveling Romans. As such they tended to house collections of local documents of interest. So his request to see the memoir of Mucianus and his travels throughout Asia shouldn't raise any eyebrows.

He glanced around at various patrons as he walked toward the counter, curious to know if one of them was the man who would pick up his letter the moment he had returned the volume he was about to check out. Whoever it was would say a lot about Timothy and his selection of associates. If what Cleo said was true, then the spy would have to be somebody high enough in the church. John or Timothy would know his identity, no doubt. Athanasius had no clue, and yet he was about to reveal himself to this agent, and this made him most uncomfortable. For in so doing, he might be revealing himself to spies from Rome or the Dei or both, if they were watching John's men.

At the counter was a civilized, older librarian whom Athanasius vaguely recognized. He prayed to Jupiter and Jesus both that the patrician didn't recognize him, and thanked the gods that he hardly ever spent time in libraries while supervising his performances abroad.

"And how can I help you, sir?" the senior librarian asked in a professional but almost too loud voice that spoke volumes about the *gravitas* that the library sought to project about itself.

"I'm traveling through Anatolia and was told I should check out a memoir by a former governor if I want to do some sightseeing. It's a travelogue by Gaius Mucius Mucianus."

"Ah, yes. Miracles in Asia Minor. If you believe in that sort of thing."

Athanasius said nothing about the editorial comment. "You have it then?"

"But, of course," the librarian said, taking a small leather strip from his counter. "It's in a private shelf in back only because we need to reserve as much space as possible on the public stacks for more popular works. Someday, when the new library goes up, we'll have room to hold 12,000 scrolls. Even then we'd fit into the smallest corner of the Temple of Artemis. Excuse me."

He disappeared for a moment, and Athanasius looked around, catching in just the twinkling of an eye the stare of a man at a table, who quickly buried himself back again in his scroll. Athanasius pretended not to notice.

Friend or foe? he wondered, and the librarian returned without the leather strip nor any volumes.

"Is there a problem?" Athanasius asked.

"Not at all," the librarian said. "One of our staff is setting them out for you at that table over there. There are a good 12 volumes, you know."

Athanasius looked over at the corner of the room nearest the statue of Athena, where a scrawny young man dropped each volume like a heavy brick, only drawing even more attention than Athanasius had already.

"Twelve volumes, you say?" Athanasius asked. John had said there were only eleven, Athanasius recalled. He supposed it didn't matter, as he was only to concern himself with volume eight. "I might have to come back tomorrow and possibly the day after just to get through half of them."

"That's usually the case, sir," the librarian said with a knowing look. "Please sit down and make yourself comfortable. Take all the time you need."

"Certainly," said Athanasius, and made his way over to the table in back by Athena, aware of curious glances. He sat down and cracked open the first volume.

The scrawny librarian worked silently nearby, rearranging stacks of scrolls and books. Every now and then he glanced over as Athanasius picked up one volume and then another, making notes on his own tablet like a traveler would to mark highlights for his journey. The volumes were arranged geographically, with sections inside further broken down to cities within the provinces that Mucianus detailed, each with a story of some miraculous spring, fish, fruit or even rock that was unnaturally large or boasted healing properties or some such.

Coming to the seventh volume, and aware of the prying eyes of the librarian, Athanasius pretended to reach for it. But in a sleight of hand he actually picked up the eighth volume instead. This one had a section in back on Cappadocia and its underground cities. Interesting, he thought, and surreptitiously slipped his letter into the section and closed the volume.

He made quick work of two more volumes before leaving them all on the table and returning to the librarian at the counter. He hoped his ruse had worked.

"Did you find what you were looking for?" the librarian asked with a raised eyebrow.

"I don't know," Athanasius said. "There are so many volumes. As you suggested, I'll probably have to come back tomorrow to finish the rest."

"But, of course," the librarian said. "I'll have them put in back now, and when you return we'll bring them out for you again."

"Thank you," said Athanasius.

On his way out he passed the man who had glanced at him and was still buried in the single scroll that had occupied him during Athanasius's entire visit.

The Artemis Wine Bar was just across the street from the library. It was an open-fronted building with outdoor dining under its wide canopy. Athanasius sat down on a straw chair at one of the small, round tables, ordered a cup of the Cappadocian special, and watched the entrance of the library.

It was almost an hour of observing patrons enter and exit the library before Athanasius saw him: the man who had been glancing at him when he first went inside. Now he was walking quickly away with his hands stuffed in the folds of his tunic, his head looking this way and that. Then a hand came out of a fold for a moment, red with the dye that Cleo had given him to pen the bogus letter he left behind. Now he knew whom the local church leaders in Ephesus had sent for the pickup, and he could follow him to John's man and avoid wasting time and risking detection at some inn overnight.

He left a tip on the table and quickly walked out of the bar onto the street and started to follow the man with the red hands. He looked like Jesus with the nail marks in his hands, Athanasius thought as he blinked in the harsh glare of the noonday sun. The light was bouncing off the whitewashed walls and surfaces of the streets. For a moment he feared he had lost the man but then saw him glancing back his way, spotting him, then starting to run.

Athanasius ran after him, trying not to cause any more of a scene, until he almost fell upon him at a corner, where the man suddenly stopped and turned.

"Relax," Athanasius told him, grabbing him at the shoulders. "Let's just walk along to whomever you are walking along to and everything will—"

Before Athanasius could finish his sentence, he heard a whoosh from overhead. An arrow suddenly struck the man in the chest and he cried out. Athanasius let go. The man fell to the street, dead.

Athanasius looked over his shoulder in time to see a Roman with a shield strapped to his back tackle him to the ground. A rain of arrows began to fall, bouncing off the shield—or the Roman.

"You follow me if you want to live, Chiron," the Roman said gruffly, pulling him up to his feet.

Athanasius got up and over the Roman's head saw the archers on the rooftops. He stared. There on the roof was none other than the monster who had murdered his mother and niece back in Corinth! The scar down his face was unmistakable, and so was the recognition in his eyes as he reloaded.

"Quick!" shouted the Roman who tackled him, and now Athanasius saw armored chariots barreling down the street from both directions. "We cut through to the alley!"

Athanasius felt the Roman shove him into a rug shop, pushing him past the various rolls and stacks of carpets. The rumble of boots and chariots stopped outside.

"This way," he said, pushing Athanasius out back into the alley.

There was a grating in the pavement, garbage strewn everywhere. The Roman pulled up the grating and barked, "Jump!"

Athanasius peered into the dark. "How far down?"

"Far enough."

Athanasius could hear the shouts, "The alley!"

They threw themselves into the open sewer and held onto the stone rim with their fingers. The Roman had just enough time to reach out with a free hand to pull the grating back over them before a legion of troops crashed out the back door of the rug shop into the alley and fanned out.

Hanging onto the grating by his fingertips, Athanasius looked over at the Roman and suddenly saw something between his breastplate and shoulder straps—the tattoo of the Dei stamped under his right arm.

"Who are you?" he said as the rumble of chariots came barreling down the alley above.

"My name is Virtus," the Dei man said as his legs swung up and kicked Athanasius in the stomach, causing him to lose his grip and plunge into the darkness below until he hit the bottom and blacked out.

20

When Athanasius opened his eyes, he found himself lying in a dank cell. Hunched over him was the man who had knocked him out. He remembered the attack on the streets above: the confrontation with the man with the stained hands, the rain of arrows from Roman snipers on the rooftops, the escape with the help of this man into these tunnels, and the Dei tattoo under his arm.

"Where am I?" Athanasius asked, sitting up.

"Where I was only weeks ago, in the tunnels beneath Ephesus," the man who called himself Virtus said.

"You," Athanasius said, touching the lump on his head. "You're Dei."

"Maybe," the man said.

"So Rome wants me dead, but the Dei wants me alive?" Athanasius said. "Why?"

"That is a mystery to me too. I simply follow orders, Athanasius."

"So you know who I am?"

"I've seen your plays in Rome," Virtus told him. "But I missed the one here before it was shut down after Caelus died."

That's right, Athanasius thought. In one way he had already arrived at the source of the recent troubles. "You know how he died exactly?"

"I killed him."

"You?"

"Not exactly. I was his bodyguard, and I failed to protect him from the Dei."

"I thought you were Dei."

"Now I am. I wasn't before. I was Praetorian. Third Cohort. Then Caelus and I were captured down here."

"Why didn't they kill you too?"

"I was of better use to them alive," Virtus said. "They knew I was a dead man if I showed my face to Rome after losing Caesar's chief astrologer. So they set me up here as a Watchman in the city. When the local governor and legions got secret communications that you had escaped Rome and killed the garrison commander on Patmos, they were ordered to drag you in, kill you without question and send your head to Caesar. Nobody was to know you were alive. The Dei intercepted the orders and sent me to protect you."

"Protect me, Virtus?" Athanasius asked. "Or to intercept me before I made contact with local church authorities?"

Virtus's face clouded. "What are you talking about? We are the local church authorities. The man who died, I knew him from The Way here. He was a good man. You should not have involved him."

Athanasius was confused by what Virtus was saying, or rather by Virtus's confusion. He actually still believed the Dei and the Church were on the same side against Rome.

"Me involve him?" Athanasius said. "Listen here, Dei Praetorian. I'm the one who never should have been involved. And from what you are telling me, neither should you."

"Then why have you brought your troubles to Ephesus, Athanasius?"

"I have a vital revelation from Rome for the bishop Timothy here and all the churches in Asia Minor."

"A revelation you say, Clement of Rome?" Virtus said in a mocking tone. He had read the name Athanasius was using in Ephesus from the papers in his pouch, which was in the corner with his belt and daggers. "And what revelation is that?"

Athanasius told him. "The Dei is an imperial organization, run by Domitian in order to play Rome and the

Church against each other in a forever war while he eliminates enemies on both sides and consolidates power."

"Lord Jesus Christ, have mercy on us!" Virtus cried out, making some movements with his hand that looked like the cross sign of the letter *Chi*.

Perhaps that was a signal between the lower ranks of the Dei to each other, Athanasius thought, and he was stunned to see that Virtus had become a true believer and yet had failed to distinguish the Church from the Dei. If so, the Dei were more deeply intertwined with the churches of Asia Minor than even Cleo intimated.

"Well, at least you believe me. So you must have had your suspicions."

"Perhaps, but I could never get over the death of Caelus and why Domitian would want his own astrologer dead."

"He didn't want Caelus dead, Virtus. That's the problem. There is something else going on in the Dei. It seems to have a mind of its own. This is why Domitian is terrified and lashing out everywhere. You tell me you had orders to protect me from Rome. I can only assume such an order is counter to the will of Caesar. Who in the Dei gave you the order?"

"I don't know," Virtus said. "My orders are left to me every morning in a wooden cylinder that looks like a twig, behind the statue of Domitian at the new temple that Caesar erected for himself."

"And that didn't offer you a clue as to the Dei's high command?"

Virtus seemed genuinely embarrassed. "I thought it was the Dei's way of tweaking the nose of the empire by carrying out its business right under its nose."

"And you never thought to lie in wait in advance and watch to see who it was who left your orders for you?"

Now Virtus got defensive. "You have a natural inclination to think like a spy, Athanasius. But I am a soldier by training. A soldier who follows orders and doesn't question his commanders."

"Well, now you know too much to do that anymore," Athanasius said. "Were you going to take me somewhere, or was someone going to come by for me?"

Virtus nodded, seeming to sense whatever kind of existence he had managed to eke out down here had now turned upside down once again. "To a warehouse on the docks."

"Which warehouse?" Athanasius asked, instantly sensing he might be getting closer to the man Cleo told him was called "Poseidon" by the Dei. "Whose warehouse?"

Virtus seemed reluctant to divulge the information. It was clearly the biggest secret he had been entrusted with by the local Dei.

"They wouldn't happen to be associated with the Club Urania or brothel boats like the Sea Nymph, would they?"

Virtus's eyes widened. "You know more than I do, Athanasius. Surely we are not long for this world." He paused. "I was to take you to Celsus Shipping and leave you in their protection."

Celsus! Athanasius felt like he had been struck by lightning.

Of course, he thought. The former consul and senator Julius Celsus Polemaenus, the local "Greek done good" here, was probably the key link between the Dei in Rome and Ephesus, the gateway to the churches in Asia. Now it all made sense: the opium, flesh and blood that trickled to Ephesus from the rest of Asia Minor was transported by Celsus Shipping to Rome to feed the insatiable Games. And Celsus, the once and future governor of the capital of Asia Minor, was going to honor himself with his own library here for his work!

"Who runs Celsus Shipping here for Senator Celsus, Virtus?" Athanasius demanded. "Is it his son Aquila?"

"No," Virtus said. "His cousin Croesus from Sardis and his sons."

Athanasius nodded. He knew that side of the Celsus clan. The original family name of Croesus was allegedly derived from the ancestors of the legendary King Croesus of Sardis, who like his modern progeny Celsus was famous for his wealth. "We have to let the leader Timothy know. You can set up a meeting for me?"

"Yes, but I'll have to leave and come back. And you'll have to be here when I get back."

"So we trust each other." Athanasius pulled out the letter from John. "Recognize the seal?"

Virtus looked at it. "I do. And I find it hard to believe the last apostle entrusted you with it."

"Well, blessed are those who believe without seeing. You'll take me to this person? You know who John's man in Ephesus is?"

"I know. I'll take it to him."

"No, the letter and I are inseparable," Athanasius insisted. "One thing we can both agree on is that the Dei did not want this letter to get to your friend. Will you take me to him?"

Virtus sighed. "I will leave and arrange a meeting at a safe house with the contact and come back for you."

"Can I trust him?" Athanasius asked.

"Yes," said Virtus. "But that's exactly what he's going to ask me about you, and I still don't know what I'm going to say."

21

Whatever Virtus said, it worked. The safe house was a villa beyond the town's Magnesia Gate at the top of the hill, in that section of terraced houses where the richest citizens of Ephesus lived. Virtus told him the story after arranging the meeting and walking Athanasius up the hill. The villa had belonged to one of the local church's most generous members and was his gift to the ministry of Bishop Timothy. It was a place where the church's leaders could meet in safety away from the bustle of the town below.

The villa reminded Athanasius very much of the hillside home he and Helena shared—or once did—back in Rome, and this depressed him. It had running water, heating systems, private inner courtyards, and a rich décor of mosaics and frescoes. It represented all the refinements of his former life, symbols of what he most likely would never enjoy again.

They were greeted by young, well-groomed members of the church who lived in the house as staff, and ushered into the largest room, where another young man was waiting for them. He was certainly no Timothy, who may have been a young disciple of Paul's when he had written his letters to the churches but was now about 70. This man was about his own age, Athanasius guessed, certainly no older than 30.

"My name is Polycarp," the young man said. "I'm the apprentice bishop to Timothy here in Ephesus. Please, come in."

They sat around a table with a burning candle in the center, Athanasius opposite Polycarp, Virtus standing by. "Polycarp, you say?"

Polycarp nodded without betraying any emotion. "I believe you have something you wanted to give me?"

"Yes," said Athanasius, handing over John's letter.

Polycarp opened it and began to read. Athanasius watched his eyes carefully, noting them darting back a couple of times to a particular line, working out the cipher in his head. He eyes grew wide in alarm the longer he scanned, despite no other change on his face. He swallowed, folded the letter and slipped it into his toga.

Athanasius could see the bishop trying to make sense of whatever it was John said, starting with whether or not to share it with him. What he said first he said to a servant. "Wine, please."

The servant nodded and departed, and Polycarp cleared his throat. "So you are Athanasius of Athens, successor to Chiron. I never did believe that when I heard it. You say the Dei is an imperial organization, and John, the man who discipled me, is inclined to agree. He wants me to consider sending you on to meet Cerberus."

"Cerberus?"

"Our most vital contact with the church in Cappadocia."

"The 'eighth church' John told me about?"

Polycarp nodded. "His identity is a closely guarded secret. Even I don't know who he is."

"Well, where is he then? How soon can I meet him?"

Polycarp shook his head. "You don't meet with Cerberus, Athanasius. He meets with you. And I'm not going to send you to him, because John cautions that you could yet be a spy from Rome sent to destroy the Church."

Athanasius glanced at Virtus, who looked equally surprised. They said nothing as the servant returned with the wine Polycarp requested. Polycarp handed cups to him and Virtus, and took a sip of his own. Then another. He was obviously unnerved by what John had written.

Virtus said, "Bishop Polycarp, I think Athanasius's theory about the source of the Dei being here in Asia Minor is correct. I'm not sure I grasp all of it. But I am certain that the Dei is not Christian."

Polycarp looked aghast. "You think it is apart from both Rome and the Church?"

"It certainly operates in Rome and clearly here in Ephesus," said Athanasius, trying his wine and finding it quite good. "But it's not imperial, as I originally thought. And it's not Christian, if we are referring to the apostles Peter, Paul and John. Its origins come from elsewhere. And I think our best lead is a local shipping operation."

"Yes?" asked Polycarp, hanging on everything that Athanasius was saying.

Athanasius was about to continue, but as he tasted the full effect of his wine, he lost his train of thought. He took another sip, pausing, swirling it in his mouth, actually enjoying it. "This wine is excellent, Bishop Polycarp. Surely you don't serve this during those mass communion services of yours?"

Perplexed at the sudden shift in the conversation, Polycarp shrugged. "I'm not an expert, really. It's not the wine we serve for communion, but it's from the same vineyard. There's nothing special about it, really. I mean, of course it is special, as a symbol of our Lord's blood spilled for the remission of our sins. But in itself I'm afraid it's quite common."

"There's nothing common about this," Athanasius said, putting down his cup. "I've tasted it before. In the Palace of the Flavians. This is Caesar Domitian's favorite brand. Where did you get it?"

"Caesar's wine!" Polycarp exclaimed. "I don't believe it. The blood of Christ and the wine of Caesar are the same? This is a cruel thought even in jest, Athanasius."

"I'm not jesting. Where does this wine come from? Somewhere in Cappadocia, yes?"

Athanasius saw Polycarp and Virtus stare at each other.

"Yes," Polycarp said quietly. "From the Lord's Vineyard."

"The Lord's Vineyard?"

"I mean the Dovilin Vineyards," Polycarp said. "They sponsor a ministry they call the Lord's Vineyard. It's an organization of Christians who trade with each other, apart from the prying eyes of the empire."

"And what does it take to join the Lord's Vineyard?" Athanasius pressed.

"You must be invited into the fellowship by a member. Man to man. They keep no lists or membership rolls. It's all very loose and not very sinister, if that is what you're getting at."

"Then why are you reluctant to talk about it?"

"I'm simply honoring the group's request that members not speak about it or its activities."

"So you are a member?"

"No, but some of my church members are," Polycarp said, getting testy. "The Lord's Vineyard operates under many guises in the empire. These groups are intended to draw attention away from the main organization, precisely because it has become a target of misunderstanding, even among Christians."

"I understand perfectly, Polycarp. The Lord's Vineyard is the primary front for the Dei within the churches in Asia Minor."

"Preposterous!" Polycarp cried out, as if personally offended.

"How does your church get this wine, Polycarp?"

Polycarp paused. "The man who gave us this house is the distributor for Dovilin wines here in Ephesus. He is a pillar in the church."

"Tell me about this pillar."

"His family used to make idols in Sardis, but when they became Christians, they gave up their trade and suffered much hardship. The Lord blessed them with new business here in Ephesus and a fleet of ships. They trade foodstuffs and wine with Rome and have bountifully blessed the church. We have all thanked God for the Croesus family."

Athanasius dropped the cup and stood upright as three armed legionnaires burst into the room, followed by an older man in a fine toga with golden trim in the pattern of the Greek key.

"Well, Athanasius," said Croesus. "My cousin the senator always believed Greeks should stick together, don't you?"

22

Croesus looked older than Athanasius had imagined, and more frail. Hardly the swarthy pirate he had expected, and for a moment, just a moment, he thought he had made a mistake. The three legionnaires more than made up for it, however. One had his javelin pointed at Virtus, another his sword to Athanasius's back, and a third was relieving a stunned Polycarp of John's letter.

"This is a private meeting," Polycarp objected in a manner that in any other circumstance Athanasius would have found laughable.

"Nothing of yours is private, Bishop," Croesus quipped. "Including your precious church."

"Surely what this man has told me isn't true, Croesus?" Polycarp pleaded. "The Lord's Vineyard is not in league with the Dei. It grows grapes."

"It grows assassins, you holy fool." Croesus turned to Athanasius. "And you've become quite the new recruit from what I hear. Senator Maximus. Commander Barbatio on Patmos. You could learn from this one, Virtus."

"Does the Dei want me dead or alive, Croesus?" Athanasius demanded. "Because right now I'm terribly confused."

"Yes, you are," said Croesus and looked over John's letter and made a face at Polycarp. "This Caesar code is unreadable without the key word. What is it?"

"Poseidon," Athanasius blurted out. "The key word is Poseidon. Ironic, yes? That is your code name in the Dei, is it not?"

Croesus wasn't amused.

"Let me show you," Athanasius said, and jumped forward to grab Croesus, spinning him around as a shield to face the point of the legionnaire's sword that had been at his own back. He then pulled out his dagger and put it to Croesus's throat. "Back away," he told the legionnaires. "Back away or Poseidon is dead."

"You really are a fool in the end, aren't you?" said Croesus, raising his own hand to his lips to kiss his ring.

"No!" shouted Athanasius, trying to pry it out of Croesus's mouth. "No poison to save you this time, old man."

"Kill me, idiots!" shouted Croesus.

To Athanasius's shock, the three legionnaires moved quickly across the rug to finish the job on Croesus themselves. Then Virtus, thinking quickly, pulled the rug out from under their feet, tripping them on their swords.

Athanasius hurled his dagger into the first legionnaire's face, striking him in the eye, and down he went. Virtus picked up the javelin that the legionnaire had dropped in his fall, plunged it into another's back, then broke it off and used the sharp end to stab the last legionnaire in the gut under his breastplate.

Polycarp, who proved cool under pressure, nevertheless looked bewildered as Athanasius tackled Croesus and struggled to keep the old man's hand out of his mouth, but he was too late. Already the eyes were dimming.

"You're going to talk, Croesus," Athanasius growled. "You know you can't escape. No poison to save you. What does the Dei want?"

"Everything."

"By putting Rome at war with the Church?"

The old man looked at Athanasius, genuinely shocked. "You really don't know, do you?" He began to laugh heinously, then coughed up blood.

Polycarp said, "He has a devil inside!"

"We are legion, Bishop," Croesus hissed. "We will take over the world!"

He then began to choke, and his head fell to the side.

Polycarp was stunned. "You murdered him!"

"He killed himself, Bishop," Athanasius said and held up Croesus's dead hand with the ring. "Smell it, it's poison."

Polycarp sniffed and turned away, gagging.

Then Virtus turned the body over and ripped away the tunic to reveal the tattoo of the Dei to his bishop, who could only stare at the black *Chi* symbol.

"I don't understand. He was a pillar of the church."

"Yes," Athanasius said dryly, "and pillars hold things up."

Athanasius helped Virtus drag the body of Croesus to a corner and began to strip Poseidon of his effects, starting with his ring. It had the *Chi-Ro* emblem, but no Greek letters nor any jewels, which indicated a mid-level officer in the Dei, but clearly much higher than the lowly *Chi* ranks.

Polycarp, who looked to be in shock, stared at the corpse of his church's key financial backer and fell to his knees in prayer, begging the Lord Jesus for forgiveness in associating with this man and his money, and vowing to renounce any hint of materialism the rest of his life as a minister of The Way.

"What are you going to do, Athanasius?" Polycarp asked weakly.

"I'm going to follow the wine to this Lord's Vineyard in Cappadocia," Athanasius announced, handing Croesus's ring to Virtus. "And Virtus here is going to follow Croesus's shipment to Rome."

"It won't work," Virtus said as he took the ring. "As soon as Croesus fails to disembark in Ostia, the Dei will know he's dead."

"Which gives us three weeks from the time you land in Rome and he doesn't," Athanasius said. "And another two weeks before express couriers can send news of it back here. Add another five days to reach Cappadocia, and I have almost six weeks."

"Six weeks to do what, my friend?" Virtus asked.

"To follow the wine."

Polycarp, who Athanasius realized was cleverer than he had thought, said, "He is going to the source of Caesar's wine to poison it."

"That could work," Virtus said, slowly nodding. "But for Caesar's wine tasters."

Athanasius decided not to reveal any details about Galen's potion, which would delay the effects on any wine taster long enough to ensure the wine made it to Domitian's lips, down his throat and into his stomach. "Leave that to me. Let's just say I am going to the source of the Reign of Terror to cut it off."

"Assassinate Caesar!" Virtus said, sounding as if the very idea was beyond the realm of the possible to mortal men.

"That's right," Athanasius said. "With Domitian gone, his designated successor Vespasian the Younger becomes Caesar, and with his reputed faith the empire becomes Christian. We can stop this forever war between Rome and the Church."

The look on Virtus's face was really quite extraordinary, as if he himself had been in old John's cave and seen the rocks split open to reveal a vision. He, too, sank to his knees in prayer. But unlike the horrified Polycarp, he sang praises at this possibility.

"Come, Lord, come!" the former Praetorian cried out to heaven, then turned to Athanasius. "But what if this plan doesn't work?"

"You'll meet up with a man in Rome named Stephanus, who will introduce you to other Christians within Domitian's own circles, including perhaps your former superiors in the Praetorian who are sympathetic. They will ensure that even if I fail on my end that you will succeed on yours."

His mission clear, Virtus came to life, and Athanasius recognized a true Praetorian.

Polycarp, however, would have none of it. "Say what you will about helping the Church, Athanasius, but you are pursuing your own personal vengeance. This plot is not inspired by the Spirit of God but by the bloodlust of your flesh. You want vengeance. You don't care about the Church of Jesus."

"Says the bishop who whores with the Dei," Athanasius shot back.

Polycarp nodded. "You are right about that, Athanasius. I have been wrong. I confess my pride in my church's standing before the eyes of Christ in the Revelation. But I see now that even an unadulterated message of faith in our Lord and his shed blood for our sins can become adulterated within the administration of our community of faith. For this I repent, and from now on, thanks to what I have seen here today, I will speak out against the corrupting influence of money in the church. But I cannot in good conscience condone what evil you harbor in your heart, Athanasius."

"What you'll do, Polycarp, is act as go-between here in Ephesus to oversee messages between me and Virtus, understand?"

Virtus nodded. Polycarp didn't look too sure.

Athanasius said, "If you love all the churches of Asia Minor and not just your own, Polycarp, then you'll help get me to the Dovilin Vineyards and connect me with this super apostle Cerberus in the underground church."

Slowly Polycarp nodded in surrender. "I will help you, Athanasius, but only to expose the Dei to the churches of Asia Minor who have drunk from its poi-

soned cup. May your plans for evil turn out for good and
the salvation of many. The Lord bless you. The Lord
bless us all. For I myself see no blessing in this venture,
only bloodshed and death."

23

His name was Samuel Ben-Deker, a Jew from Spain by way of Malta who specialized in the design and manufacture of quality amphorae to transfer wine in bulk across the Great Sea. The letter of introduction from Croesus of Ephesus boasted that Samuel's novel use of resin coating inside an amphora could improve and age wine to perfection based upon days of travel and the regional preferences of the destination. The Dovilin Vineyards could use a man like Samuel, in spite of him being yet another poor Jew. Perhaps the Lord's Vineyard could use him as well.

That was the cover story Athanasius had invented for himself.

As Cappadocia's capital city of Caesarea shrank in the distance, he huddled in the back of the covered wagon he had chartered, part of a long freight convoy from Ephesus

to Laodicea to Iconium, and examined the letter of introduction from Croesus that he had forged.

It looked authentic enough, he thought, comparing it
to another letter in Croesus's hand that he had lifted from
the old man. And the paper stock was the same, as was
the seal. Still, he worried there might be some sort of
coda or sign that these Dei used, and he was wagering
that Croesus would not use the Dei code. If Dovilin
needed such assurance, Athanasius had a second letter in
code that he could say he forgot about, which would not
only confirm the first letter but say something about Dei
business that Samuel was to deliver as well but not know
about.

The cart hit a bump, and Athanasius bounced hard and
cursed. He put the letters away and returned to the travel
guide he had picked up in town. It was a copy of the
same book in the library of Ephesus: Volume 8 of *Miracles in Asia Minor* by Gaius Mucius Mucianus. He wondered whatever happened to the former governor of
Syria, who at one time was the right hand of Domitian's
father, Vespasian. Mucianus died or disappeared decades
ago, leaving only his memoir as a primer for Athanasius
as he entered this exotic land.

He looked out at the rocky plains and pointy hills that
resembled chimney stacks. It was another world. Unlike
Rome, Christians seemed to operate quite in the open out
here. He saw fish signs proudly displayed outside inns,

shops and restaurants. And the closer to Cappadocia he got, the more prominent the Dovilin name appeared on signs, stone pylons and buildings.

He fingered the Tear of Joy necklace that Polycarp had given him to wear as a sign to the mysterious Cerberus inside the underground "eighth" church of Asia Minor. It was a silver six-pointed Star of David with a sapphire shaped like a tear in the center. He was to wear it under his tunic and let it be visible only in situations and to persons where Cerberus might reveal himself to him.

He got off at the small town nearest to his destination and began to walk with his pack over his shoulder. The fresh and fragrant scents of plants and flowers were a definite improvement from the dungeons, ship bilges and sewers that had marked his journey thus far. Turning a gentle bend, at last he saw the green valley of the Dovilin Vineyards—6,000 hectares of lush paradise surrounded by sharp mountain peaks hiding secrets dark and deep.

24

Life in Rome was becoming more tenuous by the day, thought Ludlumus, as the Master of the Games sat with his sullen and simmering Caesar in Domitian's private box at the Colosseum. That Athanasius had pulled off an incredible escape was humiliating enough, but to mock them both with the tongue of Domitian's Pharaoh Hound Sirius was over the top. Late word about the slaying of the garrison commander on Patmos, compounded with this morning's news that Athanasius was spotted in Ephesus and had eluded capture, had prompted Ludlumus to stage Caesar's favorite orgy of death in hopes the emotional catharsis would defuse a sudden explosion of murderous fury.

The mass execution was called the Death Relay, and it slaughtered a number of poor souls at once. Here the propmasters laid a special track around the rim of the arena floor, the "runners" evenly spaced, each with a

241

sword or ax in hand at the start. The trumpets blasted and off the runner raced around the track. The object was to catch the runner in front of you and hack him to pieces, thereby escaping the race and joining the survivors in the center of the arena.

As the runners dropped out, either by being hacked to death or doing the hacking, the distance between the remaining would grow. Soon there would be just two runners left, on opposite sides of the track, each exhausted. The editor of the match would then taunt them, announcing: "Now it's all about desire. Who wants to live more?" It was painful to watch the remaining two runners speed up and slow down, each on the verge of collapse, trading places so far as closing the gap, until one gave up and died in spirit before he died in the flesh.

Sometimes, like today, to make things more interesting, Ludlumus would alternate spots at the beginning of the race between Amazonian women and male dwarves, to ensure the long strides of the Amazons would lead to quick dwarf deaths, and then leave the women to kill each other off until one was left to live another day, if only that.

As one dwarf after another fell and the Amazons began to hunt each other, Domitian quipped, "Those are actual dwarves down there, Ludlumus? You didn't switch children for them or anything? There doesn't seem to be a lot of fight in them."

Ludlumus glumly said, "It's all real, Your Excellency."

"Good. I was beginning to wonder if the race was fixed."

There was little Ludlumus could say except to point out the imperial bow and arrows beside Domitian's chair. "You want to finish off a couple as is your custom?"

Domitian said nothing but picked up the bow and an arrow and took aim at the arena floor.

Ludlumus had made sure the bright yellow uniforms of the Amazons made them even bigger and clearer targets. Caesar hated to miss in front of an audience, and he wasn't as good a shot as he imagined himself to be.

Domitian let the arrow fly to thunderous cheers, and the Amazon target looked over her shoulder and sprinted only to be hit squarely on the back and splatter on the track. That left three Amazons to chase each other, at greater distances apart, which would drag this out a bit more.

"Good shot, Your Excellency," Ludlumus said as Domitian sat down, refreshed by his kill and thirsting for more blood.

"I want Athanasius dead, Ludlumus."

"Orion spotted him in Ephesus. He's our top assassin in Asia Minor. It's only a matter of time."

"Orion killed the wrong man, Ludlumus."

244 | THOMAS GREANIAS

"An unfortunate snag, Your Excellency. But with the help of local governors and legions on the lookout, Orion will quickly hunt him down and bring him to us in time for a spectacular end to the Games this summer."

"No, Ludlumus," Domitian cut him off sharply. "You had your chance. Your entertainment failed miserably. I want Orion to kill Athanasius on sight and ship his head back to me in a box. No fingers. No tortures. No public spectacles. I want his head for me to look upon with my own eyes. Only then will I know that this little Greek clown is dead, dead, dead."

25

It was late afternoon when Athanasius turned off the country road and onto a long private drive lined with stately cypresses. The end of the gravel drive opened like a dream to reveal the majestic Dovilin villa surrounded by its mystical vineyards.

The Dovilin family, from what local gossip Athanasius had procured from tradesmen on his way in, had made their fortune in land holdings and bought and built up their celebrated vineyards after the Judean War. Now the family, through hired management, had turned it into one of the empire's most well-respected and lucrative wineries, an unspoiled paradise far from the cares of the outside world.

A big, beefy servant named Brutus welcomed him at the door with an instant expression of suspicion and disdain.

Athanasius stammered as if intimidated and in a shaky voice said only, "Do-Dovilin."

Brutus grunted, and Athanasius looked past the circular sofa and carved wooden benches of the reception atrium while Brutus began to sift through his pack without apology. Finding nothing—Athanasius had buried a smaller second pack with his Roman uniform, sword and interrogator's knife kit, along with his Dei ring and money, under a boulder he had marked between the last town and the villa—the slave returned the sack, and a young woman emerged from under a large arch wearing an expensive stola and Egyptian sandals.

"Well, hello there," she said as if he were some unexpected surprise.

Athanasius could smell her perfume even before she stood before him and looked him over with approval. She was attractive enough. Everything about her seemed to mimic Roman fashion but was overdone: the dress, the hair piled on top of her head and dyed honey gold, the bracelets and bejeweled pendant holding her outfit—and bosoms—together. Just who was her audience out here in the sticks? Surely not stragglers such as Samuel Ben-Deker.

"You are Dovilin's wife?" he stammered, as if awed by her beauty.

She laughed. "His daughter-in-law. My name is Cota. My father-in-law is in the main courtyard. Is he expecting you?" She paused, as if asking for his name.

"Samuel, Mistress Cota. Samuel Ben-Deker." He thrust his letter of introduction into her hand.

"Wait here, Samuel Ben-Deker," she said with amusement and vanished with the letter.

The man who entered the atrium moments later was in his seventies with short-cropped, grey hair in the Roman style and a tanned face. He looked prosperous and confident in his light and tailored tunic. The oversized furniture, busts, urns and decorative amphorae among the marble columns and rippling white drapes framing endless vineyards only accentuated the wine merchant's wealth.

So this was Dovilin, Athanasius thought. But was he also the leader of the Dei in Asia Minor? His ring certainly indicated so. It was almost exactly like Chiron's, with the *Chi-Ro* symbol flanked by the Greek letters Alpha and Omega. All it lacked was the tiny amethyst inside the *Ro* loop at the top.

Dovilin gazed at his unexpected visitor, taking in the cheap tunic and sandals of a runaway slave or poor freedman. But his businesslike demeanor revealed this wasn't the first time a man in rags had appeared at his doorstep. "Your name is Ben-Something?"

"Ben-Deker," Athanasius stammered and acted shameful and overwhelmed in this display of wealth. "Samuel Ben-Deker."

"Yes, another Jew. You are also a follower of Christ?"

Athanasius nodded. "I pray you may be able to spare me room and board."

"Young man, surely you see the winery across the vineyard. Present yourself to the offices. My son runs the business and does the hiring and firing. But I'm afraid you picked the wrong time of season. We're two months from harvest, which is when we do the bulk of our hiring for the fields."

"It's not work in the fields I seek, sir."

"You don't look skilled for anything more…"

"Amphorae," he said, nodding to the letter of introduction from Croesus in Dovilin's hand. "It is in the final vessel of its journey that the juice of a grape can ripen to perfection or turn to vinegar by the time it reaches the lips of an important customer."

Dovilin paused, as if to consider whether or not to accommodate his friend Croesus, because he certainly didn't seem to think much of Samuel Ben-Deker. "Come with me into the courtyard."

Athanasius followed Dovilin through one grand atrium and hallway after another until they reached the large courtyard where a middle-aged man with a long beard was seated. Apparently Athanasius had interrupted a meeting Dovilin was engaged in.

"Bishop Paul, this is Samuel Ben-Deker. He comes by way of our friend Croesus in Ephesus."

The bishop had an oily expression and examined him coolly. "You don't seem like one of Croesus' boys."

Athanasius took a risk and made the sign of the cross with his hand, watching Bishop Paul exchange glances with Dovilin, who looked up from the letter of introduction.

"Croesus says you lived in Malta, Ben-Deker?"

"Yes, sir," Athanasius said. "Several years, and before that Spain, working under the vine for General Trajan's family in Hispania Baetica."

"Then you'll know his nephew and vineyard manager Marcus Ulpius Antonius?"

Athanasius stammered. "I am sorry, sir. I do not know him."

"Good," said Dovilin. "Because Trajan has no nephew by that name, and I don't know who runs his vineyards. But whoever it is does a piss-poor job compared to ours." He laughed with Bishop Paul, and Athanasius managed a weak smile. Then Dovilin stood up and said, "Ben-Deker, drop your tunic."

Athanasius froze. "I'm sorry, sir?"

"You heard me, Jew, drop your tunic and loin cloth now."

Athanasius heard a giggle in the distance and caught Dovilin's daughter-in-law, Cota, watching from an arch, and now she had a dark-haired girlfriend with her, who also giggled. Feigning humiliation—it wasn't difficult—Athanasius removed his tunic, stepped out of his loin cloth and stood naked before Dovilin, Bishop Paul and a duly impressed Cota.

Dovilin and the bishop, however, were not so impressed, even angry.

Dovilin said, "You call yourself a Jew and yet you are not circumcised?"

"My mother was a Spaniard, sir," he said, quickly putting on his loin cloth and tunic, at which point Cota disappeared out her archway. "Aren't we all free in Christ?"

Dovilin seemed to admit there was little argument to that, but Bishop Paul said sharply, "Don't you dare quote Scripture to me, boy. Do you understand? Can you even read?"

"No, sir. But I hear, and faith comes from hearing the Word of God."

"I told you to stop quoting Scripture, Ben-Deker," the bishop said, emphasizing Samuel's Jewish surname. "I have my own test for you."

Athanasius feigned confusion. "I am being tested? I do not understand."

"You don't have to," Dovilin said calmly. "Just answer the good bishop. He is the leader of the church here in Cappadocia and only wants to keep wolves away from the sheep."

"Wolves?" Athanasius said in surprise.

"Yes, Ben-Deker," said Bishop Paul. "Now answer me this: Who killed Jesus? The Jews or the Romans?"

Athanasius paused as the bishop gave a satisfied nod toward Dovilin, who was watching him closely. It was a cruel test, Athanasius realized, to put upon poor Samuel Ben-Deker. Obviously, as a nominal Jew, he had to say the Romans. But his understanding of the church in Cappadocia was that the Christians here blamed the Jews, or rather their religious leaders, and this was a source of division.

He was about to say, "Both," when the impatient bishop started badgering him. "Come now, Ben-Deker, this isn't a trick question," he said. "Not for a real Christian."

"Neither the Romans nor the Jews killed Jesus," Athanasius said suddenly, a thought striking him from out of the blue.

"Neither?" the bishop replied and looked at Dovilin in amusement at this unusual response. "Then who did?"

"Jesus chose to lay down his life for us all."

Dovilin looked genuinely surprised, the bishop outraged. He didn't like the answer, but apparently couldn't refute or berate him for it either.

"Who taught you this?" he asked.

Athanasius didn't really know. He couldn't remember the particular passage from the Christian scriptures he had pored over back on the Pegasus before meeting John. But he had definitely picked up the subtext, and he now recalled something about their God whispering timely answers to Christians when questioned by Roman officials.

"The Holy Spirit," he began and was cut off.

"The Holy Spirit?" the bishop said, incensed. "You are an uneducated, unwashed Jew from Malta, a potter who works clay."

Athanasius could restrain himself no longer. This bishop was an absolute fraud and knew it. No wonder he didn't want Christians quoting Scripture—he considered it a weapon to be used, not a revelation of truth. Athanasius knew the type well—the Roman augurs and oracles were full of Bishop Paul's kind. The only way to deal with self-appointed gatekeepers of truth was to stick them with their own Holy Writ in front of other believers.

"We are all earthen vessels," he replied. "God is the potter, we are the clay."

Dovilin started to laugh, delighted to see his red-faced bishop at a loss for words. "I see your proud attitude has gotten you into trouble before, Ben-Deker. You should watch that mouth of yours," he said good-naturedly. "Let's see what you can do with your hands. I'll have Brutus take you out to the winery."

Athanasius nodded, and Cota appeared again. "I'm going out there now, Father. I can take Samuel."

"Well, do it now before the winery closes for the evening, and have Gabrielle put him up for the night and then put him to work in the morning."

"You really want to hand him off to that little whore, Father?" Cota asked. "I thought we could put him up out back with the First Fruits."

Athanasius's curiosity was piqued by Cota's references of this "whore" and these "First Fruits," but he wasn't surprised by Dovilin's firm reply, directly addressed to him.

"You may have a sterling introduction by my good friend Croesus, Ben-Deker," Dovilin said. "But we operate by biblical principles on my vineyards. Every man starts from the ground up like our grapes. You will reap what you sow with your work, and we'll see what kind of seed you really are."

"Oh, thank you, sir. Thank you," Athanasius said with as much sincerity as he could fake. "I will not let your kindness and generosity down."

"See that you don't, Ben-Deker, because nothing goes to waste here. Even the bad grapes are used to fertilize our fields. Bad for the wasted skins, good for our soil."

26

The winery itself was on the other side of the vineyard from the Dovilin villa, separated by six hectares of grapes. As he and his escort Cota walked the gravel path between the house and the winery, Athanasius saw the spectacular two-story façade cut right into the rocks of the mountains. The façade, with its arches and inset frames for statues, was positively scenographic, just like the stage buildings behind the orchestra for his productions in the theaters.

"That is the winery ahead?" he asked, dumbfounded and not feigning it.

"Yes," Cota told him. "Behind it is our stone wine cave where we store our finished product before distribution. Upstairs is the office. Our vineyard manager oversees the harvest, fermentation and field workers. My husband, whom you'll meet, oversees sales and distribution."

"How much wine do you produce each year?" he asked, doing his best to get some information out of her during this opportunity.

"Almost ten thousand amphorae per year."

"Ten thousand!" he exclaimed. This was multiple times anything even the Palace of the Flavians could serve up in a year. "Who drinks it?"

She laughed. "You and me, of course. The bulk of our shipments go to the churches of Asia Minor for communion worship. My husband knows all the numbers, but I doubt he'll share the particulars with you."

Cota herself didn't seem to be in any hurry to introduce him to her husband, and she asked him if there was anything in particular he wanted to see.

"I find it best to simply follow the wine," he told her.

"Then follow me, Samuel."

She led him into the mouth of one of two cavernous entrances, where huge stone treading lagars had been dug out. Here men from the fields dumped their baskets of grapes, and then women pressed the grapes down with their feet.

"We call this first or sweet press," Cota explained.

"The good stuff," Athanasius quipped.

He watched the juice run off down wide troughs into drains that went into special basins for fermentation deeper in the cave. After the free juice poured off, the women stepped out of the treading lagars, which were now filled with the waste of the grapes called the pomace.

"Mind if I look closer?" he asked Cota.

"Not at all, but do be careful," she cautioned, although he couldn't imagine why.

He looked into a lagar that had been filled with red grapes. The pomace was blackish grape skins, stems and seeds that contained most of the tannins and alcohol. The juice from this pomace was the brand bound for Caesar's palace, he concluded, and then examined a lagar for white wine production. Here the debris was a pale, greenish-brown color, which contained more residual sugars.

"You must save the green stuff for some special dessert wines," he started to say when the entire tunnel began to shake.

"Step away, Samuel!" Cota shouted, and pulled him back by his tunic as the ceiling seemed to cave in.

For a moment Athanasius thought the whole mountain was collapsing upon them. The rumble was deafening. With amazement Athanasius watched large flat boulders as wide and long as the two main lagars descend from the cavern ceiling from large wooden capstans, pulleys and ropes. Then he saw how they defied gravity: teams of six men each were stationed at the spokes of two great horizontal turnstyles, pushing them in order to control the descent of the boulders until they pressed flat on the lagars. Suddenly a second burst of vast quantities of blood-red and pukish green pomace sprung forth from the lagars toward even larger fermentation pools beyond the first.

Cota laughed as Athanasius caught his breath. "We almost lost you, Samuel, and you haven't even started yet!"

He nodded at the boulders. "You've got screw presses too. These are very rare."

"So is that," she said, and he realized she was looking at the Star of David with the Tear of Joy around his neck. She began to fondle it. It must have fallen out of his tunic when he had bent over the lagar. "Did a girl give you that?"

"It's been in my family forever," he replied and slipped it back under his tunic.

She looked relieved, then went on. "The cave provides the structure for the mechanisms. The free juice produces our highest-quality wine in the smallest quantities. But the screw press squeezes more juice and profits for good-quality wine in larger quantities. Now watch this, because this might be your job if my husband doesn't like you."

The boulders began to quake in the lagars again, and the men at the turnstyles were back at their positions, straining harder than ever to raise the stones like the mythological Sisyphus pushing his great boulder up the mountain only to see it roll back upon him. As soon as the boulders were back in place above the lagars, teams of scrawny young men, some mere boys, jumped into the lagars.

"Clear!" came the shout.

Supervisors pulled back planks that Athanasius hadn't noticed before—they were stained by countless pomace grindings—to reveal holes at the bottom of the lagars. Then the scrawny sweepers began to push the remaining pomace down the holes.

Athanasius glanced at Cota and bent over the nearest lagar to look down one of the holes. Through it he saw the pomace dropping into vast pools of water in a cavern below.

"Fermentation pits for lora," he said. "The bad stuff."

"We make no bad wine, Samuel," she sniffed. "We give the gift of wine to those who could otherwise not afford it."

Athanasius now understood. Lora was an inferior wine that was normally given to slaves and common workers. It was simply a mix of leftover pomace and water. Disgusting stuff, recalling the one time he asked a servant to allow him a sip. It could hardly be called wine at all.

"Let me guess," Athanasius told Cota. "I'm looking at the Dovilin brand of communion wine down there. Water soaked in grape skins. That's how you fill 10,000 amphorae."

"I like it," said a voice, and Athanasius turned to see big Brutus looking down at him with a frown.

Athanasius nodded. "My favorite," he said, and winked at Cota. "I don't know how the other half takes it so strong."

"Mistress Cota," Brutus said, "your father-in-law would like to see you later when you are finished with this one."

"Well, I'm not," she told him. "Not yet. But soon. I have to take him to Vibius. Go on."

Athanasius watched the scowling slave leave and said, "I see Dovilin's eyes are on everybody here."

"This way," she told him as another shift of men from the fields came in with fresh baskets for the presses and the entire process started over again. "One last stop at the Angel's Vault."

The Angel's Vault turned out to be in the second of the two wine caves behind the winery's façade in the cliffs, and Athanasius realized the two caves formed a V and connected at a guard station with three great vault doors and two armed guards. One door led back to the pits and presses from which they had come. The second door, according to Cota, would lead them to the Angel's Vault and the commercial storefront of the winery.

"What about this one?" Athanasius asked her, pointing to the third door that opened into a particularly black, narrow and harrowing tunnel.

"That's the hole to hell, Samuel. I do hope Vibius doesn't send you down there."

Athanasius followed Cota through the second tunnel that would lead them back outside through the main winery entrance. Here the walls were lined with amphorae, and Athanasius sensed immediately that this was what he was looking for in this entire mission to Cappadocia.

"They haven't been sealed yet," he observed.

"This is the final fermentation before we seal the wine," she told him. "The freestanding amphorae you see are the reds, which we keep at higher temperatures in the cave. The amphorae that are half-buried are the whites, to keep them cooler."

Athanasius immediately focused on the freestanding reds, scanning to see any markings or imperial insignias that would indicate they were bound for Caesar's palace. "So decorative, with all kinds of marks and labels."

"Master painters from the caves," Cota told him, as if reciting a rehearsed line all the Dovilins were forced to repeat to buyers. "God speaks to many artisans down here."

Athanasius nodded at the artwork that could be considered Christian to some, especially those involving fish and grain, shepherds and sheep. Then he caught a row of black vases in the Spartan style with red gladiators.

"These look imperial," he said.

"They are," she said, and looked this way and that quickly, her voice lowering to a conspiratorial whisper. "They say the wine in these amphorae pass through the lips of Caesar himself."

"Impressive," Athanasius said. "But risky. What happens if he doesn't like it, or even falls ill?"

"We make sure that can never happen. That's why the angels take their sip first."

Athanasius started. "Angels?"

Cota nodded, as if sharing the secret of the ages behind the great Dovilin wines. "Something about the air in the amphora," she said. "Too much of it and the wine turns to vinegar. Not enough and the wine is too bitter. So for the final fermentation we leave the amphora open just enough for the proper amount of air to escape. We like to say it is for the angels to take their sip of the spirits, their 'angel's cut.' Then we seal the amphora shut with a special piece of cork and ceramic capping."

"Like this one?" Athanasius asked, picking up the cork capper from an amphora to Cota's dismay and sniffing it. "I see you use resin as a sealant. Smart. The resin preserves the wine once sealed and flavors it with the

proper fermenation, provided you know what you're doing. What is this indent on top of the cork with the Dovilin emblem?"

Cota took the cork from Athanasius and quickly
placed it lopsided atop its amphora. "There is something
in the resin," she said. "Once the cork is sealed, it cannot
be tampered with in any way, or the cork discolors. If it
is not discolored, the palace staff then use a thin iron
hook to pierce it and pull it out, and the wine is ready for
serving."

"So who applies the proper mix of resin?" he asked.

"The whore of hell," she sniffed. "I think I hear her
now."

They moved on, but Athanasius made sure to remember the pattern and décor of the amphorae bound for
Rome. It was here in this chamber, before the amphorae
were sealed, where he would poison Domitian's wine.

He tried to keep up with Cota, who breezed through
the main wine cave toward the exit without explanation.
Their tour, it seemed, was over. Along the way he noted
similar patterns on the amphorae here as in the Angel's
Vault, and they seemed to have more markings for
weight, price, destination and such.

He realized he might have to use these sealed amphorae as his key to identify those bound for Domitian, then
go back and poison an identical and open amphora in the

Angel's Vault, then switch them. Simple but not easy, he suspected.

They had arrived outside in the courtyard below the towering façade as the Dovilin winery was closing up for the day. He noted the servants moving in and out of the cave, as well as security: almost a dozen ex-legionnaire types doing nothing much but standing around and looking tough.

"This way," she said, tugging his hand. "The office is upstairs."

They climbed a short flight of stone steps to the second story of the façade, where an open arch led into an impressive office with a table and fine furniture, but no husband.

"Vibius?" she called out.

Athanasius heard muffled voices. They seemed to be coming from behind the wall of shelves with scrolls, which Athanasius assumed to be commercial contracts and delivery schedules, sales receipts and records.

Cota cocked her ear, and her eyes narrowed. Her lips formed a thin, grim line, and she marched to the wall and pushed something that opened it to reveal another room behind it.

Now the voices were loud and clear—a young woman's and a man's, presumably Cota's husband. There was a definite slap, then the girl's voice cried out: "Stop it, Vibius. You know I am only trying to help the vine-yard."

Vibius said, "I will help the vineyard, and you will do what I want."

"I know what you want, Vibius, and you'll never get it with me."

"You little whore," he said. "You've given yourself to every rat in the streets. Now you want to get holy with me? I think not."

"Vibius!" Cota screamed, and Athanasius followed her inside to see her husband threatening this girl with long dark hair, her hand at her face where it had been struck.

Vibius turned and looked at his wife and the stranger with rage. "What do you want?"

"This is Samuel Ben-Deker. Your father wants you to put him to work."

Athanasius could feel Vibius's stare. "Are you sure you haven't already, Cota?"

"Vibius!" she screamed again, so that all inside and outside the winery could hear.

But Vibius was unmoved. "Take this one to suitable quarters tonight and see if you have any use for him to-morrow," he ordered the girl, who half-turned her face to reveal a ghastly split cheek that made Cota gasp.

"Yes, sir," she said and in defiance gave Vibius a mock Roman salute.

He brought up his hand to strike her again but thought better of it when Cota sternly repeated to him, "Vibius, your father."

"We'll go out the back way," said the badly beaten girl, and walked through an archway into the Angel's Vault toward the secondary vault doors that led to the caves deep inside the mountain.

Athanasius turned to Cota. "I'm to follow her into that?"

"Where else for you, Ben-Deker?" Vibius said. "Now leave us."

Feeling very strange, as if he had been to this place before, Athanasius followed the girl into a stone cave that led only to darkness. The long shafts of light from the sunset that had streamed across the floors of the winery office began to disappear as the vault door closed behind him.

"The Dovilins order the wine vaults sealed off every night from the inside as well as the outside," the girl explained and turned to face him. "Don't worry about the dark. I know the way. By the way, Samuel Ben-Deker, my name is Gabrielle."

Suddenly he stopped, watching the last shaft of light touch her bleeding face and illuminate it like a halo of light, before the vault door plunged them into darkness.

It was the girl from his dreams back in Rome.

<u>27</u>

That evening Dovilin thought he had better see how things went with the new Jew and sent Brutus to find Vibius. It was Cota who showed up in the courtyard.

"Where's my son?" Dovilin asked her.

"You know you should be asking one of the Sweet Grapes girls if you want to know what my husband does at night, Father," she replied flatly.

Dovilin had neither the energy nor time to reply. His son's marriage was what it was. For himself, he would have gladly taken care of Cota's needs were it not for his firm belief, more stoic than Christian, that feelings of eros were better channeled into business and accumulating wealth. It was a lesson he had somehow failed to pass on to his son, as Cota was quick to remind him all too often. "Just tell me about Ben-Deker. How did things go?"

"Fine," she said, although Dovilin knew there was more that she was holding back. "Vibius didn't like him, of course, but he didn't stop your little whore from taking him to the caves for the night to sleep with all your other slaves."

Dovilin thought he understood now. "I don't like Gabrielle either, Cota. None of us do. But the vineyard needs her. The family can master the science of wine production, but the creation of great grapes is an art. She understands the soil, the sun, the wind and water like nobody else."

"She has help with that, Father, you know it," Cota said darkly. "Deep down in the caves."

He nodded. "Perhaps. But it is her tongue that saves us in the Angel's Vault, during the final fermentation. Hers is the last tongue to taste our wine before it is sealed and shipped and then opened before even Caesar. It's never let us down."

"Or never let you or Vibius down, Father?" Cota replied, insinuating rumors that Cota knew were utterly false but which Dovilin did not refute, if only to make Gabrielle an outcast not only among the employees of the Dovilin Winery but the Christians of the underground church in the caves.

Dovilin was ready to send her away. "Is there anything else you wish to tell me about Ben-Deker?"

"His Star of David is something a man like him would never wear for himself. It has a Tear of Joy inside."

Dovilin stiffened. "Tear of Joy, you say?"

"A crystal of some kind."

"What color?" Dovilin pressed.

"I think it's a sapphire. For a man like Samuel, it must be his most priceless possession. He'll have to watch himself in the caves."

"Yes, yes," Dovilin said and waved her off. "You can go."

He cursed, pulled a cord and waited impatiently for Brutus to appear. He felt a rare drop of perspiration on his forehead and wiped it off. His slave appeared in the courtyard and said, "Master."

"Brutus," said Dovilin, scribbling a coded text on a small strip of papyrus, rolling it up and slipping it into the stylus with which it was penned. "I need a Mercury courier and horse immediately to deliver this message to Rome: We have Athanasius."

<u>28</u>

Athanasius stumbled down the dark and seemingly endless cave after the young woman, his hands feeling the walls as they narrowed, tripping over jagged rocks as he tried to keep up with her.

"Where are you?" he muttered and then slipped, tumbling over a ledge and into space until he landed flat on his back, the wind knocked out of him.

"Samuel!" the woman cried out from afar.

Samuel? My name is Athanasius.

His head was lost a haze of confusion. He was Athanasius of Athens, famed playwright in Rome until everything was taken away from him by the imperial conspiracy Dominium Dei. Now he was on the run, hunted across the sea by the assassins of Rome, taking refuge the darkest corner of the empire in Asia Minor, here in the underground cities of Cappadocia.

Yes, he thought as he began to inhale and exhale again. Samuel Ben-Deker was only a name he was using here. It wasn't his real name. And yet Gabrielle was the real name of this woman he had just met in the flesh, a woman he once dreamed about back in Rome long before his present tribulations.

Nothing makes sense anymore. I've literally fallen into my nightmares.

He saw Gabrielle high up on a ledge above him with a torch. There were hundreds of torches now, flickering throughout a great cavern of rocky pillars and bridges, and levels and levels of ledges and caves. This was where the Christians hid themselves and lived like animals. Now he was one of them.

He gasped, trying to get his breath back as he took in this incredible world beneath the mountains. There were hundreds of workers marching home from the fields outside—thousands—carrying their torches, singing hymns and exiting the cavern into still more caves, tunnels and other parts unknown. He had never seen or imagined such a sight in his life.

"Samuel Ben-Deker," said the voice of Gabrielle. She was close now, and he looked up to see her angelic, blood-streaked face. "You won't be long for this world if you don't watch your step. Stick to the marked paths."

He followed her across a bridge over what appeared to be a bottomless pit to hell.

One wrong step, indeed, he thought, trying not to look down.

"There are several cities down here that have been used over the centuries to hide people from the wars above," she told him. "Now we Christians hide from the Romans."

Their fear, he thought, was completely unjustified. The Romans wouldn't send good men down these hell-holes simply to go after Christians. For one thing, he could clearly see a vast defense network of traps throughout the many levels as they walked. There were large round stones ready to drop and block doors, and at the entrance of every new tunnel he noticed holes in the ceiling through which defenders on the level above could drop spears. But the biggest deterrent he could see was the first he had succumbed to: the narrow corridors in the tunnel systems and the even narrower bridges and ledges along the walls of the great caverns. Roman fighting strategy was to move in groups, which wasn't possible here, making them easy to pick off.

"All you've managed to do is carve out elaborate tombs for yourselves," he told her. "Why do you even go outside to work the fields for food if this is all you have to live for?"

She stopped before the entrance to a rather mysterious, glowing cavern. "If this life is all we have to live for, then we are indeed to be pitied among men. But the life

274 | THOMAS GREANIAS

that we lead, we live for the Lord. Come, I will show you."

Inside the glowing cavern Athanasius discovered a church sanctuary used for worship. Several hundred Christians held flickering candles, singing hymns to Jesus. Bishop Paul conducted the worship from the front, and as Athanasius followed Gabrielle to the back of the deep cavern, he had to concede that perhaps the good bishop did perform some actual work around here. He later found out that it took about a week for the bishop to complete a single communion service for the entire church, rotating nightly among smaller church clusters like this one, grouped by families and local communities.

The singular thing he noticed about all the faces illuminated by candlelight was how young all these Christians were. Besides Bishop Paul, Athanasius had to be the oldest person present, and he himself was barely an adult. One apparently had to be young to be a Christian, because one had to stand on one's feet for the entire service after a long day's work.

Athanasius stood next to a watchful Gabrielle while Bishop Paul read from an epistle of the Apostle Paul's that Athanasius could not recall from the scrolls in the Chiron trunk aboard the Pegasus.

"Like a thief in the night the Lord will come when you least expect him, and there shall be a tribulation such as the world has never known nor ever shall. Those in fields must flee to the mountains from whence comes their help, and in darkness wait for the angels to separate the wheat from the chaff. So prepare your oil lamps and stock your grain, for you do not know how long before the earth is scorched and the ground made holy before the bride of Christ, which is the Church, can walk like Lazarus into the light of a new heaven and earth."

Some elements of what the bishop said sounded familiar, but it felt like a mish-mash of other epistles from Paul, Peter and John and did not have what Athanasius learned early on in his playwriting days was the "ring of truth" to it. That is, regardless of whether one believed the fiction, one grasped that its internal logic was sound, that it had integrity. This reading did not have integrity for some reason, and it took a while before he figured out why.

He leaned over to Gabrielle, who seemed rapt in attention at every word from the bishop like the rest, and whispered in her ear. "Didn't the Apostle Paul say something to the effect that Christians should reject any supposed letter from him saying that Jesus has come back or when he would come back?"

"Yes," she said softly, barely moving her lips and staring straight ahead. "But then Bishop Paul is a liar and an apostate, and this scripture he is reading is not of God but the devil."

Once again he was completely flummoxed by this girl. On the one hand, she was the loyal vineyard manager of the great Dovilin Vineyards. On the other hand, unlike the Dovilins, she seemed to be cut from the same cloth as the other true believers he had encountered in Tribune Marcus, the Last Apostle John and young Bishop Polycarp. Like oil and water, the two didn't mix, and yet here she was, an angel in his way, thus far preventing him from reaching his goal in the wine cave and poisoning the amphorae bound for Domitian.

Now Bishop Paul with great excitement introduced a special missionary from the Lord's Vineyard.

"As we all know, God gave the Dovilin family a vision to plant the Lord's Vineyard in both grape and truth. At the same time, the Lord spoke the same message to many other leaders of the Church in Asia Minor. This message was that if we are to prepare the world for the Lord's return, we must influence the Seven Hills of Rome. These seven hills are trade, government, the military, architecture, literature, the arts, and the Games. This is our spiritual battlefield, and the Lord's Vineyard is here to raise up those who would put on their spiritual armor and go out to scale these mountains for Christ. One such warrior from among you has seen the work of the Lord with his own eyes and come to share his testimonial with you."

A strapping, self-professed young thespian stepped forward. His name was Narcissus, and he began to talk about all sorts of signs and wonders.

"Rome is on fire for the Lord!" he told the gathering, apparently unaware of the irony that the last time Rome was truly on fire, Nero blamed the Christians and used them as human torches to light his gardens at night. "You have heard the news of wars and rumors of wars, but you have not heard what is quietly taking place behind the scenes. Senators, generals, even those among Caesar's household are coming to the Lord! They are asking for our prayers of protection for them as they seek to influence the empire for Christ."

There were murmurs and praises.

Athanasius was all ears now, waiting for names. Surely Narcissus would talk about Flavius Clemens and his widow Domitilla and their boys Vespasian and Domitian. Perhaps he would even mention Athanasius of Athens as a great and secret martyr for Christ.

"I myself was counted worthy to share my own faith with the greatest thespian of our generation!" Narcissus said. "In a private audience with none other than the comic Latinus I personally shared the Good News, and he accepted!"

Latinus! Athanasius burst into a loud laugh that drew stares as he quickly coughed and cleared his throat and said, "Amen!"

Others chimed in as well, but Gabrielle held her stare at him.

Latinus was certainly on fire as a homosexual, and his hedonism back in Rome had made even Athanasius's pale by comparison. Athanasius could only imagine which bathhouse this "private audience" took place in. This Narcissus stooge was a fool, and the Lord's Vineyard a complete sham.

"The fields are white for harvest!" Narcissus concluded. "And it is my prayer that after this harvest, more will join me as I mount my hill, and those others on other hills. Together we can change the world for Christ!"

I know a faster way, Athanasius thought to himself, and it's through the Angel's Vault.

The reading of scripture and testimonial over, the service would now end with Communion. Bishop Paul stationed himself at the exit of the cavern with a large goblet of wine. "The blood of Christ," he said each time a supplicant came forward and took a sip. To his right stood good, strapping Narcissus with a loaf of bread, breaking off pieces and adding, "The body of Christ" with dramatic flair. The supplicants consumed the bread on their way out.

For many of these poor souls, Athanasius realized, this might be their only meal of the day. Including, it seemed, himself. He was actually impatient for the line to move forward. When he reached Bishop Paul with his large goblet of wine, the bishop looked at him with disdain and almost pulled the cup away from Athanasius's lips. Athanasius could barely hide his own disdain for the tasteless lora wine. Fortunately, the bread turned out to be substantial enough to satisfy the pang in his stomach as he chewed it slowly on his way out of the church cavern and into the caves.

Gabrielle was further down a long corridor where small groups of people conversed with each other, but not with her. Athanasius heard whispers of "whore," "Jezebel" and "Babylon" as he tried to catch up to her.

"Gabrielle, wait. Where are you going?"

She stopped and looked at him. "To say my prayers and retire for the night. We have much work in the fields tomorrow."

By "we" he felt she actually meant to include him.

"As Dovilin knows, I'm not a field laborer," he told her. "But I can help you with the storage and transport of wine if you let me see what you're doing with the amphorae in the Angel's Vault."

She ignored his remark and asked, "So what did you think of our Communion?"

Athanasius realized she was looking at his Tear of Joy necklace, which once again had fallen out of his tunic, mostly likely when he bent over to sip from the Communion cup. She wasn't interested in talking business. The interminable subject of God and doctrine seemed to be his only way to her heart.

"I didn't expect the bishop to take the words of Jesus literally about the bread being his body and his blood wine," he told her. "I would have thought it obvious to the disciples at the Last Supper that Jesus was not in the bread he broke for them nor the wine he poured for them. They were symbols. But it's certainly a great doctrine for the Dovilin brand of Communion wine among the churches of Asia."

She looked him in the eye and said, "So near and yet so far you are, Samuel Ben-Deker. Like the Dovilins you would use Jesus to change the world according to your will, not the will of God."

"Only because God hasn't changed a thing," he told her, and put his hand on her wounded cheek. "How good can God be if he allows such evil to happen to you and to me?"

She let his hand linger on her face for a moment before lifting it off with her own small but strong hand. "I can see you haven't forgiven whomever you feel has wronged you, Samuel. But you must. Just as God has forgiven us through Jesus."

He caught her glancing again at his Tear of Joy necklace and wondered for a moment if this man Cerberus he was supposed to meet in this literally underground "eighth church" of John's revelation was in fact a woman. He decided to push the conversation.

"To forgive is divine, Gabrielle, but I am not. I cannot live here in a hole like you, working for hypocrites like the Dovilins to enrich them while they fleece Jesus's sheep instead of feeding them and then sleep in soft beds at night without a care in the world. There is no peace in that."

"And what do you propose doing, Samuel?"

"Jesus drove out the moneychangers from the temple. I would follow his example."

"Jesus didn't hurt or kill anybody."

Athanasius paused. "Who said anything about killing anybody?"

She looked at him again with her big, dark eyes, smoldering in both passion and pain. "You look like a man who could kill, that's all."

Her words stopped him cold. Nobody had ever said that about him before, and he wondered if he had indeed changed so much in the weeks that had passed that as much was true and visible to others if not to himself. "I only mean to infer that it will take more than whips to drive the Dovilins from this land."

"And for this you need access to the Angel's Vault?" She looked at him suspiciously.

"Yes," he told her flatly. "I cannot comprehend why you defend the Dovilins."

"Exposing your hatred is not defending the Dovilins, Samuel. There are plenty of open alcoves in the bunk caves for the seasonal vineyard workers. You look tired, and tomorrow I will start you in the fields. We must soften the soil of our hearts as much as the soil of the vineyard."

This I cannot do, he thought as she walked off and was swallowed up yet again into the darkness. Soften his heart when Rome had none? He could see the faces of Domitian and Ludlumus and now Dovilin before him. What frightened him was how hard it was to see the face of his beloved Helena in his mind's eye, only her statue in Corinth, and even that was fading away like the image of his mother and family.

Soften his heart? If he didn't hold onto his hatred, he feared he would no longer be able to recall even that.

29

Athanasius couldn't sleep all night, so there were no dreams or even a nightmare to pass the time. Instead he had to lie awake inside a cavern with dozens of strangers, many of whom smelled worse than he did, waiting for the first stirrings of the caves before dawn.

In the morning he followed a few officious cave men who seemed to know where they were going toward the surface. Like the angels who rolled away the stone at the tomb of Jesus, they opened what appeared to be the underground city's major gate, and he hurried outside into the vineyards, taking in the faint light of day and fresh and dewy air in great gulps like a man who barely survived suffocation.

At last the master Vibius arrived on a fine stallion and dismounted while a slave took the horse to the small winery stable. Then other slaves, including big Brutus from the villa, began to open up shop. Another servant put a spread of fish, cheese and eggs on the table under the olive tree, and Athanasius understood this was meant for the workers to come and help themselves as they reported for work and went out into the fields.

"You, Ben-Deker," Vibius said, pointing at him.

Athanasius froze.

"You may give the blessing."

Athanasius began to breathe quickly. His mind raced to remember the prayer that Jesus taught his disciples. Something about blessing God's name and daily bread. But it was too long. So he simply bowed his head like the others were doing, trying to come up with something. He slyly glanced up to see Vibius staring angrily at him.

"Heavenly Father, bless this bread we are about to receive, and your servants the Dovilins for sharing their blessings with us who deserve no good thing. Amen."

Vibius grunted, and a legionnaire coughed. All heads save Vibius's were still bowed.

Had he said something wrong?

Big Brutus leaned over and whispered, "In Jesus's name. Amen."

Athanasius spoke up and concluded, "In Jesus's name. Amen."

The heads came up with smiles, the hands unclasped, and the food was quickly consumed.

Athanasius watched everybody get to work, but there was no sign yet this morning of Gabrielle. He saw Vibius walk up the narrow flight of steps to the second-story offices of the winery. He could go up there and ask what to do, but the wine cave was open before him, and now was a perfect opportunity to look inside and act lost if found.

The wine cave was cool and dry inside, with rows of amphorae lining either side. He loitered by the rows, trying to figure out which labels were bound for Rome. He found a row of six black amphorae with red gladiators, exactly like the ones in the Angel's Vault, and wondered if these could be the imperial vessels. He crouched down and tried to make heads or tails of the markings. There was the Dovilin insignia, both at the bottom of the amphora and on the cork seal on top. Where were the other markings?

He finally found them, cleverly hidden in the pattern of the Greek key that circled the neck of the amphora. These amphorae were marked for Ostia and then Rome's city port on the Tiber and finally the Palace of the Flavians, marked with the Seal of Caesar.

All he had to do now was find a counterpart amphora in the Angel's Vault, an unsealed amphora where he

286 | THOMAS GREANIAS

could poison the resin around the cork stoppage and then cap and substitute it for one of these.

"What are you doing?"

Athanasius stood up to see Gabrielle standing before him. He glanced beyond her at the back of the cave and the tunnel from which she had emerged. "I hear Caesar in Rome has a private tunnel like you between the Colosseum and the palace. We should all be so lucky."

"We all work hard here," she said. "Biblical principles, you know. There is no slave or free here. No male or female. No Jew or Gentile. We are all equal before Christ."

"I think the Dovilins believe some Christians are more equal than others."

"And you, Samuel. You seem to be avoiding work in the field this morning."

"I told you, Gabrielle, I work with amphorae like these to improve the taste and preservation of wine. This is where I belong. I'm no ordinary field laborer."

She took his hands and looked at them. "That's for certain. I doubt you've ever done any heavy lifting your entire life."

"I most certainly have," he told her. "Every time I take a piss."

She laughed for the first time with him, truly laughed, and her smile somehow broke his heart. Maybe it was the cut under her animated eyes, so full of life and yet filled with sorrow. She had an effect on him that no woman ever had before, including Helena, and it made him uncomfortable and curious all the same.

"Follow me, Sampson, and we'll see how strong you are."

Much to his disappointment, she took him far away from the winery, past rows and rows of vines to the middle of the vast fields.

"The Dovilins are in the business of celebrations," she told him. "Communions. Weddings. Banquets. Baptisms. Everything and anything. Those celebrations begin with wine. Jesus turned water into wine. It was his first recorded miracle. It was at a wedding. We can't turn water into wine. But we can turn grapes into wine. Good wine starts with good grapes. Good grapes start with good vines."

"Yes," Athanasius said. "Jesus said, 'I am the vine. You are the branches. Without me you can do nothing.'"

Unlike Bishop Paul, she took no offense at his display of knowledge. But neither was she impressed. "Without the vine there is no wine, Samuel. My primary job as vineyard manager is to forecast the harvest. The Dovilins don't like surprises. We must predict how much fruit we're going to be getting come harvest."

So that's why she was the vineyard manager, Athanasius realized. Despite the contempt with which everybody seemed to regard her, her methodology for forecasting grape yields—and improving them—was simply too valuable for the Dovilins to ignore. It was a talent Vibius clearly lacked, as well as everybody else around here. Suddenly Athanasius wondered not how Gabrielle got her job but how the Dovilins' business could ever thrive without her.

"So how do you do that?" Athanasius asked.

"You are going to count the clusters for me, Samuel."

"Me?"

"Look," she said, and lifted a branch on the nearest vine. "See these flowery little buds? These are the ovaries. They develop into grapes. Now count them."

Athanasius got down on his knees in the dirt and with his hands lifted several branches on the vine and counted. "This one has 14 clusters."

"You missed some, Samuel." She lifted another branch. "This one has sixteen, see?"

He saw. He looked under the last branch she had lifted and accidentally broke it off. "Oops."

"You might as well be dropping gold so far as the Dovilins are concerned," she cautioned him. "You don't want to cost them money in your counting."

He sighed. Counting grape clusters was not what he had in mind in traveling all this way to Cappadocia. This morning he was further away from the wine cave than he was upon his arrival, doing mindless work for this maddening girl who was barely a woman and who in her Christian charity defended these Dovilins who beat her down along with everybody else in this forsaken valley.

Perhaps she was a dead end, a waste of time, and he would have to pursue a less direct yet faster route to the Angel's Vault.

"So how long do I do this?" he asked her, already thinking that Dovilin's daughter-in-law Cota might be his better bet inside the winery.

"Until you reach the end of the row," she said, pointing down the long line of vines. "Then you go down all the other rows and count how many clusters there are and write them down."

She handed him a leather strip with a lead puncher to mark numbers and walked away.

"There are going to be grapes on the vines by the time I finish counting," he called out after her. "No, there won't be any grapes, because they will have already been picked!"

He watched her disappear into the distance between the endless rows of grapes. He was already sweaty, and the day had barely begun.

"I saw that," said a gruff voice, and he turned to see Vibius on his horse looking down at him. He was pointing to the ground, where the broken cluster lay. "I'm taking it out of her pay, Ben-Deker. Now get to work."

Athanasius got down on his knees and started on the next vine, carefully lifting one branch to count a cluster, and then another, as Vibius and his horse breathed heavily over his shoulder.

30

The assassin known as Orion had been on quite a death run lately since Corinth thanks to Athanasius of Athens, and he looked forward to its finish as his horse took its water in Caesarea and then galloped on its final leg toward the Dovilin Vineyard.

First came his orders in Corinth, which were to assassinate the Greek and his entire family. But the local legions botched the job by moving in too soon on the estate. All they managed to do was burn the family alive and let Athanasius escape. But Orion did manage to catch a glimpse of this Athanasius, which made him indispensable to the operation in Ephesus after Athanasius killed the garrison commander on Patmos.

Now Athanasius had not only escaped the trap set in Ephesus, he had also slaughtered the Dei's key man there, Croesus, who was cousin to Senator Celsus in Rome. The shipowner's swollen and almost unrecognizable corpse had bobbed up in the silted harbor after coming loose from its anchor. He had allegedly taken off the day before on a ship to Rome. Orion was already following reports of a man jumping caravans on the way out of Ephesus toward Laodicea, and he had followed the trail to Iconium when he crossed paths with a messenger from the Dei's man in Cappadocia. They knew each other, exchanged information and figured things out quickly.

This Samuel Ben-Deker was in fact Athanasius of Athens. The Greek had brazenly decided to move up the chain of the Dei by killing Croesus in Ephesus. Now he had set his sights even higher, targeting Dovilin in Cappadocia.

All of which made Orion consider the possibility that Athanasius was more than what he appeared to be. No man was that favored by the gods. To escape the Tullianum, slay a tribune and Senator Maximus, escape Rome, escape Corinth, and then break into the prison on Patmos and kill its commander?

Athanasius had to be getting help from somewhere. But where? Certainly not from this Lord Jesus Christ worshipped by the Christians. From Rome? The Dei? The Church?

Orion flicked the ear of his horse with his whip and they picked up speed. He decided it didn't matter now. Athanasius was a dead man. Still, it always helped to know who ultimately wanted the target dead—or alive—

if only to tip him off about any other orders that might include his own death.

That was the problem with being the man who tied up loose ends for Rome, Orion thought. It made him one too.

31

Gabrielle was a dead end, Athanasius concluded after several hours of counting clusters. He was no nearer to poisoning Domitian's imperial amphorae in the winery nor to the identity of his alleged contact Cerberus in John's so-called "eighth church" at Cappadocia. But between the fields and caves and some bartering, he had been able to scrounge up the various ingredients required to make his poison for Domitian. He also had come up with a plan to break into the Angel's Vault that night without the help of Gabrielle, who was marching toward him along an irrigation ditch between the vines with a furious brow on her dirty face.

She hasn't even seen my progress yet, he thought, and already she is angry with me.

"Congratulations, Samuel Ben-Deker," she informed him. "You've been promoted."

"To the winery?" he asked quickly.

"Oh, even better: the Dovilin estate itself. You're joining the First Fruits."

"First Fruits?"

"The elite household staff chosen to support the Dovilins and the ministry of the Lord's Vineyard."

He couldn't hide his disappointment, and this seemed to surprise her.

"Your prayer is answered, Samuel. No more hellholes like the rest of us. You get to live at the estate, serve the visiting dignitaries and drink the same wine as the Dovilins."

"Why me?" he asked her.

"Well, you're not a woman, Samuel, and you're certainly no follower of Christ," she explained. "So why shouldn't the Dovilins judge you worthy enough to join them? Now get yourself to the stables behind the villa. Leave your counting scroll. I'll be your relief for the rest of the day."

He watched her sink her knees into the wet soil by the ditch and start counting to herself. She looked like a little girl, so small and frail and yet made of iron. He stood there a while, wanting her to say something else, anything. But she didn't, wouldn't even acknowledge he was still lurking. Finally he walked away across the vineyard toward the villa.

When he reached the stables behind the Dovilin villa, his pack from the caves was already waiting for him in a large bunk room built to house a dozen or so of the "First Fruits," who were all muscular, clean-shaven and well-scrubbed young men in crisp staff tunics. The head of staff was big Brutus himself from the house. Athanasius wondered if he had gone through his pack again, but when he opened it he found his small lead vial of poison still in its hidden pocket.

"We have everything you need here," said a lilting voice, and Athanasius closed his sack and turned to see Cota, Dovilin's daughter-in-law and Vibius's wife, looking at him with an arch smile and holding out a folded tunic for him. "Even a bathhouse. Let me show you."

Aware of the stares of Brutus and the other First Fruits, he followed her out back to indeed find a bathhouse and beyond it the outdoor kitchen where the young women of the estate prepared the food.

"You'll need a good bath before dinner, Samuel. It's time to get the dust of the field off that body of yours. Some Roman officials have arrived, and you'll help with the service."

Athanasius nodded, although the mention of Roman officials worried him. "I appreciate the honor of working at the villa, but I am afraid I am depriving you of my greatest gift."

"Now what might that be, Samuel?" she asked with exaggerated interest.

"If we could meet privately in the Angel's Vault tonight, perhaps I could show you."

She frowned. "What could you show me in the Angel's Vault that you couldn't show me out here?"

"What I can do with your amphorae," he told her innocently. "I know a way to create an amphora with walls half as thin and twice as strong. Smaller amphorae on the outside allow as much or more wine on the inside, and enable Dovilin Vineyards to transport almost a third as many amphorae for the same weight and price as yours do now."

"That is interesting," she said, absent of any interest in the subject at all, but moving closer to him and putting a finger on his chest. "What else could you show me?"

"If you would be amenable to opening just one amphora, I could see if you are coating the insides with the proper quality and quantity of resin. I have a formula that not only preserves the wine during transport but can help in aging it properly during its travels."

"I do think taste is paramount," she said, licking her painted lips. "You'll let me taste this resin of yours?"

"Absolutely, Mistress Cota. I want you to be satisfied with my labor above all else."

"Well, then, let me see what I can do, Samuel. And if this new formula works, and I am satisfied, then perhaps we can discuss it further with my husband and father-in-law."

Athanasius put on a big, earnest smile. "God bless you."

"Now let Cassiopia help bathe you, and Brutus can massage those hard, tired muscles."

"I don't think that's necessary, Mistress Cota," he said shyly. "But a bath would be nice."

And it was, regardless of the limited affections of Cassiopia, clearly under orders from Cota. The heated water and oils soaked into his skin that had been caked with dust and dirt over the weeks, and he realized how much hot water was the very definition of civilization. Then he thought of Gabrielle working his relief in the fields, answering to Vibius at the winery and Bishop Paul in the caves. When he stepped out and into his new wardrobe and sandals, he felt so clean on the outside and yet still so filthy inside. In short, he felt very Roman, and thus, he supposed, better prepared to meet Dovilin's guests.

They worked in threes, these First Fruits, so that night Athanasius set the triclinium while Brutus and a young man named Claudius poured the wine for Dovilin and his two guests, the well-connected legates from the XII Fulminate and XVI Flavia legions in Cappadocia. A third guest, who apparently accompanied one of the legates, stood at attention in a corner, staring at Athanasius.

It was the Roman assassin from Ephesus, the one with the gash down his face from forehead to chin. The one who earlier in Corinth killed his mother and his niece.

From the moment their eyes first locked, Athanasius thought he was dead. But the man said nothing, simply stood at attention in the opposite corner of the room, staring at Athanasius and making it clear that he knew exactly who he was staring at.

"You have to learn to rule the world," Dovilin was telling his guests.

The two Romans looked at each other, mystified.

"We already do, Dovilin," said the legate from XVI Flavia. "The Roman empire and its influence stretch across the entire earth."

Athanasius caught a glance from Dovilin, and now had to assume that the old man knew everything: that Croesus, Samuel Ben-Deker's sponsor, was dead, that Samuel Ben-Deker wasn't who he claimed to be but somebody else entirely, and that this assassin standing in the corner had already informed him that he was Athanasius of Athens.

"Your fortresses, roads, ships and government, yes, of course," Dovilin went on with the Romans. "But it's the hearts of men I'm talking about."

"I think I know what you mean, Dovilin," Legate XII theorized as Brutus and Claudius poured rivers of endless Dovilin wine into their bottomless cups. "Vespasian's genius was in improving the provincial infrastructure here in Asia Minor and thus facilitating our defense of the eastern frontier, all without firing an arrow."

Legate XVI echoed his agreement. "We must always be ready for war with the Parthians over Armenia. But Domitian is too preoccupied with the Christians."

"Maybe," said Dovilin with a worldly, patrician air that promised the perspective of the bigger picture. "But he has carried on his father's plans for the construction of road networks in Asia Minor for troop movements, and the increased settlements associated with your expanded military bases have done more to open up commerce than anything else, enriching us all."

That was the magic word, Athanasius thought. Commerce. This was the true work of the Lord's Vineyard.

"All of you are more than military men. Your families are wealthy, beyond the equestrian ranks. Like General Trajan, your wealth and power here can grow far beyond your service to Rome."

Now the two legates were extremely interested, hanging on every parsed and patiently strung word coming from Dovilin's lips.

"Your families have olives, oil and grains. Mine has wine."

"I see how you can sell much Dovilin wine through us to our legions and the local governors of Asia Minor,"

said Legate XVI. "But I fail to see how much you and
your household staff could purchase from us."

"You forget the Christians in the caves all over Cappadocia, gentlemen. Hundreds of thousands. Individual-
ly, they have little in possessions or money. But as a
whole they are a market bigger than any single capital in
Asia Minor. Who best to serve them than your family
businesses? We all benefit, and Caesar will reward you
like he has others who do business with me."

"This is true," said Legate XII. "The Flavians know
the East, and three governors so far in Asia Minor have
been drawn from our ranks."

Throughout this exchange, the assassin from Ephesus
hadn't blinked once, Athanasius thought, his eyes still
fixed on him as one of the servant girls brought in some
sweets for dessert and slipped Athanasius a note.

The assassin saw Athanasius palm it.

"Then here is to all of you and your promotions," said
Dovilin, holding up his cup. "And to your XII Fulminate
and XVI Flavia legions."

To which they all cheered each other and drank.

Athanasius quickly glanced down at the note. It simply read:

media noctis inclinatio

So Cota wants a midnight rendezvous at the Angel's Vault, Athanasius thought. When he looked up again, the assassin in the corner was gone.

It was past midnight when Athanasius hurried outside the villa toward the stables, long after the legates had left with plenty of amphorae of wine, but presumably leaving behind the assassin to make short work of him. How? Was his long presence at the meeting and sudden disappearance meant to torture him? Whatever Dovilin's intentions, it was certain he was not meant to survive this night.

Athanasius calmly walked into the bunkhouse, bracing himself to meet his assassin, but found nobody waiting for him. He grabbed his sack and went back out.

He could hear the girls washing the ceramics and utensils of the supper and chatting with each other at the kitchen, and he could see Brutus off by himself smoking some kind of rolled-up leaf and looking at the sky.

He quietly worked his way around the bunkhouse to the back and merged with the shadows between the vineyard rows. Once he was a safe distance away, he broke into a run. In the morning the Dovilins would know he was gone for good. None of that mattered anymore, though, because if he survived what he had to do, he was never coming back to this place.

As Athanasius was fleeing the estate, the assassin Orion took his seat with Dovilin in the villa's courtyard. He real name was Patraeus, and he was upset that Dovilin had not allowed him to kill Athanasius on sight. Now his target was out of sight, and Dovilin not only seemed unconcerned but intent on wasting even more time by pouring them both more wine.

Dovilin said, "I thought Athanasius was killed as Chiron in Rome a month ago."

"No, sir. He escaped somehow and killed the garrison commander on Patmos and then made it to Ephesus and again evaded capture."

Dovilin sipped his cup thoughtfully. "That doesn't sound terribly efficient of our organization, does it?"

"He clearly had help from the inside, sir," Patraeus said, and finally took a sip of his cup. He preferred to avoid any wine while on a hunt, and the Dovilin brand was reputed to be more powerful than most, but it appeared he would insult his host otherwise.

"Inside where, Patraeus?" Dovilin demanded. "Inside the Dei? Inside Rome? Inside the Church?"

"Very hard to tell which is which these days, sir."

"Isn't it?" Dovilin agreed, seeming to relax. "I knew it was Athanasius the moment I saw him on my doorstep."

Patraeus sincerely doubted that. "Then why didn't you kill him?"

"I will," he said. "As soon as he leads us to the true identity of Cerberus."

"Look, sir. I was supposed to kill him on sight, send his head back to Rome in a box."

"You'll get your head to send to Domitian in the morning, Patraeus, and I'll get Cerberus."

Patraeus opened his mouth to say something when he felt a tug inside his throat. Everything inside him began to constrict, and he dropped to his knees gagging.

Poison!

"You have been as much a help to the Dei in your death as you were in life, Patraeus," Dovilin was saying, although the words began to slur in Patraeus's head. "This poison came from a tiny vial in Athanasius's sack. I believe it was intended for our Lord and God Domitian. From your delayed reaction, it appears to be a Dei formula that would have circumvented the palace wine taster and reached Caesar's lips…"

By then Dovilin's words were but a distant hum, his presence a mere shadow, leaving only a final, fleeting thought to escape with the assassin's spirit.

Loose ends.

32

Athanasius made it to the olive tree in the courtyard outside the winery, aware of two snipers walking along the second story of the façade. He could see their silhouettes in the moonlight. But that appeared to be all the security there was, just a couple of guards on the lookout ready to sound any alarms. He then saw a dark figure in the mouth of the winepress cave below—Cota, waving him over. She seemed to be holding a basket.

It was too far and he risked being spotted by the snipers once he left the cover of branches. So he waited until the nearest sniper turned his back, then he darted to the cliff, kissing the wall as he worked his way to the winepresses. The loud chirping of locusts covered the sound of his steps. Once inside Cota couldn't wait and wrapped her arms around him.

"Such speed and stealth, Samuel!" she said and pressed her lips to his face.

He took her by the hand and led her toward the vault doors in back, where a torch flickered on the wall. "The faster we get to the Angel's Vault, the more time we have together. Are there guards?"

"Only locks," she said breathlessly, "and I have the keys."

He grabbed the three on a ring she dangled out of her hand. "Samuel!"

He smelled the alcohol on her breath. It would make things easier for him shortly, but not now. "Quiet, Cota, and I promise you a revelation."

"Oh!"

He opened the vault door at the back of the winepress cave and found the interior guard station empty as promised. He tried to open the heavy door to the Angel's Vault, but the first two keys didn't work. He tried the third one. With a sharp push he finally turned the rough tumblers and it opened.

He took up the torch, stepped in and saw the amphorae lined up like the treasures of a pharaoh's tomb.

"Get comfortable," he told Cota, who seemed both perturbed and yet aroused by his take-charge manner.

"Samuel, you are full of surprises," she said as she spread linen and a few small pillows across the floor.

"A man has to preserve an air of mystery, you know," he said as he kneeled before one of the imperial amphorae and opened his sack. He dug his hand in to find his vial of poison but couldn't feel it. He dug further.

"What are you looking for?" Cota asked. "I'm right here."

"I had an exotic aphrodisiac from the Far East I thought we'd try with some of this wine," he said, shaking out everything from his pack on the floor in a panic. "You don't think anybody in Rome would miss it if we helped ourselves to a couple of cups from an open amphorae, do you?"

Cota didn't reply.

"Do you?" he asked again, and turned around in time to see Vibius raise a thick forearm holding a mallet.

"Actually, I do," Vibius said, bringing the mallet down on his head.

He was back in the dark of his nightmares again, this time no Gabrielle to be found. He was gagging on refuse, unable to breathe, an unbearable pressure upon his back. He felt like he was about to explode. Suddenly a halo of light appeared around him, the dark shadow rose, and he raised his head up out of the pomace of the lagar to gasp for air as grape skins and pulp filtered down through holes into the cavern below. In front of him he could see a horrified Cota on the ground in tears while her husband Vibius barked orders to Brutus and the guards manning the screw press.

"Again!" he shouted.

Athanasius heard the creak of the capstan, pulleys and ropes as the boulder above him began to lower, shaking the lagar below him. He wanted to crawl out, but he had no strength in his legs, and feared his body would be cut in two.

"Please, Vibius!" Cota screamed as the boulder came down.

Athanasius buried his face in the rotting grape pulp, turning to flatten his head as much as possible, bracing his shoulders and hips and praying his bones didn't smash to dust under the weight bearing down upon him.

It pushed him down, unbelievable pressure, and he worked his tongue to free an airhole in one of the drainage holes to breathe. His temples were in a vise, and he was sure his head was about to split open like a melon, and then he heard a crack and feared the worse.

Vibius must have heard it too, because the screw press wheel began to turn and the boulder lifted off Athanasius's body, broken for sure.

"Well, it looks like you won't be walking out of here alive, Athanasius. So why don't you tell us what you're after."

He could barely open his jaw, and when he did, he spat out grape stems and seeds. "Domitian," he groaned. "Poison."

"And you realize what that would have done to us, don't you?" Vibius shouted in his face. "The Roman legions here would wipe us out. All of us. Including the underground church. Is that what you wanted?"

"No."

"Well, let me tell you what I want, spy. I want you to tell me who Cerberus is."

"I don't know."

Vibius dangled the Tear of Joy necklace in front of Athanasius's face as he lay in the pit. "I think you do."

"He doesn't," said a voice, and Athanasius glanced up to see Gabrielle with a crossbow. He blinked twice, because he didn't believe it, and then she actually shot an arrow into Vibius's arm. "Samuel, move!"

He felt the rumble above and with all the strength he could muster rolled out of the lagar and got up on one knee. He started to wobble as Vibius pulled the arrow out of his shoulder and came at him with it.

"The Dei says die!" he shouted.

Athanasius ducked and straightened his knee out enough for Vibius to trip over it and fall into the lagar.

"Stop!" he called out to Brutus and the rest at the wheel.

But his cry only made them stop too suddenly. The windlass snapped, and the boulder dropped on Vibius, crushing him. His blood spurted out, pooling down the drains to the fermentation pits.

"Vibius!" Cota screamed, running over. "Vibius!"

Athanasius staggered to his feet, amazed he could even stand upright. He saw Gabrielle in the back by the gate to the tunnels, waving him over. "Hurry!"

Brutus and the guards stood in shock, and Athanasius knew why. It wasn't his head that was going to roll; it was going to be theirs. Unless they brought his to Dovil-in first.

"Run, Gabrielle!"

He chased her into the dark, cursing himself for his failure to kill Domitian by poison and praying Virtus was having better luck in Rome.

33

A handful of anonymous but aristocratic Romans were waiting for Croesus when his commercial flagship Poseidon anchored in Ostia. But the slain shipowner and Dei chief from Ephesus never appeared. So their small line of regal chariots departed along the Appian Way back to Rome, where Virtus, who had spotted them from aboard the ship before it arrived, followed them by taxi to a plain, four-story building not far from the Palatine. He checked into the inn across the street and made sure to get a room with a balcony view of the building.

For several days Virtus watched the golden chariots and litters that rode in and out of the house in Rome, where rich and powerful members of the senate and Roman society came to pray with one another and pay tribute to the Dei. Among them he noted Senator Celsus, cousin of the slain Croesus of Ephesus, and Senator Sura, father of the master of the Games Ludlumus. But there were many more as well, and it was the lesser-known junior members that he did not recognize that worried him most, and he did his best to memorize their faces.

After two weeks he became familiar with the cycle of groups and began to get a better picture of the circles in which the Dei had influence, many of which were dia-metrically opposed politically and culturally. Others seemed to have strong ties to the wine, oil and commer-cial shipping industries. He noted no outward forms of identification, and no large group meetings. Only these small group meetings held weekly.

Fairly acclimated to Rome again, Virtus was now ready to make contact with this man Stephanus whom Athanasius had told him about, and to place the servant of Flavius Clemens inside the palace with the help of his Praetorian comrades. Not that any of this would be nec-essary, of course. Athanasius was the smartest master assassin that Virtus had ever met, and the power of the Lord was with him. No doubt he already had everything in Asia Minor well in hand.

34

Deep within the bowels of the mountain range, Athanasius and Gabrielle moved through twisting corridors, chased by Dovilin's men who now wore Minotaur masks to hide their identities among the sleeping Christians now awakening with screams. Gabrielle led the way down a grim shaft, helping them to temporarily lose the Minotaurs.

"Where are you going?" he asked her. "You're taking us down, not up."

"I'm taking you to Cerberus," she told him.

They ran through a narrow, winding passage that ended in a large, circular cavern. They carefully made their way around the edge, then Gabrielle held up her torch to reveal an abyss ready to swallow them whole.

"I can see why the Roman legions don't come down here," he breathed.

"Stay close to the wall."

They followed the ledge to a series of narrow steps that took them down to yet another ledge, which led into a tall tunnel. He could hear the sound of water and they soon entered a terraced cavern with waterfalls all around. He looked up to see water spilling out from two levels up and disappearing into cavern depths below.

"This way," she said, pushing them through a flooded tunnel.

"Does this ever fill up?"

"Often," she said, as they slogged through the waist-deep water.

The tunnel opened up and sloped down into a large grotto.

"Slide," she said, jumping down.

He followed her down the water chute through a series of pools, before they were caught in a power channel at the bottom. He thought they were going to drown as they tumbled toward the bowels of the deep, but then almost as suddenly they broke the surface of a serene under-ground lake and climbed out.

"We're close," she said.

"I should hope so," Athanasius replied with breathless incredulity, thinking this made his escape through the Great Drain look like bath play in comparison.

They entered a great and solemn cavern, with golden stalactites creating columns from the floor to the ceiling.

They almost looked Doric in style, these natural formations, Athanasius thought in wonder.

There in the middle of the columns, lying on blankets and hides next to a natural spring, was a very old man with very dark skin. In his youth he must have been quite strong. But in his old age, his legs had withered somehow and he was lame. This pit seemed to have been his home for years, and the only way he survived, Athanasius guessed, was with the help of Gabrielle.

Gabrielle said, "This is him, Cerberus. Samuel Ben-Deker. But I heard Dovilin's son call him Athanasius."

Athanasius stood flat-footed as Cerberus looked him over with ram-like eyes. "Welcome, Athanasius of Athens," he said, his voice like the rumble of the waters in the cavern. "You have the key to Rome, I have the key to Asia Minor. Let's see why the Dei never wanted us to meet, but the last apostle did."

35

Cerberus seemed all too aware that his time on this earth was quickly drawing to a close, and he wasted no words. "I'm called Cerberus, because like the three-headed dog of Greek mythology who guards the doors to Hades, I guard the three doors to the Dei, the secret of its origins. You, Athanasius, though you do not know it, guard the secret to its destiny."

Athanasius, sinking down on his knees beside the old man, said, "I want to know everything."

"The first thing you must know is that the Dei is only thirty years old, but the powers behind it are much, much older," Cerberus told him. "I come from a family of star-gazers and assassins, cousins to the Dovilins. We have been assassins for hire, run out of Cappadocia, since the days of the Hittite kings, and before that Egypt. My side of the family took a different turn when my great-grandfather followed the stars to Bethlehem to assassi-

319

nate Jesus at his birth on orders from King Herod. But three stargazers from the East convinced him otherwise, and my family ever since has served the Lord."

Athanasius nodded. "But not the Dei."

"No. As I told you, the spirit of the Dei goes back centuries, to before the pharaohs of Egypt and the fall of Atlantis, all the way to the creation of the universe. They follow the stars in everything they do, from the founding of Rome to great military campaigns to the planting of crops."

Athanasius looked at Gabrielle. "Forecasting. You chart the stars to grow grapes."

"We use the seasons and cycles of recorded history to make better guesses for farming," Cerberus said. "Not to chart our lives. A man reaps what he sows, regardless of what the stars may say. Which is more than I can say for the Romans, who conscripted my services during the Judean War thirty years ago."

"Vespasian," Athanasius said. "The first head."

"You were right, Gabrielle," Cerberus said. "He is quick to connect the dots." Cerberus took a breath. "Yes, Vespasian, and then his son Titus. They wanted to know their enemy's intricate Jewish calendars and Sabbaths and use the stars against them. Then, after destroying Jerusalem, they brought the treasures of the temple to Rome and erected a vast coliseum, the Flavian Amphitheater. All this you know now. But what you don't know is that the Dei was forged in the ashes of the Judean War between three men: Vespasian, Dovilin and Mucianus."

Mucianus! Athanasius thought. Surely it was no coincidence that the last apostle John directed him to the memoirs of the former Syrian governor in the library at Ephesus.

"Mucianus was the mastermind who put the Flavians and Dovilins together," Cerberus said. "Domitian's father Vespasian had been given a special command in Judea by Nero with orders to put down the Great Jewish Revolt almost thirty years ago, and Mucianus supported him with arms and troops and passage across the Anatolian plains. After Nero died and there was civil war for control of Rome, Mucianus marched on Rome on behalf of Vespasian with an army drawn from the Judean and Syrian legions—and Dovilin mercenaries and assassins. Meanwhile, Mucianus had Vespasian travel to Alexandria, where he was proclaimed emperor, and secure control of the vital grain supplies from Egypt. Vespasian's son Titus remained in Judea to deal with the Jewish rebellion."

"Where was Domitian in all of this?" Athanasius asked. "He had to have been a teenager during the Year of Four Emperors."

"Under Mucianus's protection in Rome while Vespasian was in Egypt," Cerberus said. "Domitian was the nominal head of Rome in the months before his father finally arrived to claim the throne. But for all practical purposes Mucianus was the de facto emperor of Rome."

"What happened to Mucianus later on? He seems to have disappeared from Roman life entirely, leaving only his travelogue of Asia Minor."

"That is a very good question, Athanasius, and you must find the answer, because the Dei has evolved considerably from Mucianus's original three-fold purpose," Cerberus explained. "The first purpose of the Dei was to establish a secret Praetorian to ensure the continuity of the Flavian dynasty. Until Vespasian, the Praetorian had been known to select rather than protect their Caesars, and dispose of them at will.

"The second purpose was to reverse the supply lines that Vespasian and Mucianus had established for the military during the Judean War and bring the spoils of the provinces back to Rome. Commerce, as you may have detected, is the heart of the organization, and the Dovilins were given a free hand with land in Cappadocia so long as they could also provide bodies.

"The third purpose, and most sinister, was to create a vast counter-insurgency to pacify the Church."

Athanasius wasn't sure he understood. "Pacify the Church?"

"The horrors of the Judean War and the fanaticism of the Jews at Masada frightened Vespasian," Cerberus said.

"He knew that wars fought with ideas are different than wars fought with spears. He worried that the Christian faith had become a virus after the destruction of the temple, leaping from Jews to Gentiles like some plague that could engulf the empire now that it was no longer ethnocentric. So he wanted to encourage a civil war within the Church between Jew and Gentile to further isolate Jews in Asia Minor. Then he wanted to use the Dei within the Praetorian in Rome to infiltrate the disciples of the apostle Paul who had taken root under Nero."

Athanasius nodded. "So for thirty years the Dei was an imperial network to spy out and pacify the Church from within," he said. "Until Domitian changed the game by using the Dei to assassinate Roman officials— his enemies—and publicly blame the Christians, pitting the Church against the State. Why?"

"The stars, of course," Cerberus said. "Domitian's birth chart proclaimed the date of his death. His father, brother and the rest of the Dei believe the stars are destiny, and therefore Domitian had none. I suspect he killed his father and then killed his brother, and has been killing anybody else who believes the prophecies."

36

Back in Rome, Domitian was listening to his replacement for Caelus drone on about this moon and that sign. His name was Ascletario, and Ludlumus had dug him up from somewhere in Germania. He was fairly well-known around Rome and had moved up in prominence after Caelus's demise. His specialty was interpreting signs and dreams, and already Domitian didn't like what he was hearing inside the basilica at the Palace of the Flavians.

"I must stand by my previous assessments," Ascletario concluded.

Domitian had summoned the astrologer after yet another spate of lightning strikes across Rome and the rest of the empire. So much so that he awakened from his sleep just the other night and cried out for all to hear, "Let him now strike whom he will!" That very night the capitol was struck by lightning, as was the temple of the

Flavian family, and even the palace itself. Come morning the Praetorian had discovered that the tablet inscribed upon the base of his triumphal statue had been carried away by the violence of the storm.

As if that were not enough, the next night he dreamt that Minerva whom he worshipped above all else had declared to him that she could no longer protect him, because Jupiter had disarmed her, and that now he would have no sanctuary from the wrath of heaven.

Thus Domitian had hastily convened this audience with Ascletario to interpret these events and his own subsequent fate, especially in light of the impending date of September 18, which was little more than a month away.

"Tell me again what you think it all means, Ascletario," Domitian demanded. "And where this all ends."

"What it means is a change of government is coming soon to Rome," Ascletario said. "Where it ends with you, Your Excellency, is in the beginning."

The astrologer then produced Domitian's own natal chart, as if Domitian hadn't had it burned into his nightmares since childhood.

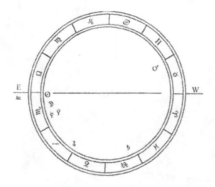

"As everyone, including your father Vespasian, has known, the moon and sun are in dangerous positions relative to Saturn and Mars. This has been fixed forever and cannot be changed."

"Even by Caesar of Rome, the Lord and God of the universe?" Domitian demanded.

"Yes, Your Excellency."

"Tell me, then, you who claims to know the future," Domitian said. "To what end do you think you should come yourself?"

Ascletario calmly replied, "I shall in a short time be torn to pieces by dogs."

Domitian laughed. "No, Ascletario, you won't be torn to pieces by dogs, because I will prevent that. But you will die today." He nodded, and his Praetorian took position on either side of the astrologer. "Kill him, and then burn his corpse."

37

Athanasius listened intently to everything Cerberus told him about the Dei, its origins with Vespasian, Dovilin and Mucianus, and its changing nature under Domitian. All of which made him consider the scions of Dovilin and Mucianus.

"Dovilin's son, Vibius, is dead," Athanasius told him, waiting for a reaction from Cerberus but seeing none. "So I don't know where Dovilin goes from here."

"I do," said Cerberus, and removed a letter from beneath one of the blankets upon which he lay and handed it to him. He almost knocked his small oil lamp over in the process, which seemed to be an accident waiting to happen.

The letter was an elaborate invitation, the kind Athanasius used to receive back in Rome, hand-delivered by messengers in crisp white tunics and metal-studded belts.

You are invited to the Harvest Banquet at the Dovilin Vineyards on August 18 to celebrate the Harvest of wines and the work of the Lord's Vineyard. You will not want to miss it.

Of the hundreds of Christian leaders that the Lord's Vineyard has discovered in its first 30 years, only a few are receiving this invitation. The most successful, experienced and highly placed believers in trade, military and government are invited to attend the tenth annual Harvest Banquet.

This invitation-only event is one of the most significant of its kind. Your life will change forever. So please mark your calendar and clear your itinerary for August 18.

The Dovilin Family Vineyard is one of the most beautiful locales in all of Asia. Outstanding musicians will lift your spirits to the stars. You will experience unforgettable fellowship in safe, secure surroundings with committed Christians.

You will meet God as never before.

The invitation listed what it called famous Christians who had attended previous Harvests, but Athanasius didn't recognize any names and was unimpressed.

Where was the name of strapping Narcissus on the list? Indeed, elitist nonsense of this sort was rare even in Rome.

"Domitian's rule is more a meritocracy than the Church's," he told Cerberus, handing the invitation back.

But Cerberus refused it. "You'll need it to get into the banquet."

"I can't go back there. She can't go back there. We're going to Rome, where the Dei will least expect us, and where Domitian is."

"But you don't know who the Dei is today," Cerberus said. "Dovilin is the only one of the three still around, but he now takes orders from Vespasian's son Domitian, and Domitian may still be taking orders from Mucianus's son or successor the way he did when he was nominal Caesar in Rome thirty years ago. You must find out what has happened to the third line in the Dei trinity. That is key, Athanasius."

Cerberus pressed his arm for emphasis.

"If you find the successor to Mucianus in the Dei or his heir, Athanasius, you will find the man who truly rules the Dei today—or will tomorrow. The true Chiron. The linchpin of the Dei. If he is removed, the Dei falls apart. If he is not removed, you can remove Domitian but the Dei will continue, perhaps stronger than ever."

"And you really think I might find him at this Harvest party Dovilin is throwing?"

"I think you might recognize a face from Rome that neither I nor Gabrielle nor anybody in the churches of Asia Minor would," Cerberus said.

Athanasius immediately thought of Senator Celsus, who was his strongest link to this Mucianus successor. He could have been the one who gave the order to kill Caelus, although Athanasius could not reason why.

Cerberus said, "Getting into this banquet will be a lot easier than circumventing the Praetorian at the Palace of the Flavians."

"It's getting out I'm worried about," Athanasius said. "I still don't know how."

Cerberus said nothing as Athanasius watched Gabrielle walk around the far perimeter of the cavern, listening.

"Who is Gabrielle, Cerberus?" Athanasius said in a low voice, leaning toward the old man. "What is she to you?"

"Gabrielle's grandmother was a maidservant spoil of war for Vespasian during the Judean War. When she became pregnant, she hid her condition for as long as possible but was found out and killed. But the baby, Gabrielle's mother, was delivered. I took care of her until she married. Her husband died, however, and then she died giving birth to Gabrielle. I have watched her ever since, except for the year when the Minotaur men took her and sent her off to work the temples and pleasure barges. She jumped a ship and came back to help me and those who would stand firm in the spirit of the Lord and not by might or power."

Athanasius felt the hair on the back of his neck rise at this revelation, and a chill ran down his spine. Then he remembered Cleo's story aboard the Sea Nymph: Gabrielle was the girl who got away.

"She's a Flavian!" he told Cerberus, who nodded. "And she doesn't even know it, does she?"

"No."

"But the Dovilins do, don't they? And hate her for it."

Cerberus didn't answer him, cocking his head. "They're coming. "

"Who is coming?"

"Dovilin's men. And they'll want blood."

"Cerberus!" shouted Gabrielle, running toward them. "Two groups from two separate tunnels!"

"Go out the tunnel behind me, Gabrielle. You must take the Angel's Pass if you are to escape."

"The Angel's Pass?" she repeated. "We are better off fighting here."

"Take her," Cerberus told Athanasius. "I will fight."

"You'll die!" Gabrielle said as men in Minotaur masks burst into the cavern aiming crossbows.

Athanasius nodded at Cerberus, who lifted a blanket to reveal his own unusual crossbow with arrows dipped in mud. Athanasius understood and grabbed Gabrielle.

334 | THOMAS GREANIAS

"You'll see him on the other side of life soon enough. Let's go!"

He pushed her into the mouth of the tunnel and looked back to see the lame old man calmly take his oil lamp and touch it to the floor. Walls of flame suddenly rose along lines of the flammable mud drawn across the floor.

"Cerberus!" Gabrielle cried, reaching toward the cavern while Athanasius pulled her back.

Then the old man raised his crossbow and released an arrow that struck the ceiling. Even from the tunnel Athanasius could hear the dome of the cavern crackle, and suddenly the whole thing caved, burying Cerberus and the Minotaur men and sending plumes of dust into the tunnel.

"Hold your breath!" he shouted, pushing her down the tunnel as flaming rocks fell like stars from the sky.

Leaving the collapsed cavern of death behind them, Athanasius and Gabrielle raced across a rock bridge spanning a wide abyss and arrived at two passageways. One was tall and narrow, the other short and wide.

"Which way to this Angel's Pass?" he asked her.

Her face looked vacant, confused, as if she couldn't accept that Cerberus was gone, her life at the vineyard gone, everything gone.

"Gabrielle!"

She came to life again and looked at the passageways. Then she put her hand to the rock, feeling it. "The short one. I feel a breeze. The Angel's Breath. It leads to Angel's Pass. We have to follow it all the way out. If we stray, we're lost."

They crawled through the tight passage, and Athanasius felt like he was back in the lagar with Vibius putting the screw press to him. The tunnel began to twist and turn, narrowing further as the breeze turned into a loud whistle.

"What is it?" Athanasius asked her.

"I hear water. We're close."

Moments later they crawled out into the light of day, collapsing onto the rocks outside and allowing the cool water of the babbling brook to sooth their scratched and bruised legs.

Gabrielle was shaking in tears.

Athanasius put his arms around her and held her tight, hiding his horror at the touch of her back, where he could feel the deep gashes and welts from her days in the ships and cities. She had come back to this place, but there was no place for her here anymore.

"I need your help, Gabrielle."

She turned on him, her dark eyes flashing passion, and pounded him on his chest. "Haven't you done enough? Vibius is dead! Cerberus is dead! You were supposed to expose the Dei to the Church, not expose the Church to the Dei!"

"I need you to help me get into the Harvest Banquet in two days."

"So you can kill more?"

"So I can find the Dei's true link to Rome, this Muci-anus successor. I know he or one of his representatives will be there. Until we know who runs the Dei in Rome, the church there and all the churches here in Asia Minor are in danger. The apostle John knows this, Polycarp in Ephesus knows it too, and so did Cerberus. The church here can't go back to living in holes and pretending that this is not so."

"I'll help you, for the sake of the Church," she said, her eyes still moist. "But if you ask me, I think you're the third head of the Dei."

"You know that's not true."

"Maybe not," she said. "But the way death surrounds you, it might as well be.".

38

Once again Helena had been summoned to join Caesar for dinner at the palace. She feared the worst, expecting to find the head of her beloved Athanasius served up for them on a silver platter. When she arrived at the private dining room, however, she discovered the death they were to celebrate was that of Caesar's latest astrologer, Ascletario. And Domitian was nowhere to greet her, only an ashen Latinus.

"What happened?" she asked the comic.

"The emperor ordered Ascletario to be burned alive today," Latinus told her. "As he was not feeling well, he sent me over to enjoy the entertainment for myself. Everything was in order for the performance. There was a small crowd, the body was bound and laid upon the pyre, and the fire kindled. It was all hugely predictable, I thought, when suddenly there arose a dread storm of wind

337

and rain, which drove all the spectators away and extinguished the fire."

A bad omen, to be sure, Helena thought, but to ruin dinner for Domitian? "So that was it?"

"No!" said Latinus. "His body was still on the pyre when a pack of passing dogs ran out and tore it to pieces! It was just as Ascletario had predicted!"

Helena covered her mouth. She didn't know whether to laugh or cry.

Latinus nodded. "I know! It was something out of one of Athanasius's plays."

It was! she thought. It was a sign!

She suddenly felt dizzy, however, like she would vomit.

"Dear Helena, I am so sorry," Latinus said. "I didn't mean to bring up…"

She shook her head. "I'm not well. Excuse me."

She ran past a column and down a marble corridor to a guest bath and promptly threw up into a basin. She breathed heavily, trying to steady herself, then vomited again. Oh, how the acid burned the back of her throat. She spat out what was left from her mouth, and then washed her face in a fresh bowl of water.

A dread now replaced the explosion of joy she had experienced only a moment ago. Even if Athanasius were still alive, she thought, and even if he were to return triumphant to Rome by some miracle, how can I ever face him in my condition?

A storm of anguish and grief churned inside her as the belief sank in that no matter what her beloved's fate, her own hopes for a brighter future were nothing now but an illusion.

She poured the cool, clean water over her face, and then looked up into the brass mirror to see the distorted reflection of Ludlumus and froze.

"So the goddess is with child," he told her in the mirror. "It's Domitian's, isn't it?"

She said nothing.

"Poor Athanasius really did leave nothing behind, did he?"

"Stop it, Ludlumus," she said and turned to face him, still feeling flush. "I know he's still alive. If he were dead, Domitian would have shown me his head. He's alive."

"And so is Domitian's heir in your belly, Helena. I'd keep that to yourself for as long as you can."

"I'm planning to," she said, then paused. "Why should you care?"

"I'd hate to see you come to any harm at the hands of the empress Domitia or the widow of Flavius Clemens. After all, if you bear Domitian's heir, he hardly needs the spare. Young Vespasian and Young Domitian are as good as dead. I should think their mother would do all she could to prevent that, use whatever means at her disposal to save her children."

Helena said nothing, only watched his long face as he studied her.

"But would you do likewise, I wonder? After all, if your beloved Athanasius ever did show up, would he even want you now? Regardless of whatever happened after September 18, to ask a man to stare at the little face of his enemy the rest of his life is probably asking more than any man could give. Then again, you are the great Helena. For you, Athanasius might do anything."

She felt her throat tighten and turned to vomit into the bowl of water. Gagging, she looked up into the brass mirror. Ludlumus was gone.

<u>39</u>

No one arriving at the Dovilin villa that night for the Harvest Banquet would have guessed from all the festive lights and music that the host's only son had just died, thought Athanasius as he emerged from the cover of the grapevines. His face was shaved clean and he was back in his polished tribune's uniform, with a swagger to match. None of the staff gave him a second look as he rounded the bathhouse and passed by the outdoor kitchen to enter the back of the villa. There he quickly picked up a cup of Dovilin wine from a floating tray and joined the guests swirling about the courtyards, fountains, flautists and harpists.

It was as if Vibius, scion of the great Dei co-founder Dovilin, never existed. Athanasius wondered what that would mean for Cota now, and could only hope he wouldn't see her this evening, or rather be seen by her.

No doubt Dovilin already sent her away or banished her from public display.

Everywhere he looked there were oversized amphorae, some open and some sealed, lined up for effect before they departed with the guests back to wherever they all came from. He was scanning the main courtyard to see if there were any faces from Rome he might recognize when he heard a voice from behind him say, "Tribune!"

Athanasius turned to see the very legate he had served at the dinner only days before in this house. His uniform, too, bore the rank of tribune. "Tribune," Athanasius reciprocated with a mild salute of his cup before he drank.

"Do I know you?" the legate asked. "You look familiar."

Athanasius shrugged. "I first joined up during the Dacian War and served with the Praetorian in Rome, Third Cohort. How about you?"

"I'm with the XVI Flavia legion now. So you served under the Prefect Aeolus with the Praetorian?"

"No," Athanasius replied as calmly as he could, and quickly decided to lift Virtus's background. "Third Cohort under the Prefect Secundus."

The legate, who introduced himself as Gracchus, seemed satisfied enough. "I thought I knew everybody from the Roman faction here tonight," he said. "What brings you to the Lord's Vineyard?"

"This," said Athanasius and held up his wine in such a way as to display his Dei ring.

Gracchus's look was priceless. "General, sir. I am sorry."

"No apologies necessary, Gracchus. We need to be vigilant. You asked me why I'm here. I'm here to observe. I'm here to observe you, Gracchus. I'm here to observe the work of the Lord's Vineyard. I'm here to observe everything. I miss nothing. Neither should you. Keep your mouth shut and your eyes open. If there is anything out of the ordinary, report it to me immediately."

"Yes, General."

"Now go see if Senator Celsus or his representative from Rome is here. Tell him only that this tribune would like a word with him by that bust of Dovilin over there near the harpist."

It was all the man could do to keep from saluting as he disappeared.

Athanasius swallowed hard and walked over toward the bust of Dovilin, as if to admire the craggy face, warts and all. He took another sip of wine and casually glanced around in time to see old Dovilin himself take a position before a large tapestry draped dramatically over the columns of the peristyle on the other side of the courtyard. The tapestry displayed a map of the empire, but it was divided along lines Athanasius had never seen before.

There was a gong and the music stopped, as did all the clinking of cups and trays shortly thereafter. All eyes focused on Dovilin as he cleared his throat.

"Welcome to the Harvest!" he announced. "Tonight we celebrate our wines and the work of the Lord's Vineyard. Of the hundreds of Christian leaders we have discovered throughout the Roman empire in the past 30 years, only a few of you have been invited here tonight. You are the successful, experienced and high-placed believers in trade, the military and government. We are an invisible world army led by Christ, and tonight our ranks grow yet again."

Several dozen young men and women were brought forward for debut, a fresh crop of new recruits for the Lord's Vineyard. Athanasius could only wonder how many of them, if any, understood they were enlisting in Dominium Dei, let alone in what capacities.

"These young men and women will be joining you on your journeys back to your God-given stations in Roman society. God does as he wishes with the armies of heaven and the peoples of the earth. We are the new chosen. God has chosen us to do His will on earth as it is in heaven. As above, so below."

"As above, so below," the guests responded in unison.

Dovilin said, "Now come lay hands on your new soldiers and pray for them as they help us build Christ's kingdom."

Athanasius watched as the guests stepped forward to join their intended foot soldiers for Jesus and place their hands on the young heads and shoulders. As they closed their eyes, Dovilin led the prayer, and Athanasius realized with some satisfaction that the local Bishop Paul, being but a bit player, was nowhere to be found among the august ranks of these super-Christians.

"Lord Jesus Christ, son of God," Dovilin prayed. "Thy kingdom come, and Thy will be done on earth as it is in heaven. Bless your servants gathered here tonight. Protect them in the presence of their enemies. For theirs is the kingdom and the power and the glory forever. Amen."

With that, smiles and tears broke out all around along with another round of music, food and wine. Athanasius glanced about and then saw none other than that scoundrel of an idolmaker from Ephesus, Supremus, waddling over to him. Surely he was not the link to Senator Celsus's interests with the Dei in Rome.

Supremus didn't recognize Athanasius until it was too late and Athanasius had jammed the point of his dagger in the fat man's stomach.

Athanasius whispered, "Quiet, Supremus, or I'll gut you like a fish here and now."

Supremus nodded slowly.

"Now let's walk over to a more quiet atrium, talking like two old friends, which of course we are, aren't we?"

Supremus nodded again as Athanasius put his arm holding his wine cup around the idolmaker's shoulder, while his other hand with the dagger sank deep into the folds of the Dei rep's tunic. Athanasius led them in a friendly stroll to an empty atrium off the main courtyard that was dimly lit by only a few flickering candles.

"Athanasius!" Supremus exclaimed, suddenly lowering his voice when Athanasius put the blade of his dagger to his throat. "You're alive!"

"I've come to claim my royalties for my merchandise, Supremus. I've come to claim my money. Where is it? Perhaps in the pockets of Senator Celsus and the Dei?" Athanasius dug the blade deeper into the idolmaker's flabby throat.

"Please, Athanasius. You know I am nothing. I do as I am told."

Athanasius was worried the man in his panic might raise his voice, so he pushed him against the heavy drapes in the back. If he had to, he would muffle the idolmaker's cries, wrap him in the drape and drive his dagger through to kill him.

"Then tell me what you have been told, Supremus, and who has been doing the telling, and I may yet have mercy on your miserable soul and let you live."

Supremus nodded. "I will show you. I must reach for my pouch."

"Slowly," said Athanasius, pushing the dagger further into the fat as Supremus's chubby arm reached into the folds of his tunic and produced two figurines, one thin and one round.

"See?"

Athanasius glanced at them but held the blade firmly. "I see them. Oedipus and the Oracle. What I don't see is your connection to the Dei."

"No, no, Athanasius. You do not see. Look closer."

Athanasius kept his dagger to the throat and with his other hand picked up the round figurine and looked at the carving on the orb. The oracle was supposed to be cut to look like Caelus, before he was slain. But this oracle looked different. "Who is this?"

"That is Peter the apostle," Supremus said. "The tall, thin one is Jesus."

"Jesus?" Athanasius said, and looked at what should have been Oedipus and saw the head cut to show the long hair of a Nazarene. "If there's a new comedy to skewer the Christians, I want to know who wrote it."

"No comedy, Athanasius. These are not for the theaters. These are for the churches."

"The churches?" Athanasius repeated, and Athanasius immediately thought of old John the last apostle, young Polycarp and Gabrielle. "The Dei is more stupid than I thought. The churches will never accept idols."

Supremus shrugged. "You know I only make what is ordered from Rome."

"And who is doing the ordering, Supremus? Tell me now. Is it Senator Celsus?"

Supremus shook his head. "No, Celsus takes his orders from Senator Sura."

Athanasius stopped. "Lucius Licinius Sura?"

Supremus nodded, beads of sweat rolling down his jowls.

"Sura, the father of Lucius Licinius Ludlumus, the master of the Games?" he pressed, staring at Supremus's frozen face, watching the light go out from his eyes and blood dribble from his mouth.

Supremus began to lean into him, and Athanasius caught him right below the dagger protruding from his back.

No!

Athanasius lowered the heavy corpse to the floor and burst between the drapes in time to see a figure flee through an archway and disappear.

How much had he heard? Athanasius decided it didn't matter. He had no choice but to go for Dovilin right now before it was too late.

<u>40</u>

Dovilin was seeing off a diplomat from Spain when a servant handed him a note that bore the seal of Caesar himself. "Who gave you this?" he demanded.

The servant shook his head. "One of the guests gave it to me and said the man wants to meet you in the bath-house out back."

Dovilin didn't like it. But there was no mistaking the authority of the letter. "Get Brutus," he told the servant, and by the time he reached the back of the villa near the outdoor kitchen, Brutus was waiting, all battered and bruised from the events of the week. Dovilin had to keep him out of sight, or he'd scare the guests.

"Go look into the bathhouse and see who is there," Dovilin ordered.

Brutus nodded and disappeared. A moment later he reappeared to report the bathhouse was empty.

Dovilin frowned. "Then I will go inside and wait, in case anybody is watching us. But you will keep watch out here and intercept anybody who attempts to enter the bathhouse. Understood?"

"Yes, sir," said Brutus.

Dovilin glanced about and could see nothing beyond the bathhouse but the dark rows of his vineyard rolling beneath the stars to the brightly lit winery on the other side, where crews were loading amphorae onto the supply wagons of his guests. The lights and shouts gave him some comfort as he entered the bathhouse.

It was empty, just as Brutus reported, with a couple of stands holding a dozen candles whose light bounced off the bathwater and threw wicked shadows. Dovilin would wait here only a few minutes, enough for whomever hoped to trap him to come to him, then go outside once Brutus had him.

Dovilin looked up in time to see a shadow fall from the ceiling, sending him to the floor and banging his skull against the mosaic tiles. Dovilin tried to shout, but a hand covered his mouth and he felt the sharp point of a cold blade to his throat.

The shadow above him put a finger to his lips.

Dovilin made out the uniform of a Roman tribune and a shiny face in the flickering light that he recognized as Samuel Ben-Deker, or rather Athanasius of Athens.

"You!" he said and stopped as the dagger dug deeper into his throat.

"Tell me!" Dovilin felt the ring on Athanasius's fist dig into his face. "Who is the son or successor to Mucianus in Rome? What connection does the Licinius family have to Mucianus and to you?"

"Brutus!" Dovilin screamed before his head was slammed into the floor again.

Hurt and dizzy, Dovilin heard a shout outside and saw Athanasius jump to his feet as Brutus burst in with a crossbow. Athanasius backed off, hands up.

"Now, Brutus, before it's too late!" he screamed, and gave the code word. "Melt!"

Brutus nodded, lowered his crossbow and shot him in the chest.

Dovilin felt the arrow pierce his flesh and opened his mouth to smile at the confused Athanasius. "You showed us Cerberus," he hissed, and began choking on his own blood. "You showed us Angel's Pass. Romans...will kill them all...because of you."

Then, like a scarf, he felt his spirit escape into a dark tunnel that ended in a black abyss.

Athanasius looked down in shock at the corpse of old Dovilin and then up at Brutus, who had just used up his one shot and knew it. Athanasius hurled his knife at the slave, but Brutus was out the door, shouting warnings. By the time Athanasius rushed outside the bathhouse, he heard screams from the girls at the outdoor kitchen and more coming from inside the villa. He took a step forward when the ground shook from a tremendous explosion, and he fell into the gravel as a burst of light filled the sky.

The winery had exploded in flames.

Athanasius got to his feet and looked across the vineyard at the billows of flames and smoke shooting out of the façade from the cave in the cliffs.

They've blown the winery! On purpose!

Suddenly a streak of flames shot across the vineyard over his head to the red-clay tiles on the roof of the villa.

Melt! That was what Dovilin screamed. It must have been some kind of pre-determined order to self-destruct. *The guests and slaves!*

He ran into the villa and found chaos everywhere, as smoke and flames from exploding amphorae formed curtains of heated confusion. He heard coughing and saw Cota crawling on her knees beneath the smoke, trying to find a way out, then seeing him with fear and confusion on her face as he took her hand.

"Out the back!" he told her, and began to drag her to her feet.

Athanasius pushed Cota out toward the kitchen and stables and looked back to see the entire villa in flames on a scale that dwarfed the tragedy of his own family's villa back in Corinth. And this time it wasn't the Romans who ordered the destruction; it was Dovilin himself.

Dovilin would rather kill himself and everybody with him than name the third member of the Dei trinity, Athanasius realized with a shock. *This is going to be much harder than I imagined, maybe impossible.*

A distressed and incensed Gabrielle was waiting for him back in the vineyard as he brought out Cota and a stallion that he had seized from the barn before it went up in flames. Gabrielle immediately attended to Cota, taking moments to glare at him and the scene of destruction behind him. "Congratulations, Athanasius. Now that we have no one to lead the church of Asia, it's yours for the taking."

"This was Dovilin's doing. How is she?"

"She'll live. That's more than I can say for the innocents in that inferno!"

"You know that wasn't my intention. Look, Brutus is gone, the word is out. Someone must have seen us escape through the Angel's Pass, Gabrielle. Rome's legions now have the key to enter the caves that they've been looking for, and I've given it to them."

He looked at her and knew from her expression that there was nothing he could say or do to comfort her. She was completely beyond the reach of his power of words, and right now he was at a loss for them.

"I'm sorry, Gabrielle," he told her.

She said nothing, only looked at him with horror, like he was one of those masked Minotaurs that they had escaped in the caves.

"You know what to do, Gabrielle," he told her as he mounted the stallion. "You know the caverns and all the traps. You know how to collapse the tunnels. You have to block the Romans if they try to invade the underground cities."

"You can't leave us now!"

"I have to get to Rome and make this right."

"Make this right?" She was crying tears of rage now. "We need you here now, more than ever!"

"There is nothing more I can do for you here, Gabrielle," he said, steadying his stallion as it whinnied to escape the heat. He knew, however, he couldn't leave her without any hope. "But if you and those in the caves can hold out for 40 days, we all might see a Christian world."

Her wet eyes looked doubtful, and he could swear that she was crying tears of blood.

"Fast and pray for a new world order," he told her with little conviction, and then kicked his horse to life and rode off into the night toward Kingdom Come.

With little hope for the underground church in Cappadocia that he had just left behind, Athanasius let pure, righteous rage fuel his race back to Rome. Rage at the Dovilins and the Christians here like Gabrielle who did nothing to oppose them, let alone Rome.

Athanasius now realized he had it all backwards. He thought the Lord's Vineyard was all about the flow of Church influence into the world. In fact, it was the other way around. The Dovilins, with Dei help, had turned the churches of Asia into a market for their goods, primarily wine, foundational to the Communion ritual. That's how they made money. The token shipments to Caesar were just that. Everything else came from the flesh and opium trade.

Quite ingenious and outrageous.

They were literally selling the Christians back their own sweat. The tithes and offerings that went to churches to pay for the wine were going into the pockets of the very family exploiting them all. A family cited for their Christian faith and blessings. They were profiting off the church.

No wonder old John's Book of Revelation depicted Jesus standing outside the Church, knocking on its door. The Church today was probably the last place on earth anybody would find Him.

<u>41</u>

Stephanus was shaking as the Praetorians marched him through the private residences of the Palace of the Flavians to Caesar's bedchamber. Caesar had finished his midday bath and was freshly dressed in royal robes and enjoying his sweets when Stephanus was escorted inside.

"Ah, Stephanus, I haven't seen you since you worked for my cousin the consul," Domitian said, referring to Flavius Clemens whom he had executed. "You'll have to see the boys while you are here."

"If Caesar allows it," Stephanus said humbly.

"So what's this I hear that about my niece Domitilla persecuting the loyal servant of my late cousin for defrauding her?"

"I stole nothing, Your Excellency."

"Of course you didn't, Stephanus. Why would you? The Flavians have been kind to you, even the traitors like my cousin. Did she do that to you? You seem to be in some pain."

Domitian was referring to the bandage wrapped around Stephanus's left arm.

"An accident, sir. She meant no harm."

"But, of course she did, Stephanus. On the other hand, I will offer you generosity and grace. You will continue to do the work of correspondence between Caesar and his niece Domitilla and her sons. Only now, like the boys, you will live here and not that island to which I exiled my niece."

"Thank you, Your Excellency. Thank you," Stephanus repeated when the prefect of the Praetorian, Secundus, marched inside the bedchambers without warning.

"Your Excellency, I am sorry to be so bold, but there is news out of Asia Minor."

Stephanus drew back so as not to be in the way, nor give Caesar easy reason to dismiss him. Perhaps this was news that he too had to hear. News from Athanasius or about him.

"Your assassin Orion is dead."

"Dead?" Domitian repeated. "He can't die. He's the one who does the killing."

"It gets worse, sir," Secundus went on. "The Dovilins are dead too."

"The Dovilins!"

"Everybody's dead."

Stephanus wasn't sure if that meant Athanasius too, but it looked like Domitian had trouble standing as he began to pace the room.

"So Athanasius is dead too."

"We think so, Your Excellency. We don't know."

"Don't know?" roared Domitian, and Stephanus drew back in genuine terror. "Don't know!"

Secundus kept his ground. "It's impossible to identify the remains of so many, Your Excellency," he said. "But spies have disclosed to your legions the location of the so-called Angel's Pass into the mountains of Cappadocia."

Stephanus saw fire suddenly flare up in the emperor's otherwise dull eyes. "Angel's Pass! At last!" Then he paused to summon up royal authority. "Orders are given to XII Fulminate and XVI Flavia legions in Cappadocia to use the passage of the Angel's Pass to commence full-scale invasion of the cave systems surrounding the former Dovilin Vineyards. They are to exterminate the Christians inside, every last man, woman and child, in reprisal for their attacks upon Rome and its representatives."

"Hail, Caesar!" saluted Secundus and left, leaving Stephanus alone with his new employer.

Domitian continued to pace and spew words of wrath, as if he didn't see him. Finally, he spotted Stephanus and barked, "You! What are you still doing here? Leave me!"

"Yes, Your Excellency," Stephanus said and scrambled out.

A few minutes later he passed Secundus near the offices behind the palace, and the prefect acknowledged him with a cool nod.

Virtus was right. He was in.

<u>42</u>

Aboard the Sea Nymph en route to Rome, Athanasius reviewed the encrypted message and map from Virtus that Polycarp had given him back in Ephesus. Using the Caesar shift code to decipher the message, Athanasius learned that the conspirators in Rome were clear about the general plan to assassinate Caesar. But they were confused about some of the particulars. This was fine with Athanasius, as he wanted to reveal the details in person and only at the last possible moment to avoid any betrayals from a Dei infiltrator.

The key information in the report was that Virtus had met with his former superior in the Praetorian, the prefect Secundus, and secured his word that while the Praetorian wouldn't support the assassination of Domitian on September 18, they wouldn't stop it either.

So Virtus would be free to enter the imperial bedchamber while Caesar was out and remove the dagger

Domitian had hidden under his pillow. It was important for Caesar to be defenseless when Stephanus entered the bedchamber later in the day, claiming to have uncovered a conspiracy, and then stab him to death with his own dagger, thus avenging the death of Flavius Clemens.

The dagger would be hidden under the bandages around Stephanus's left arm. His wound was a ruse to lower Domitian's defenses for when the moment finally came.

Stephanus had visited Caesar often enough to draw a detailed map of the bedchambers, which Athanasius now studied.

The biggest doubts the conspirators in Rome had, according to Virtus, concerned the timing of the attack, and whether to do it while Domitian was in the bath at midday or later on at supper.

Athanasius planned to tell them upon his arrival that the attack would take place at precisely the prophetic hour of 9 o'clock that morning, but that Domitian should be informed beforehand that the hour had passed and it was 10 o'clock. That would let Caesar's guard down even more, and in elation of having survived his doomsday hour be more vulnerable than ever to surprise.

The important thing at that point, Athanasius concluded, was to steer Domitian to the illusory safety of his bedchambers, get Stephanus in, then lock the doors from the outside, which Virtus said Secundus assured him could be done.

His hostess Cleo entered his cabin on the Sea Nymph. "All work and no play for the tribune has the girls worried you prefer the Nubian oarsmen."

"You know I need to be focused," he told her, turning back to the crude map of the palace around Domitian's bedroom that Stephanus had drawn for Virtus.

But Cleo didn't move. "Like your focus on Gabrielle?"

Athanasius pushed himself back from his scheme and looked at Cleo. He had told her what had happened. "Say what you have to say, Cleo."

"I know her too, Athanasius. She would not have done all that she did for you if she didn't love you, and yet you left her behind with your mess."

"Which mess, Cleo?"

"The ruins of the Dei and the underground church in Asia Minor," she said. "You were a dead man when you crossed my litter on Patmos. I helped you get to Cappadocia as much as John and Polycarp did. Now thousands of innocents are about to suffer because of your vendetta against Rome."

"I have done great wrong, Cleo, I confess it now. I can no longer call myself an innocent man. But make no mistake, the underground Christians in Cappadocia were suffering long before I walked into their caves, and regardless of my own vendetta, Rome has had one from the start. I changed none of that. But that doesn't mean I can't change something. If all goes well, there will be a new Caesar."

"And if you fail to kill Domitian?"

"You'll stay anchored off Ostia, and I will escape with Helena."

"What if she doesn't want to escape with you?" Cleo asked. "We don't really know how eager Helen of Troy was to return to Greece."

"She'll come with me," Athanasius insisted. "She'll run with me."

Cleo sighed. "I suppose I would if I were in her place," she said. "But what if you kill Domitian and it still accomplishes nothing? You said you also have to kill whomever you believe to be the Dei successor to Mucianus."

"And I will, as soon as I find him," Athanasius said darkly, unrolling his collection of interrogation knives. "My old rival Ludlumus has no problem with self-expression, but I think he can be persuaded if needed to reveal everything he knows about the Dei."

43

September 18

Domitian was rudely awakened in the dead of night by another nightmare of Minerva warning him that she could no longer protect him. He bolted upright in his bed, dagger clutched to his chest, which was covered in sweat. He felt a trickle down his cheek, gingerly touched it with his finger and saw blood. He jumped out of bed, ran to the brass mirror and in the candlelight saw the festering ulcer on his forehead that he had been scratching.

"Minerva!" he cried out, pleading before the statue of the goddess. "Would this be all to befall today!"

He stared at his fading reflection in the mirror. His prophesied hour of doom at 9 o'clock this day was all of nine hours away. How was he supposed to breathe in the meantime? If blood must be spilled on this day, the day that he had dreaded his whole life, Domitian concluded, then perhaps Jupiter would accept another sacrifice in his place. Perhaps an innocent prophet would do, as he had used up most of the vestal virgins.

Yes, it was his only hope now.

Domitian splashed water on his face, dabbed his forehead with a towel and then pulled a cord to summon his chamberlain. By the time he had picked up his dagger from the floor next to his bed and placed it safely back under his pillow, he heard a knock.

"Enter," Domitian said as Parthenius walked in.

"Your Highness," Parthenius said cheerfully, pretending as if this midnight rousing was common and that the day ahead would be like any other.

"I need that astrologer we arrested," Domitian told him. "Not the one from Germania. The other one."

"Which one, Your Highness? There are so many in custody."

"The Armenian, I think," Domitian said, irritated. "I want him to stand trial so I can pass an impartial and just sentence this morning. Prepare an executioner for 9 o'clock."

"But, of course, Your Highness. I will have everyone assembled in the throne room."

"No, the basilica. I will have Jupiter and Minerva at my back as I dispense divine justice." He then handed his wooden tablet with a list of names to Parthenius. "And I want every name here rounded up so they can all be executed at the same time."

He watched the door close behind Parthenius and then collapsed back on his bed, dagger clutched to his chest, lying very still until he could hear only his own uneven breath praying to Minerva.

44

It was well past midnight when Athanasius left the ship at the port of Ostia, made his way across the piers and found a taxi on the Appian Way. There was lightning across the sky, and Athanasius had heard there had been quite a lot of it lately in Rome, and that it had spooked Domitian and therefore all of Rome with him.

"The Apollo Inn," he told the driver and settled back into his open-air carriage, trying to control his concern about Helena's fate since he had been gone. The only message he received from Virtus in Ephesus was that everything was in motion here in Rome with regards to Domitian, and that was days old.

Nothing about Helena.

He wanted her out of Rome before everything went down and the decades-in-the-making business of September 18 would finally be over. She would be safely out of the picture so that Domitian or Ludlumus had no leverage over him before they were both killed.

His path was fixed. God forgive him, if that were possible at this point.

But he could not allow himself to consider life after Domitian, or contemplate the hope of his Christian allies of a Christian world—despite their savior's own words that his kingdom was in heaven, not on this earth. Nor even his own hope of a life reunited with Helena, of the freedom to think his own thoughts, to write as he wished, to maybe settle down and have children in this seemingly God-forsaken world.

No, he could not allow such hopes to occupy his mind, any more than he could allow the fears if he failed.

He could only focus on the task at hand—exposing the Dei and assassinating Domitian in one fell swoop. Two birds with one stone cast at Rome.

And he was that stone.

He couldn't feel. Couldn't waver. Couldn't look back.

Still, he wondered how Gabrielle and the others were doing.

No, he had to put thoughts of her and the poor souls in the caves away. He had to focus on Domitian as a lifeless corpse, a god fallen.

He had to focus on killing a god, and in so doing giving all Rome hope.

The taxi turned down a hill and then a wide, well-lit boulevard to reach the Apollo. It boasted a lively tavern on the street, and a courtyard leading to an entrance to the rooms above in the back.

"This is it," he said to the driver, holding out payment, his hand trembling ever so slightly.

"Ask for Venus," the driver said, motioning to the whorehouse next door. "You won't regret it."

Athanasius watched him move down the road and pick up some sailors who could barely hold themselves upright. The taxi then headed back to the piers.

Athanasius walked around the back through the gate into a courtyard with fountains and fire pits, and then inside the small room with a counter. He ignored it and headed up the stairs to room 34.

There was Virtus, looking distressed. Behind him was a woman, a nursemaid in a smock, covered with blood. And there was another woman in the bed, moaning, clutching her stomach. Blood was running across her body. Athanasius immediately ran to her bedside.

The woman's face was contorted by pain, but it was clear that it was Helena.

Athanasius sank to the floor beside the bed.

Virtus closed the door behind him and spoke in a low but urgent tone. "She's been stabbed."

"I can see that!" Athanasius barked. "Helena! Helena!"

She opened her eyes. "Athanasius, it is you? You're alive. You cannot see my shame."

"Who did this to you, Helena? Tell me."

"No, Athanasius, let me die. Leave me!" she wailed, while the nursemaid put a hand over her mouth to quiet her.

"How could you let this happen?" he growled at Virtus.

"She did it to herself, to kill the child."

Athanasius stared at him. "What child?"

"The one growing inside her belly. Domitian's child."

Helena looked like she had died, and Athanasius tried to shake her when the nurse pulled him away. "She's still breathing. She'll survive. So will the child. She missed with the knife, but the cut is deep."

Virtus said, "We can only pray for her now. There is much to discuss but so very little time. Everything is happening so fast."

But Athanasius was furious. This was a disaster, and he hadn't yet stepped foot in Rome. Helena was pregnant with Domitian's child, and she had tried to take its life along her own. Now this nursemaid and others were involved, and what was supposed to be a quiet reunion had turned into an unfolding tragedy.

Athanasius could hardly speak. Still, Virtus was right. There was no time. The wheels of fate were in motion, and if he didn't roll with them, he would be ground to dust. "Let her sleep. But if things go badly, she needs to be ready to leave with me on the Sea Nymph later today. Now let's go find the identity of Mucianus's successor in the Dei."

Virtus paused. "You are chasing ghosts, Athanasius."

"No, Virtus," Athanasius told him, whipping out his sword. "I know where Ludlumus lives. We will take him and make him talk."

"That's the thing," Virtus said, stammering, and Athanasius could feel the bad news coming. "Ludlumus is dead."

45

Pliny the Younger liked to retire early and rise early. He was fast asleep when his bed shook and he opened his eyes to see a figure standing at the foot of his bed with a sword to his throat. "Boo!"

Pliny was about to cry out when he felt the point of the blade at his throat and saw the ghost put his finger to his lips. And then, as his eyes adjusted to the dim light of his room, he recognized the figure and shook at the sight of the ghost, come to take him down to Hades with him.

"Athanasius!" he said in a low, horrified whisper. "They killed you, not I! It wasn't my fault! I did my best to save you!"

"We'll see about that," Athanasius said. "Get dressed."

The Tabularium was the national archives of the Roman Empire, housing its official records and the offices of many city officials. It was built into the front slope of Capitoline Hill, just below the Temple of Jupiter and next to the dreaded Tullianum prison from which Athanasius had escaped on a similar night like this not that long ago. Looking more like a fortress to hide Rome's secrets than a basilica of information, Athanasius thought, the Tabularium's imposing three-level façade was built from blocks of grey, volcanic peperino and travertine stone.

"He allegedly was torn apart by his own animals under the arena floor this morning," Pliny was telling him about Ludlumus as they entered the empty Forum square. "An accident, they say, something about an unbolted gate in the tiger pens. I simply assumed Domitian was behind it. All sorts of crazy things have been happening lately, and now you show up, back from the dead, dressed up as a tribune."

"Well, you are the ghost hunter." Athanasius could see the single-door entrance at the bottom of the Tabularium's tall, fortified base. At the top of the base were small windows cut out of the facade, and above them the Doric and Corinthian arcades.

"If there is any trace of the ghost of Mucianus, we'll find him here," Pliny told Athanasius. "I'm curious myself, especially with the demise of Ludlumus and your connection of his father to the Dei. You know, I've consulted with him in the past about ghosts. And now you show up with all these revelations. Maybe something really is going on today. It brings back all the chills of Pompeii."

But Athanasius was still looking at the squat Tullianum prison next door, wondering whatever happened to old smashface the warden, before turning his attention to the two guards outside the entrance to the Tabularium.

The guards recognized Pliny on sight and allowed them inside without trouble. As they passed through the interlocking interior vaults of concrete, Athanasius felt his pulse quicken at the thought that he was on the verge of discovering the secret fate of Mucianus while bracing himself for the probability that all tracks of the Dei ghost had been erased and that he, Virtus and Stephanus were running blind into what promised to be an epic, historic morning, however Rome stood at the end of the day.

"Over here is where the deeds, records and laws are housed," Pliny said as he followed a particularly austere corridor to a large vault, where they found a skeleton of a clerk with hollow cheeks. "Hello, Hortus."

Hortus didn't appear surprised to see them here at this hour, and Athanasius suspected that most senators did their archive skullduggery themselves at night rather than send their staff by day.

"I need some old documents for Senator Sura in order to update them and submit them for approval to the senate. I need everything for these seven years."

Athanasius watched Pliny sign a wax tablet and list the band of years starting with the Year of Four Emperors.

The clerk looked at the tablet, back to Pliny and then to him, the mysterious tribune who said nothing. Hortus seemed surprised by the wide band of years. "This will take some time," he said, "and higher-level authority."

"I have my supervisor's authority, Senator Nerva," Pliny said and presented an identification token.

Hortus nodded.

Athanasius watched the ghoul disappear to the back and asked Pliny, "You trust old Nerva?"

"Yes, and you're going to have to, because if you do kill Domitian today, you'll need Nerva's help to confirm the succession of Young Vespasian. He's old, has no heirs and is trusted by competing factions to do the right thing in line with the law during times of crisis."

"Maybe," Athanasius said. "What are you hoping the clerk turns up?"

"If Senator Sura, Ludlumus or any member of the Licinius family had any official business with the Mucianus family, the papers would have been filed here," Pliny told him.

"And if their business wasn't official?"

"Regardless of the true nature of their arrangement, to conduct any trade in the empire would require paperwork, Athanasius. We can infer quite a bit from it. We're not an entirely criminal government, you know. There are good men in Rome."

Hortus apparently was one of them, returning with a thick stack of documents, which Pliny took to a small table for review.

"Official state business," Athanasius authoritatively told the clerk, who had probably seen quite a bit of "state business" in this dungeon and slowly nodded.

"Thank you, Hortus," said Pliny, returning the material all too quickly. "We have what we need. Goodbye."

Athanasius followed him out of the vault and back down the long tunnel. "What did you find?"

"Nothing," Pliny said. "That's the problem. The business records have been sanitized. But I have another idea."

They descended a flight of gloomy stairs into the bowels of the Tabularium, and then yet another flight even further below until they reached a vast suite of interlocking vaults.

"Birth and death certificates," Pliny explained. "These are usually missed when commercial records are altered, and we may find something about either the Mucius or Licinius families that will tell us something about what happened to Mucianus."

Athanasius, now thinking about Helena alone and bleeding back at the inn in Ostia, said, "Time is running short."

"Then we split the work and double our time," Pliny said before they presented themselves before another pinch-mouthed clerk, who if possible looked to have even less flesh on his bones than the one upstairs.

They worked through two stacks while the clerk kept a beady eye on them. By the time word of this research reached Domitian or the Dei, it would be too late: Domitian would be dead and Nerva would rally the senate to bless the succession of Young Vespasian to the throne.

"Jupiter!" remarked Pliny, and then covered his mouth.

Athanasius leaned over to look at what Pliny had discovered. But it didn't look like any birth or death certificate Athanasius had ever seen before, although he hadn't seen many.

"These are adoption papers," Pliny whispered. "Adoption papers between the Mucius and Licinius families. It changes the name of Gaius Mucius Mucianus's son from Lucius Mucius Ludlumus to Lucius Licinius Ludlumus."

Athanasius stared. "Ludlumus was Mucianus's son! But now he's dead. Who did it, and who might have taken his place?"

Now it was Pliny who looked like a ghost himself, white as a sheet. He gulped and said, "I'm afraid it could be the lawyer who handled the adoption."

Athanasius looked at the signature and seal at the bottom of the certificate. It read Marcus Cocceius Nerva.

Senator Nerva!

Athanasius grabbed the official adoption certificate, slipped it under his breastplate, and said, "We've got to get out of here."

Pliny was only too quick to agree, leaving the papers behind them for the clerk as they rushed out of the Tabularium.

Athanasius raced back to Ostia on one of Pliny's horses as the first hint of sunrise began to break across the horizon, his mind racing faster than the horse as he pondered the significance of what he had discovered at the Tabularium. Ludlumus was the son of Mucianus, whose fate was still unclear at this point. Perhaps he had died long ago at the hands of Ludlumus, much like Domitian killed his own father.

The death of Ludlumus, however, was more problematic. Was it at the hands of Domitian, in which case everything should proceed according to plan? Or was it at the hands of Senator Nerva, who could rally the senate to install not Young Vespasian but the Dei's designated successor in the wake of Domitian's demise? In the first case, Nerva was simply a lawyer who knew how to keep state secrets, however terrible. In the second case, he was Chiron and the true leader of the Dei all along.

Whatever the case, thanks to the adoption certificate of Ludlumus in his possession and Pliny's help on the senate floor, the Church could connect Senator Nerva to the Dei, along with Senator Sura, Senator Celsus and others, exposing them all and securing the succession of Young Vespasian.

Meanwhile, he and Helena would be long gone from Rome.

Upon reaching the inn at Ostia, Athanasius raced up the stairs behind the courtyard and down the hallway to the room with Helena. But when he burst inside, she was gone, the bed and furniture turned upside down.

He scanned the debris looking for clues and then saw it—a note pinned to the wall by a dagger. He ripped the note off and read it:

We meet in the arena at 9 o'clock and trade the document you stole from me for Helena.

It was signed *Chiron*.

46

All of Rome was in a fog that morning, a kind of meteorological and supernatural stupor. The streets were thinned of the usual crowds, and the overcast skies more ominous than ever. What faces Athanasius could glimpse looked vacant under the occasional flashes of lightning. The hour of dread had finally come, and by the way they shuffled along the Sacred Way near the Flavian Amphitheater, everybody knew it, as if their sole purpose was simply to reach the next hour.

Athanasius looked up at the empty, ghostly Colosseum rising into the mist. One of the statues of the gods ringing the arches of the second story seemed to move. Athanasius caught his breath but didn't miss a step. So there were sharpshooters trained on him before he even entered the stadium. But then he never imagined Chiron was going to let him walk out of here alive.

He stepped under the arch at Gate XXXIV, one of the 76 public entrances into the Colosseum. It was the only gate from which the chains had been unlocked today. The peeling sign beside it proclaimed, "Death Guaranteed!"

Athanasius entered the maze of empty passageways and ramps under the stands, which were supported by hundreds of towering arches. There were no souvenir sellers, sausage vendors or fortunetellers to slow his march to the runway that would direct him to his section. A moment later he emerged at the end of the tunnel into tier 1 and beheld the vast arena, with nothing but Helena in the center and empty stands all around.

"Helena!" he shouted, sprinting his way toward the emperor's box. "Helena!"

He hauled himself over the bronze balustrade and landed on the soft sand of the arena floor. He started toward her when she screamed.

"Athanasius, stop!"

Suddenly the sand before him shifted and an entire section of the floor collapsed to reveal a great pit filled with roaring lions trying to claw their way up. And if they had the usual ramps, they could have.

Athanasius stepped back and looked across at Helena, who was shaking on the other side of the pit. He then looked all around the ghostly stands, waiting for a hail of arrows or the appearance of Chiron. But none came down.

Slowly he began to circle around the pit toward Helena when he felt another vibration under his feet and stopped. Sure enough, the dust began to swirl again as another trapdoor opened and a platform rose with a towering figure in a white toga.

"I am risen!" Ludlumus proclaimed with outstretched arms. "I am risen indeed!"

A fury of thoughts and emotion engulfed Athanasius. Ludlumus alive? So his rival had faked his death to set this board and place these pieces. But what was the next move? What was his game?

"Behold the beast!" Ludlumus cried out, pointing to the pit. "Behold the Whore of Babylon!" He waved his arm at Helena. "And behold the rider on the white horse," he said, pointing straight at Athanasius. "The one who has come to save them who shall instead be cast into the pit of fire!"

Athanasius half expected an eruption of flames to explode from the pit, but Ludlumus probably intended to save that effect until after he had cast them to its bottom, their flesh torn to pieces by the lions and their eyes looking up to him like he was some malevolent god.

But this god wasn't omniscient, Athanasius thought, hoping that the thought and care Ludlumus put into this production had made him oblivious to the ground being pulled out from under him at the palace. Once Domitian was gone, Ludlumus would be history too.

"More games, Ludlumus?"

"The greatest of all, Athanasius. We are surrounded by a great cloud of witnesses, don't you see?" He gestured to the ghostly stands under the overcast sky. "You have finished the race and entered the Hall of Faith. Welcome to the afterlife."

The sand shifted again, and a gladiator and Praetorian were launched into the arena. The Praetorian was in chains and gagged, the gladiator holding a sword to the soldier's throat. From the engravings on his breastplate, Athanasius could see the gladiator was one of Domitian's. Then Athanasius saw the eyes turning wild under the helmet of the Praetorian and recognized Virtus.

They got him before he could steal Domitian's dagger.

In that instant Athanasius knew that his plans had failed. If they had gotten Virtus, then they had gotten Stephanus, and Domitian was alive this very hour.

"He too was lost," Ludlumus laughed. "But, like you, now is found."

47

In the basilica at the Palace of the Flavians, surrounded by great statues of his contemporaries the gods, Domitian again picked at the bloody ulcer on his forehead as he listened to testimony on behalf of still another astrologer. This one was an Armenian who dared to agree with his late predecessor Ascletario that the recent rash of lightning in Rome augured a change in government.

What it really augured, Domitian knew, was the soothsayer's untimely end.

It was the only certainty of the hour that Domitian knew he could control.

Ironically, it was the prosecutor Regulus who was defending the astrologer, or rather his astrology. The poor fool misinterpreted the obvious signs of Jupiter's displeasure at those who would challenge his son Domitian as Emperor and twist the stars to suit themselves like the infernal Christians and their rising Age of Pieces, the cosmic symbol of their Christ Jesus.

"This man merely repeated predictions that have long since warned Caesar of what year and day he would die, and even the specific hour and manner," Regulus said, looking up from a papyrus with lunar tables. "All he added was that the moon is in Aquarius and that today's fifth hour, beginning at nine o'clock, is especially dangerous and could augur transition. But he also concluded that Caesar would be safe if he lived to ten o'clock."

Domitian was tired of this astrological minutia. For years he had known just how unusual were the twin events of Mars setting on the Roman horizon with the moon at its lower culmination, both within minutes of each other. Especially as the moon's position in Aquarius was exactly the same as Saturn at the time of his birth on October 24 almost 45 years ago. While this happened every month, the connection with Mars setting as the moon passed its lower culmination made it an astrologically noteworthy event.

He looked down into his empty wine goblet and then to Julius, his food-and-wine-tester, who ceremoniously poured him the last of the proven, poison-free Dovilin wine in the palace. In recent weeks he had half-hoped his former dog walker would turn purple and die after losing his beloved Sirius.

Domitian turned to Regulus and said, "However he covered his ignorance, it doesn't negate the fact that he predicted a change in government, something that could only happen with my demise."

"On the contrary, Your Highness, he said it was your prophecy as Lord and God that would determine the outcome."

"My prophecy?"

Regulus cleared his throat, fully aware he was voicing what nobody else would, and yet claiming they were not his words from his own mouth but those of Caesar himself. He picked up a tablet and read from it.

"Caesar himself was overheard yesterday refusing a present of apples and telling his servant Julius, 'Serve them tomorrow, if only I am spared to eat them. There will be blood on the moon as she enters Aquarius, and a deed will be done for everyone to talk about throughout the world.'"

"My word! My word!" Domitian stood up, beside himself. "Silence!"

The basilica was quiet.

"What time is it? What is the hour?"

Julius conferred with another member of the staff who ran out, then returned and whispered in his ear. Julius announced, "The time is 10 o'clock, Your Highness."

Domitian collapsed into his chair and exhaled. The hour had passed! He had survived! The gods were indeed greater than the stars!

He looked across the small group of magistrates in the hall and noted their dismay, even horror, at this reality, and stood up to address them.

"The deed has been done today that the world will talk about. Emperor Domitian Flavius is a god who defies the stars, and whose reign shall be forever. And the deed shall be memorialized with blood on the moon in Aquarius, beginning with the execution of this astrologer and all astrologers who would worship the stars instead of their Caesar. Kill him. I'm off to my bath."

And with that, Caesar walked out of the basilica with a new bounce in his step and deaf ears to shouts from behind.

"But Your Highness!" Regulus called out.

Domitian could feel a second wind enter his body, a second spirit, a new life. To have this weight removed from his shoulders! To have the unequivocal salutation of the gods!

"I will feast tonight on the blood of my enemies!" he told his entourage of attendants as he walked, the old energy of hatred focusing his mind now that the fog of dread had lifted. "I have my list, and my Praetorian will have names."

I knew you would protect me, dear Minerva, he prayed to himself, then turned a corner to find Parthenius his chamberlain waiting for him. Domitian stopped, as did the several attendants who had followed him out of the basilica.

Parthenius said, "Your Highness, a person has come to wait upon you with a document about a matter of great importance that simply cannot be delayed."

Domitian frowned. That Parthenius refused to name this person in the company of the others informed Domitian that this matter was indeed important. But could it be more important than his bath? He felt like Jesus rising out of his tomb, and now he wanted to plunge into the waters of his bath like a baptism to symbolize his rebirth. At the same time, Domitian understood that word of his survival had probably scattered the panicked roaches from the shadows into the light, and he should make haste to crush them all.

"Then I will retire to my chamber," he announced, dismissing the others and following Parthenius inside.

It was his servant Stephanus who was waiting for him with a letter, and his arm still looked no better with its bandage.

"I told you that you should have one of my doctors check that out," Domitian told him as he took the letter and began to open it.

"I think I shall," Stephanus said.

Domitian looked up to see that Stephanus had actually unwound the bandage, but there was no wound. Then he saw the dagger in Stephanus's hand before it stabbed him and he screamed, "Minerva!"

He lunged for the dagger he kept under the pillow of his bed and found the sheath. But it was empty!

Stephanus pulled out the dagger and was about to strike him again when Domitian tackled him to the floor. He dug his long fingers into Stephanus's eyes and ripped them out, making Stephanus howl and release his dagger.

Domitian grabbed the dagger and slashed Stephanus's throat, screaming at the top of his lungs to his Praetorian outside, "Help! Help!"

He felt a stab at his neck and saw Stephanus reaching up to him, an eye hanging out of its socket, his mouth awash in blood. Domitian kicked him like a dog, grabbed the statue of Minerva and smashed it on his head.

"Die, you Christian scum! Like your master my cousin! All of you! Die!".

<u>48</u>

Athanasius had returned to Rome with the express purpose of seeking vengeance on Ludlumus and Domitian, reuniting with Helena and getting their life back. Fulfilling his obligation to the Christians by assassinating Domitian and installing Young Vespasian was simply the cost of doing business and doing good for the people of Rome as well as the Church.

But that plan, he knew as he stood in the middle of the Colosseum facing Ludlumus, was blown.

Ludlumus had faked his death, Virtus had been caught, and Domitian still had a knife under his pillow to defend himself against Stephanus, assuming Stephanus hadn't been captured and killed already. Instead of changing the government of Rome and installing a Christian emperor, Athanasius had only ensured an extension of Domitian's Reign of Terror and retribution on the Christians he had sworn to help.

Still, there was no sight of Stephanus. If they had Virtus, why not show Stephanus too? Perhaps Stephanus was still at large, and a confrontation in Domitian's chamber imminent. If so, he would have to entertain Ludlumus long enough for Stephanus to take his stab at Domitian. It might be an even fight now, if Domitian had his dagger, but at least it would be a fight.

Athanasius looked at Helena, who put on a brave face even as her body trembled. The best he could hope for now was to make the exchange—the adoption papers for Helena, maybe Virtus too—and escape Rome before the wrath of Domitian came down.

"Welcome back, Athanasius," said Ludlumus. "Or should I call you Clement, Bishop of Rome? That is the name you took in Ephesus, isn't it, before you killed our man Croesus?"

Athanasius noticed Virtus motioning with his eyes to the pit, where grains of sand continued to fall like water to the bottom where the lions roared. It might be worth a try to push Ludlumus over while Virtus broke free, but it was hard to believe Ludlumus had not anticipated such a move. He stepped forward in the sand, and, sure enough, an arrow suddenly landed in front of him as a warning. He glanced over his shoulder at the empty stands, wondering where the sharpshooters were hiding.

Athanasius pulled out the certificate of adoption and paused. "Your plan has failed, Ludlumus. Even if Domitian lives, he'll know who you really are. You're a dead man. You should leave Rome immediately."

Ludlumus roared with laughter. "You don't disappoint, Athanasius. But once again you're gravely mistaken. The only surprise is going to be on your assassin Stephanus. I simply wanted the document to blackmail Nerva and ensure he sees to it that the senate confirms Vespasian the Younger as the new emperor. Now you've made even that a question mark."

Ludlumus produced a dagger, and from the imperial insignia Athanasius knew it could only belong to Domitian. So Virtus had removed it from the emperor's chamber after all.

"Yes, Athanasius, I wanted him dead too."

Virtus, meanwhile, shifted in his chains, the gladiator behind him shifting with him but keeping the blade close to his throat.

Ludlumus said, "Of course, it will be a tragedy if Domitian survives now because of you. He's going to slaughter Young Vespasian and name the baby in Helena's womb his official heir, his true blood. She'll be as safe as Venus, and you'll be food for worms. You and your friends in Cappadocia. Oh, yes, thanks to you and that little whore of yours, we now know about the secret Angel's Pass inside the mountains."

"What game are you playing, Ludlumus?"

"The greatest game of all." Ludlumus beamed in triumph. "Do you really think God spared your life in prison by having a Jesus-like figure Marcus take your place to die here in this arena? I sent Marcus through the Dei, threatening him with the lives of his wife and children. It was for them he died, Athanasius, not you."

"To what end, Ludlumus?"

"To get you to John on Patmos, and get him to implant you within the church in Cappadocia. He guessed it from the start, I suppose."

"I don't believe you."

"Believe it, Athanasius. The miracle is that it worked in spite of your schemes. First in your arrogance with Domitian's dog, which told him you were alive. Then your handiwork in Corinth, and again in Patmos. Domitian's legions would have killed you in Ephesus were it not for my intervention through the Dei."

"Your intervention?"

"It was I who gave Croesus orders to send Virtus to reach you before the Romans killed you at your drop-off outside the library. You returned the favor by killing Croesus, and setting your sights on the Dovilins, which was the same end I had for you: to use the Dei to compromise the church in Cappadocia, then go after Domitian and replace him with his nephew and establish a new Christian empire. So you see, dear Clement of Rome,

Jesus was never the author and finisher of your faith. I am."

The inflection on the divine "I am" sent a shudder down Athanasius's spine. The overcast skies above seemed to roll back like a scroll to reveal nothing but a pitch blackness beyond, darker than anything he had ever imagined, as if all the stars had fallen away and with them any flicker of hope.

"And what did my so-called Lord and God Ludlumus intend for his servant Athanasius?"

"To bring you back here at the end of your quest to unmask Chiron. And I now present him to you. He is you, Athanasius. You are Chiron. You have always been."

"I am not, Ludlumus. Your overestimate my influence—and yours—over hearts and minds."

"Hardly. You saw the effects in Cappadocia of my epistle to the Thessalonians as Paul, the one that Bishop Paul read to the church that created such a stir."

"You wrote that?"

"Yes, and you too might write something people might actually worship. Everything you ever imagined as a playwright—glory, immortality—I can give it to you."

Athanasius looked at Helena's hopeless expression, and then at Virtus, whose darting eyes indicated he was ready to make his move. "If you were behind that bogus letter, Ludlumus, it did nothing but inspire many of the

Cappadocians to quit working the fields and hole up in their caves with their stockpiles of foodstuffs."

"Exactly. How else were the Dovilins to control the masses except through fear? Fear kept the Christians in their caves. Fear works, Clement. All of our Roman religion depends on fear of the wrath of gods. From that fear of wrath come all our temples, sacrifices, feasts and commerce. Without fear of what is to come in the afterlife, Rome has only the blade to motivate people in this life. If Christianity is to become the state religion, we must take the fear of wrath from your John's Book of Revelation and use it to fashion a true religion from the superstition of Jesus and the notion that his death and resurrection somehow appeased God's wrath once and for all."

"I thought Rome wanted to destroy the Church."

"No, Athanasius. The superstition of men can't be razed like the temple in Jerusalem. It is a fire. It can only be directed or corrupted."

It was all becoming chillingly clear to Athanasius now. "So my plan to kill Domitian and replace him with Vespasian the Younger in order to create a Christian Rome is the plan of the Dei, and has been all along."

Ludlumus nodded. "The Dei no longer wants to destroy the Church. It wants to corrupt the superstition, turn it into a real religion and merge it with Rome to last a thousand years. For that to happen, it must demand some sort of sacrifice to appease the wrath of God and his final judgment so eloquently depicted by your friend John. The sacraments, rituals and worship must be commercialized—wine, idols, temples and the like. Then they can be politicized and socialized as the official state religion of Rome. Loyalty will be one and the same to Caesar and Jesus."

"So you don't intend to kill me."

"Kill you? You're far too valuable to Rome for that."

"And what's in the New Rome for you, Ludlumus?"

"Young Vespasian will be Caesar, and I will be *Pontifex Maximus,* the head of the Church. But I will rule the empire through the young emperor."

"Like your father ruled through young Domitian before Vespasian arrived in Rome."

"And betrayed my father for his loyalty by killing him," Ludlumus hissed. "Now I will do likewise, and not just to Domitian. Your friend John likewise will never leave Patmos alive. He will expire on his own, leaving me and Young Vespasian as the titular religious and political figureheads of the Roman Christian Empire. And your friends in Cappadocia—they can't hole up in the caves forever under siege by our legions. At some point they'll run out of food, then the legions will enter through Angel's Pass and pick them off. We are done with the last apostle. It's time for the first apostate."

"Meaning you," said Athanasius.

Ludlumus smiled. "As *Pontifex Maximus,* I will merge the Church with Rome. The empire will render unto Caesar what is his, and unto me what is mine."

"And if I refuse to bow to you?"

"Then you die right here, right now," Ludlumus said. "Consider my offer, Athanasius. Rome could use a man like you. Come to think of it, it already has, Chiron."

Something terrible stirred in Athanasius at the moment as Ludlumus's taunting cut him to the heart. It wasn't rage or hatred. It was a kind of sentence in his spirit that had been rendered, a realization that Ludlumus his enemy was absolutely correct: Athanasius had indeed discovered the final secret of the Dei: that his idea of a Christian Rome was Ludlumus's and Rome's all along— and certainly not Jesus's, who plainly said his kingdom is in Heaven. If he was guilty of nothing else, it was his attempt to use the Church to his own ends. If his enemy was certainly not the better man here, neither was he.

"Now!" came the shout, but it did not come from Athanasius. Virtus, still bound, charged Ludlumus with his entire body, slamming Ludlumus over the edge of the pit and tumbling in after him.

Athanasius rushed to the pit and looked down to see the lions in a feeding frenzy, their roars barely drowning the screams of Ludlumus.

"Virtus!" Athanasius called down.

"I'm not long for this world, Athanasius!" Virtus cried out. "But I will follow Ludlumus who has departed already! To God be the glory!"

Then his voice was cut off, suddenly, and the roars began to fade.

Now Athanasius heard sobbing. He looked over to see Helena crumbled like a pillar of salt in the middle of the arena. He scanned the stands around them and threw himself on her to shield her from a hail of arrows.

But the arrows never came.

Athanasius held her and looked out at the empty stands. If there were snipers still out there, they had decided to hold their fire.

"We must leave immediately, Helena. I have to get back to the palace."

But she wouldn't move. "Domitian forced himself on me. I had no choice. You were dead. You must forgive me."

"I know, Helena. There's nothing to forgive. I love you. Now we must go. I have to save Stephanus."

"Save Stephnaus, Athanasius, or save her?"

"Her?"

"Ludlumus told me about your whore in Cappadocia. Gabrielle."

"What are you saying? She was a girl I met who helped me."

"Liar!" Helena screamed. "You've known her your whole life. Before you even came to Rome. I heard you call her name in the night while you dreamed in our own bed!"

She pushed him away and marched out toward the Gate of Death.

"Helena!" he called after her.

But she didn't stop. Nor could the wheels that he had set in motion. He knew he had to get to the palace, to finish what he had started. He knew the moment to choose was before him: his love of Helena or hatred of Domitian. But it was for the love of Helena he hated Domitian and had to see him dead.

Athanasius ran down the long private tunnel from the emperor's box at the Colosseum to the Palace of the Flavians. The Praetorian Guard at the other end didn't stop him as he exited into the lower offices of the palace. Nobody did. It was as if they were mere observers and, however the drama ended, would carry on the affairs of state without pause.

He raced up the narrow staircase he had memorized from Stephanus's map and could hear Stephanus's cries even before he came upon the small group of palace staff and gladiators outside the locked bed chambers of Caesar.

There wasn't a single Praetorian in sight save Clodianus, one of Virtus's co-conspirators. Clodianus was closest to the door, sword out, as if he didn't know whether he was supposed to keep Domitian from coming out, or his assassins from swooping in. Then there was Parthenius, who had led Domitian into the trap, along with his freedman Maximus. Saturius, Domitian's principal chamberlain, stood apart, ashen and paralyzed. Most of all, there was the palpable fear in the air that Domitian would appear and none would have the courage to cut him down.

Athanasius, hearing curses and threats from Domitian, knew he had to act fast. He was as guilty as any of these conspirators, more so even, regardless of who spilled Domitian's blood. Striding up to Clodianus with authority, he took the sword from the guard's hand and barked orders to Saturius.

"Unlock the doors!" he shouted. "Now!"

Saturius fumbled with the key. When he finally managed to slide it into the lock, Athanasius pushed him aside and burst into Domitian's chambers.

Stephanus was lying on the floor, his eyes gauged out, choking on his own blood, gasping for breath. Standing over him was Domitian, bleeding from his stomach, dagger in hand. He barely had time to stagger back before

Athanasius charged him straight on with Clodianus's sword, angled down from his shoulder.

Domitian gasped as he stared. "Athanasius!"

"I told you I'd be back to kill the gods," Athanasius said, plowing his sword through Domitian's throat and pinning him to the wall. "You first."

The jaw of Rome's Lord and God dropped, his blood spraying over Athanasius, who didn't withdraw his sword until he saw the light flicker out of the emperor's eyes. He then removed it, and the lifeless body slid to the floor.

Silence descended on the bloody scene as Athanasius dropped to his knees next to Stephanus. It was clear he was dead. Athanasius gazed at the ghastly hollows where shining eyes had been, put his hand upon the cracked skull and honored him by committing his spirit to God the Father in the name of Jesus.

Then, as if the stillness was their cue, the crowd outside burst into the room, weapons at the ready. They all descended on Domitian's corpse like vultures to each take their stabs, if only to satisfy their own fears that the despot was dead.

49

The blast of mournful horns and lowered flags announced the death of Caesar by the time a dazed Helena reached the Sublicius Bridge. It was now packed with people liberated from a suffocating cloud of uncertainty.

She, however, was now bound to the black abyss before her.

Domitian was dead, she knew, and so too was her future with Athanasius.

He had told her he could forgive her for her tryst with Caesar and the evil offspring growing in her belly, but she didn't believe him. If his righteous hatred could drive him to kill the father, how could he not hate their child every time he looked at his face? How could he love her every time he looked into her eyes? How could he protect the child or its mother from the Flavians—

Young Vespasian, his mother Domitilla, and Domitian's widow Domitia?

Her foolish lover may have changed Rome's religion, but he had only traded one Flavian Caesar for another, doing nothing to change their future.

Then there was the whore Ludlumus told her about. Gabrielle. Athanasius had all but confirmed his affection for her in his eyes back in the arena. Even if she had not completely replaced her in the eyes of Athanasius, that he could find hope of love in any other woman was something wholly unimaginable before he left her. Wasn't that truly, in the end, why he had raced back to confront Domitian? Not to ensure his death, nor even for this adoption certificate implicating Senator Nerva and Senator Lucindus, but this whore's safety, as Ludlumus had predicted?

He had changed.

If he could turn on Maximus, the man who had brought them together, he would surely turn on the child, and on her.

She, on the other hand, had no one to turn to now. The protection of the palace upon her through Domitian was gone. So was Ludlumus. So was Maximus. Worst of all, so was her beauty, now that she bore the scar on her belly. It was worse than a line on her face. She could pose no longer for the great sculptors of the world. She was disfigured now, hopeless, alone.

She looked down at the rippling water of the Tiber from the stone wall of the bridge. A few boats passed through, but not as many as at night. She could hear the shuffling of feet behind her, mostly the Jews from District 14 feeling safe to cross over into District 8 and the Forum now that Caesar was dead. Would they feel so happy to learn Young Vespasian would make Christianity the official state religion?

She put her hand on her belly and stepped up onto the bridge ledge. She heard somebody shouting in Aramaic, probably to get the attention of the crossing guards at either end of the bridge. They began to run toward her, but she made sure they would not catch her. She looked up at the flock of birds in the sky for one last sign, and their formation flying south only confirmed everything she feared. She lifted up her arms, as if to fly away with them, and fell into space, the rush of wind swallowing her up in everlasting darkness.

50

The new Caesar, Nerva, was seated in the throne room when Athanasius was brought before him by Secundus. Somehow the adoption certificate of Ludlumus had made its way back into his hands, and Athanasius watched Nerva touch it to a fire. The papyrus burned up, along with any possibility that Young Vespasian would see the throne of Rome.

"Bravo, Athanasius. You have indeed killed a god. The Senate has approved of your actions by eternally condemning Domitian. There will never be a temple, altar, monument or so much as an inscription erected in his honor. Those that exist will be erased."

"Along with your involvement with the Dei, Senator."

"Contrary to what you believe, I did not engineer all this. You did. The Senate wants Rome rid of the Flavians forever, which unfortunately includes Young Vespasian, however worthy he might or might not be."

"Domitian was no god, Nerva. Neither are you."

"No, I suppose not. But then I never pretended to be, and nobody has mistaken me for one, least of all my peers in the Senate. Why do you think they made me Caesar, and I accepted? You think it was some machination of the Dei? No, Athanasius. I am an old man, a caretaker of this office at best for no more than a few years. And I have no heirs, no ambitions to further my family politically or financially. I believe there can be good emperors as well as bad. Don't you?"

"Then you are a good Caesar?"

Nerva smiled at the intended sarcasm. "You think that's an oxymoron? That no such thing can exist?"

"I think the intentions can exist, but that the power corrupts. In both government and the church. God forbid when they are one.""

"Ah, yes. Socrates said only those who are willing to lay down their power are fit to have it. Like Jesus of Nazareth, I suppose. But then the Jews nailed him to a cross. Or do you think we Romans did it?"

"No, I did," Athanasius answered him. "We all did."

Nerva nodded. "Your new faith has sharpened your wit. Do you wish to convert us all now?"

"That I cannot do. I cannot change myself. How can I change the world?"

Nerva stepped down from his throne and put an arm around him. "Let's talk about that, Athanasius."

They walked to the basilica together, as if they were partners, not Caesar and the assassin of his predecessor. And no Praetorian nor anybody else followed them. Inside the basilica were additional statues and idols, but these in the form of Jesus and the disciples. One was of John, as if Ludlumus wished to use the last apostle after death. Then Mary the mother of Jesus, holding a baby. It was Helena, and the baby looked like a smaller version of Helena.

Nerva gestured toward the statues. "We picked up some things here from Ludlumus's doma that might interest you."

"Religion doesn't interest me," Athanasius said flatly. "It won't interest the Christians."

"We can make something of this tragedy," Nerva said. "The timing may be off, but Christianity will become the official state religion of the empire and extend the rule of Rome another thousand years. You can be part of this Roman Church for the ages, Athanasius. I won't even make you renounce Jesus. Simply bow to Jesus and to Rome, and you won't have to die."

Athanasius said nothing.

"Come now, Athanasius," Nerva said angrily. "I was there that night in this very palace when you kissed the feet of Rome and cursed the name of Jesus. You did it then, and I know you can do it now."

He indeed had done that. Nerva was right, Athanasius thought, and he himself so wrong about everything else. And yet, as he searched his soul, or whatever the hole in his heart was called, he realized for the first time and to his utter astonishment that this simple thing he could not do.

"My citizenship," he told Caesar, "is in heaven."

EPILOGUE

Now you know my history, Gabrielle, and my role in the Dei and in the assassination of Domitian. I am only grateful that the wrath of Rome's angels has not come to pass, and I pray that with the shift of emperors you will escape judgment.

As for me, I have indeed come to the end of my life, but I have failed to finish my race. I have fought the wrong fight and have done more evil in the name of good and of God than I ever imagined in my former life as the hedonist and playwright Athanasius of Athens.

This is my confession as Chiron, general of the infernal order that calls itself Dominium Dei.

But even if few remember the past, and the future should be forgotten by those who come after it, I take comfort in this revelation: from generation to generation, God has granted a place of repentance to all who would listen.

There was Noah who repented and was saved with the animals. There was Jonah who repented and preached repentance to the Ninevites, and they repented and were spared. Rahab, the harlot of Jericho, signaled her repentance by hiding the Israelite spies and hanging a scarlet cord in her window, saving her family from the city's destruction. This cord was a sign of the redemption that would flow through the blood of Jesus to all those who believe and hope in God.

You were that place of repentance for me.

You taught me how nature continually proves that there will be a future resurrection. Day and night declare to us a resurrection, as light gives way to darkness and darkness gives way to light. The fruits of the earth also declare the resurrection, as the seed dies in the ground only to rise up again as a vine bearing many grapes.

I may not be long for this world, Gabrielle, but thanks to you I now live for the next.

May you continue to bring forth your fruit in your season and provide shade and comfort to others. To God our savior be all glory, dominion and power, both now and forever.

Clement of Rome
CHIRON

AUTHOR'S NOTE

Many readers may be surprised to learn that the essential events and characters of *Gods of Rome* are, in fact, historical. Even the attack on the corpse of the astrologer Ascletario by wild dogs was recorded by the Roman historian Suetonius (c. 69 – c.122 AD) in his book The Life of Domitian.

The Emperor Domitian of Rome died at exactly 9 o'clock on the morning of September 18th in the year 96 AD, just as the astrologers predicted at his birth and in the manner depicted in the pages of this novel. Immediately afterward, the Roman Senate condemned his memory to eternal damnation. Domitian's name was erased from public monuments. Those who had survived his Reign of Terror took up pens to condemn him in their histories of the era, from which much of *Gods of Rome* is derived.

Domitian's successor Nerva released the last apostle John from his prison on Patmas. The former "son of thunder" lived out his remaining days in Ephesus, telling anyone who would listen to love each other as Jesus loved them.

Less certain is the fate of Clement, the Church's fourth bishop or "pope" of Rome after the apostle Peter.

Some say that Clement was the slain consul Flavius Clemens, and that their names became confused over the centuries. Or that Clement was one of his freedmen, such as Stephanus.

Others insist that Nerva's successor Trajan banished Clement from Rome, and that the bishop lived on for many years and adventures afterward in Asia Minor, performing miracles worthy of Mucianus's memoirs of the land.

In this version of events, his end came at a trial before a very conflicted Pliny the Younger, who was now governor of Bithynia in Asia Minor. This trial proved to be an eerie replay of the one suffered by an innocent playwright named Athanasius of Athens years ago before the Emperor Domitian.

But this man was different. This man would neither curse the name of Christ nor bow to Caesar to save his skin.

Unable to bring himself to condemn the bishop, Pliny made a futile appeal to Caesar in Rome, but it was denied. One can imagine the haunted governor even arranging a secret escape for his old friend. But the man once called CHIRON refused to renounce his faith, choosing martyrdom by being tied to an anchor and thrown from a ship into the Black Sea.

THOMAS
GREANIAS
RECOMMENDS

RAISING ATLANTIS

THOMAS GREANIAS

RAISING ATLANTIS

Start here if you want to get into my Atlantis series, past, present and future.

Raising Atlantis began as a hit augmented reality web series called Atlantis Mapping Project. Visitors signed up to receive "the latest breaking news from the secret U.S. dig in Antarctica." Those emails became some of the most forwarded emails in America. When *Raising Atlantis* came out as an eBook, it became an instant No. 1 bestseller on Amazon. Same with the audiobook on Audible, which honored it as "Best of Year."

Then Simon & Schuster won the rights at auction, and *Raising Atlantis* became my first *New York Times* bestseller in print. All this after Simon & Schuster had rejected the novel *three times before*, as did every other major publisher.

Fifteen years later, they're still printing new editions.

I tell this story to remind writers, artists and entrepreneurs everywhere that there is just as much value in your work—and yourself—before the world recognizes it as there is afterward.

Something we can all take to heart.

THOMAS GREANIAS

RED

"Thomas Greanias is the king of high-octane adventure!" — Brad Thor

GLARE

RED GLARE

Red Glare is one of my newest/oldest adventures. Originally a "big buck spec script" (*Variety*) in 1990's Hollywood, it hasn't reached the big screen yet. But its premise has been, er, borrowed many times. Stay tuned.

A devastating attack on post-pandemic America thrusts last-in-line Deborah Sachs into the presidency. Now she must survive assassination, find her missing teen daughter and stop her generals from retaliating on China before confirming it's responsible.

Oh, so you think you've seen the movie or TV series? More than a few times I've been at a party in LA where I've been thanked for making "such a great movie."

Ironically, the biggest headwinds *Red Glare* has faced include disbelief that a woman could be the U.S. president, Washington, D.C., could be hit by a weapon of mass destruction and China could emerge as America's No. 1 adversary in the 21st century.

The times, however, they are a changin'.

Suddenly the story feels right for such a time as now.

Booklist calls *Red Glare:* "Extremely fast-paced. An exciting adventure." No. 1 *New York Times* bestselling author Brad Thor says it's "fast, fascinating, and far too hard to put down. Don't expect to come up for air until the very last page."

THOMAS GREANIAS

DOOMSDAY ANGEL

DOOMSDAY ANGEL

Christmas 2022

Plot under wraps.

This is the one that a LOT of people have been waiting for. A lot, a lot, a lot. And because you purchased *Gods of Rome,* your eyes are the very first to behold the title and cover.

You can stay in front of the line by signing up to receive The Official Thomas Greanias Newsletter. You'll get sneak previews, exclusive excerpts, special offers and more delivered to your inbox every now and then until Doomsday.

Sign up at ThomasGreanias.com

FOR MORE ADVENTURES BY
THOMAS GREANIAS

VISIT
ThomasGreanias.com

Follow Thomas Greanias on Facebook
 @ThomasGreaniasOfficial

 Follow Thomas Greanias on Twitter
@ThomasGreanias

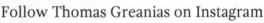

 Follow Thomas Greanias on Instagram
@ThomasGreanias

ADVENTURE FOR THE AGES™

THOMAS GREANIAS is one of the world's leading authors of adventure and the acclaimed *New
York Times* bestselling author of the *Raising Atlantis*
series, *Red Glare* and *Doomsday Angel.* CBS News
calls his books "gripping page-turners you stay up
way too late reading." The *Washington Post* says,
"Greanias writes captivating roller coasters that pen-
etrate the biggest mysteries of our times." He lives in
Florida with his family.